SIXTEEN MINUTES

ALSO BY K. J. REILLY

Four for the Road
Words We Don't Say

SIXTEEN MINUTES

K. J. REILLY

 Nancy Paulsen Books

Nancy Paulsen Books
An imprint of Penguin Random House LLC, New York

First published in the United States of America by Nancy Paulsen Books,
an imprint of Penguin Random House LLC, 2024

Nancy Paulsen Books & colophon are trademarks of Penguin Random House LLC.
The Penguin colophon is a registered trademark of Penguin Books Limited.

Visit us online at PenguinRandomHouse.com.

Library of Congress Cataloging-in-Publication Data is available.

Printed in the United States of America

ISBN 9780593620052

1st Printing
LSCH
Edited by Stacey Barney
Design by Cindy De la Cruz
Text set in American Garmond BT

For the strong, infinite, real girls in my life: Kate, Kenz, and Riv.
And for my book girls who only live on
these pages, and in my heart.

"It's no use going back to yesterday, because I was a different person then."

Alice's Adventures in Wonderland by Lewis Carroll

Saturday

PROLOGUE

When we pull into the hospital parking lot in Cole's truck, it's pitch-dark—and almost five. We spot Stevie B in the middle of the empty lot across from the emergency room doors, looking like the last man standing after an apocalypse, and our hearts soar, then tumble, then rise again when we pull up closer and see he's holding something in his arms. Cole mumbles, "Finn," and my breath catches in my throat, 'cause her name comes out of him sounding more like a whimper than a word. We don't know for sure what's gonna happen next, but the whole thing feels so dramatic. Stevie B standing there holding Finn like that, looking all shell-shocked and beat-to-shit. His mouth open, eyes big and wet, shirt untucked, hair sticking up. Finn not moving at all.

When this whole thing started, we were scared at first—*real* scared. But then this kind of mind-expanding wonder sparked, and there was something bigger, something surprising, mixed in with that fear. Something bright, without edges, that felt vast and indescribable—like the sky, maybe.

Stevie B said he felt like the Wright brothers must have felt the first time they went running down that beach in Kitty Hawk with wings strapped on their backs and their feet lifted off the ground. You know, scared to death, but full of hope too—like all of a sudden an ordinary life might become *un*ordinary because, for once, the wind promised to lift you up instead of beating you down.

We've had a whole string of those moments since Charlotte showed up in Clawson—moments when our feet lifted off the ground and our hearts stopped, then soared, then opened up bigger than we ever thought possible. And I get it now, what the Wright brothers did. Wanting to fly. Wanting to do something so big that just the thought of it paints the horizon all peachy and rose and strawberry red, like a sunrise full of promise or a field full of summer fruit, ripe for the picking.

The difference is, the Wright brothers, they were real smart and they worked for what they got. They dreamed and invented something, built something with their own hands.

But me and Cole and Stevie B, we didn't *do* anything. We just got blindsided.

And then we jumped.

Feet first. Heart second. Head a distant third.

Once we did that, we knew we were on the cusp of something either lethal or brilliant—we just didn't know which one it was, or how to tell the difference. And Charlotte, she tried to explain stuff to us. But only *some* stuff. And we tried to listen. We really did. But in the beginning, we were still stuck in the normal way of thinking, so we didn't understand most of what she was saying. Plus, it's hard to think you're destined for something big when you live in a town like Clawson. It's never been the kind of place that sprouts big ideas or smart people.

But right here and right now, as Cole runs from his truck to lift

Finn from Stevie B's arms and we wait to see how this whole thing is gonna play out, I'm wishing that Charlotte had told us how all those things that happened to us change a person. And change them forever.

But she didn't. She didn't tell us that.

Not on the day she showed up in Clawson. And not any time after.

We had to figure that part out for ourselves.

Monday

FIVE DAYS BEFORE

Cole, you're not listening," I gripe, acting like I'm put-out, but I'm not. At least not really.

Cole doesn't respond. He keeps sitting there next to Stevie B, looking off at something or someone and not listening to me. I know that's Cole's way, and besides, he's got his fingers all over my heart, so it's hard for me to get mad at him in a way that matters much.

I was going on and on about this weekend, trying to get him to agree to Friday night at the diner and Saturday at his house, but he went Cole-quiet on me and acted like he hadn't heard a thing I'd said. So I try nudging his shoulder, and that doesn't work, 'cause he only moves his feet a bit and slides forward like he's aiming to inch away from me.

"What are you looking at?" I ask, still trying to get his attention, 'cause the bell is gonna ring and lunch is gonna end soon, and I need to know about this weekend and I won't get to ask him again till tonight.

Still, there's no answer. I just get that lost I'm-in-my-own-world look of his.

I glance around the quad to the field beyond. Emma is sitting on one of the picnic tables, leaning back on her hands, flicking her hair over her shoulder, laughing at something TJ is saying, and there are a couple of freshmen over by the woods getting high, and Billy Hepner looks like he's in some kind of argument with a pair of blue sneakers and dark-wash jeans, which could be any number of people; it doesn't much matter who. The way I figure it, we're all doomed to predestined misery. The way *they* figure it—*they* being Cole and everyone else I know—this is high school and we haven't screwed up anything big yet, like our parents have, so life still has this magic to it. Like it's embedded with sparkles and fizz and possibility. I mean, Emma still thinks she's gonna be discovered and become a movie star, not a checkout girl at Binsky's, and the kids smoking weed up by the woods don't think they'll be working as guards at the prison in four years, then laid off two years after that, flat-out broke, addicted to one drug or another, with no way out, but who am I to stomp on their dreams?

I follow Cole's line of sight past all the normal stuff, looking for what caught his eye, and I see that he *is* looking at something or someone. And it's that new girl.

She showed up this morning in the front office to register for classes, and no one knows anything about her. She caused a stir, though, 'cause she's pretty in a way we don't usually see around here. Plus, she's new and shiny, and maybe not broke yet, in the way that this place breaks people.

"Who is she?" I ask Cole.

"Dunno," he mumbles, then he looks down like he feels guilty, like maybe he got caught doing something he shouldn't be doing. Like looking at the new, pretty girl with me sitting right here next to him.

"Should I be jealous?" I ask, not really serious. I mean, it's *Cole*. And me and Cole go way back, to the Elm Street playground swings and worn-down crayons and snack bags full of Goldfish crackers—the kind of stuff that ties you to someone in a way that even new and pretty can't cut through, unless it's razor-sharp.

When Cole doesn't answer, Stevie B looks over at the new girl and whistles long and low. Then in that teasing troublemaker voice of his, he says, "You might have reason to be jealous, Nell." So I give him the elbow.

"Hey!" he whines in mock pain. "Just being real, Nell."

"Be real somewhere else, Stevie B!" I say, not actually meaning it, because I know he's not going anywhere, and I wouldn't want him to anyway. Not in a million years. The three of us are plain old part of each other. It's Nell and Cole and Stevie B, like we're this triangle that wouldn't sit right if one side was missing. That's just how it is.

Right now, the three of us are sitting here on the grass under a tree, thirty yards away from everyone else who has sixth-period lunch, like we always do, and like we plan on doing every day until this spring when someone announces that high school is over. And then I suppose we'll have to find somewhere else to plant our asses.

"Cole!" I'm practically shouting now to get his attention.

"What?" he finally asks. He looks at me like he's surprised to see me. I wave at him and say, "Remember me? Your girlfriend? Name's Nell? Started dating before we were born?"

Cole says, "I *know* her, is all."

"You know her? The new girl?" I ask, more than a bit stunned. Stevie B gives me a look like he doesn't believe Cole either.

"You just said you *didn't* know her, Cole," I say. "I just asked you who she is, and you said, 'I don't know.'"

Cole gets that look again. Like he's all sunk down deep inside himself and he's gone somewhere else, with no plans of letting anyone else join him.

Stevie B asks, "From where?"

"From where what?" Cole asks, like he's so distracted he can't follow a conversation even for a minute.

"From where do you know the new girl?" Stevie B asks, annoyed.

I mean, Clawson, New York, is not the kind of town where people know people from other places. As my dad used to say, we're two hours south of nothin' and just north of nowhere. So we know people from *here*. Nowhere else. That's it. It's like there's some kind of force field around the place—or one of those electric fences they have for dogs. You know, like we have a collar around our necks and we'll get zapped if we even think about leaving. I mean, we *don't* have a collar around our necks. I'm just commenting that it has a way of working out that way. I think it's because all the dirt and small-town shit has a way of keeping you tied to a place.

My mom says I'm right, and that the binding dirt and small-town shit is called *oppression*. But Cole sees it different. He says it's the people that keep us tethered to Clawson. But that's only because if you don't count his dad, he has better people than most.

Cole looks down and mumbles, "It doesn't much matter how I know her. I just do."

All of a sudden, I feel uncomfortable. I can't explain it, but I get this crushing pressure in my chest sometimes when it feels like Cole isn't telling me something. It's not that he's lying outright. It's just that he's leaving something out. And sometimes I feel that whatever he's not telling me would change things if I knew what it was. It doesn't happen often, and I know it's probably meaningless, like I know everyone has their private stuff, but these last couple of weeks I've been thinking there's more private stuff to Cole than there should be. Like there's this whole part of him he doesn't want me to see.

"What's her name?" I ask softly.

It takes him a long minute to answer. "Anna."

Stevie B's leaning back on his elbow, looking over at the new girl with that grin he gets every September when a pretty new freshman arrives who promises to cause a whole circus full of trouble. "No way it's Anna," he says. "It's got to be Hannah or Heidi or . . ."

I give him a sideways glance, like *Why on earth would her name have to be Hannah or Heidi?*

He shrugs, then laughs. "What? It goes with Hottie, is all. You know, Hannah Hottie, Heidi Hottie . . ." Then he pulls a piece of paper out of his pocket and starts drawing a picture of the new girl wearing shiny tights and a sparkly cape and looking all fierce and sexy, like Rogue from the X-Men or the Invisible Woman from the Fantastic Four.

I punch him in the shoulder, and he makes a whole production out of it, faking like it hurt, tellin' me I messed up his sketch, and sayin', "Anna just sounds too old-fashioned. You know, like it's from a book or something. And that girl standing there is no Anna."

We all watch her for a bit, and then I say, "She got named before anyone knew how she'd turn out." Then Stevie B looks up from the picture he's drawing and says, "Hey, look at that. Hannah Hottie is walking in our direction."

Cole straightens up and brushes some grass from his jeans and looks uncomfortable, like all of a sudden his shirt doesn't fit him right or his skin's itchy, and my uh-oh meter goes into overdrive.

I watch the girl for another minute or two and realize that she's not coming over to us; she's just walking around all awkward, trying to look occupied, probably not sure what to do with herself or who to talk to, since this is her first day in this new-for-her poor-ass excuse for a high school.

I whisper, "Welcome to the bright lights and big city of Clawson, Anna." Mostly to myself.

But Cole kind of makes a sound like a grunt, low and sarcastic, like maybe he actually heard me this time. Then Stevie B puts his drawing down, hops up, and calls over to the girl as loud as he can. "Hey, Anna!"

She turns, startled, stares at Stevie B for a long minute, and looks back over her shoulder like she's not sure he means her, but then she starts to walk toward us for real.

Me and Cole are still sitting on the grass, hidden behind Stevie B, and when the girl gets close, she looks at him and says, "My name is Charlotte." No new-girl best-foot-forward sweet-as-summer-tea smile served with that either. Only words and nerves, all raw and jagged. And a statement of fact: *My name's not Anna. It's Charlotte.*

My heart starts to race, and I don't know why.

My mom says that we all know stuff we have no right knowing. Not in some weird way like from another life or anything like that. She says it's more like we all have this kind of intuition, or some kind of ability to know stuff that means something, even if we don't know what to do with it and can't understand where it came from or why we know it. And I think it's true, 'cause I feel that exact thing now, gnawing at me from the inside. Like I know something isn't right.

Stevie B looks at Cole. So does the new girl.

"This here is Cole Wilder," he says. "And I go by Stevie B."

Stevie B acts like he's proud of himself for makin' the introductions, even though he ignored me outright. For a second, Cole looks like he's about to say something, but then he doesn't. Not even a "Hey" delivered with Cole's shy aw-shucks cute-boy smile, which melts just about everyone and everything for miles around.

When the new girl first sees Cole sitting behind Stevie B, something happens in her eyes that has nothing to do with melting hearts and getting warm. Those eyes of hers turn from pale blue to dark blue to black, like winter just blasted through a month too early with unexpected force, and that thing my mom always says about knowing stuff we have no way of knowing starts dancing through my head as loud as a marching band in a Fourth of July parade. It's like the horns are trumpeting *We know stuff, Nell. Watch for it and listen!*

Whoever this new girl is, she looks scared. Scared of Cole, even. And Cole is the sweetest person I know. But she doesn't say anything. She just hurries away.

I watch Cole, and he's following her with his eyes. I've always said that he has a hunter's eyes. He sees stuff other people miss—the small stuff, like broken twigs and scat, which living things leave in their wake. And right now, he has *that* look. It's not one of the normal Cole looks, like when the left side of his mouth turns up and that shy smile starts to form right before he says something that warms your heart and turns you into a puddle that makes you say yes to anything he's asking. If he had *that* look right now, he could have said *Oh shit, Nell. My bad. That's not Anna,* and it would have come out all slow and warm and full of syrup. And I would have bought it, even though I know that Cole can twist ordinary words and make them ring true when they're not. But the look in his eyes right now is a hunter's look. And when he doesn't say anything at all, it hits me like buckshot. Because it sounds like he did. And what it sounds like he said was *Oh shit, Nell. It is Anna, and it's gonna be a problem.*

I watch the girl who calls herself Charlotte hurry toward the back door of the cafeteria, the one they prop open with a couple of cinder blocks in the summer months for air. Whoever this girl is, she's moving fast. Like she has someplace to get to. I glance down at my phone. Seventh period doesn't start for another fifteen minutes, so I figure it's more like she's got someplace or someone to get *from*.

The only questions are, Where or who?

And right now, it looks like that place she has to get from is here, and the who is Cole.

The problem is, Cole's digging a hole with the heel of his boot in the dry dirt beneath the tree we'll be sitting under until they tell us we can't. And he's not talking.

2

As soon as Charlotte leaves, Cole heads for his truck, which is parked in the senior lot with its front tires pulled way up on the lawn, just like he's parked it every single day this fall. I yell after him, "Hey, Cole! You're headed the wrong way." But he keeps walking, jiggling his keys like he can't wait to start the engine and bolt. Before he's out of my sight, I send him a text asking where he's going, but I'm watching him and he doesn't even look at his phone.

When the bell rings, I stand up and dust myself off, then head to class, pretty sure Cole's planning on cutting the rest of the day. Which means next week he'll have detention, which means he'll miss work, which means his pay'll be docked, and that spells trouble.

I spend the rest of the afternoon wondering what he's doing that's worth detention and docked pay, and trying hard to listen to my teachers drone on about stuff that has nothing to do with my life.

Then the new girl shows up in my ninth-period class.

The class is called Life Skills, and we learn about insurance and how to not go broke and how interest compounds when you earn it and when you owe it—way more when you owe it—and how we all should eat food like kale and cilantro so we don't die.

I'm downright certain that nobody eats kale or cilantro, and if they do, it doesn't stop them from dying. But I figure right now everyone in Life Skills is in the same boat as me—we don't care one bit about Ms. Daniels and her leafy greens, 'cause we're all watching as the new girl's designer jeans and polished nails and glossy lips take a seat by the window. And I'm pretty sure they're all thinking the same as me: *She's gotta be in the wrong class.* I mean, she doesn't exactly look like she needs anyone at Clawson High to teach her life skills. She looks like she has it all figured out, like she knows where to get her hair and nails done and how to get a wardrobe that includes three-hundred-dollar jeans even if you're living in some tumbledown Podunk town where a lot of the kids don't have enough food unless they happen to steal it from the school cafeteria.

Right now, I have three sandwiches and a slab of lasagna wrapped up in a slew of napkins in my backpack, and I figure that's a life skill way more valuable than the conversation we're about to have about the nutritional value of herbs and fancy vegetables. Meanwhile, all of the boys are staring at the new girl so hard it's unlikely their ears work. I know they're all wondering how good a shot they might have of nailing her if they throw out their best pickup lines. I'm guessing that none of them are thinking about getting to know her first either. She's like a shiny new sports car they all want to drive even before they've lifted the hood or checked the price tag, 'cause just looking at her shuts down most of their normal brain function.

But right now, I need to figure out who she is and what she's up to, so I ignore all the whispering and comments the boys are making and instead try to make sense of the bad feeling I have that's telling me something here isn't right.

Then the new girl takes out her cell phone and sends a text message. When Ms. Daniels doesn't say anything to her about no phones in the classroom, I figure it's because it's the girl's first day. After she hits SEND, she slips the phone into the outside pocket of her backpack. Then my ears perk up, because Ms. Daniels asks her to tell us where she's from and maybe add in a little something about herself.

That's when the new girl kind of blows everyone away. She says she's from "everywhere," then smiles coyly, like that's a place on a map. And that's all she says.

Even Ms. Daniels doesn't know how to respond to that.

When the bell rings and class ends, the new girl is first out the door. I catch up with her in the hallway, tap her on the shoulder, and say, "We didn't properly meet. My name's Nell. I go with Cole."

Get this: She asks, "You go *where* with Cole exactly?"

So I say, "Everywhere." And that kind of stops her in her soft leather boots. But then my eyes land on the necklace she's wearing. The gold chain and turquoise stone and tiny pearls catch the light as I wonder, *Who* are *you?* And when I look up, she does that thing with her eyes again, where they turn from a pale blue to deep sapphire to boiling black, before she walks away.

I lose her in the sea of kids in the hallway.

But not before I got what I wanted.

I lifted her phone from the outside pouch of her backpack, and I now have it stashed inside my left boot as I head for the exit.

3

Cole taught me how to steal stuff when we were little. He told me there were two rules.

One: Don't take anything you don't absolutely need.

And two: Don't hide it anywhere obvious.

Then he made me practice, over and over again. He taught me how to work alone and how to work with a partner and, most importantly, how not to get caught.

Which is what I'm doing right now—trying not to get caught—as I hurry to the parking lot because it's Monday, and Monday is one of the days I pick up Cole's little sister, Finn, and bring her to the park. Mrs. Wilder works as a secretary at the prison, answering phones and typing stuff for the warden—who she hates—but the job comes with health insurance and it pays decent. Which means I can't mess this up and be late, because Finn hates it when I'm late, and she'll stomp and fold her arms and pout all afternoon and make a whole meal out of it with her mom. So I'm watching over my shoulder, hoping Charlotte doesn't figure out about me jackin' her phone, come running after me, and hold things up.

When Finn was born, she had to be hooked up to breathing machines, and had all these wires and tubes sticking into her tiny arms and nose, making her look more like a newborn hamster/evil science experiment than a human baby. Cole and me, we just stood there with our faces pressed against the glass partition they had to protect her from the outside world—the two of us standing in that hospital hallway, staring at her in that bassinet as those machines pushed air into her lungs.

Then Cole, he told me he'd give Finn his lungs if he could. And I believed him, 'cause I felt it too. Like, even though she was barely a week old and wasn't even my real sister, I wanted to break through that glass and protect her from all the bad stuff life was shoveling at her. So I told Cole that if he gave Finn both of his lungs he would die, and that was messed up, because kids need a lot more to get by in this world than just air. Then I told him that it would be way smarter if him and me both gave her *one* of our lungs. That way, all three of us would live and Finn would still have a best friend *and* a brother.

We were only twelve then and pretty much didn't know how things worked in this world, but Cole agreed with me that him not dying and Finn still getting two working lungs seemed like a much better option—and he acted like me offering up my lung like that was plain old normal. And that's how it felt to me too. Just plain old normal. So that was the plan me and Cole made right after Finnegan Shay Wilder was born: one lung from him and one from me.

A few months after that, Cole's dad left because he couldn't take it anymore. Working two jobs and having a sick kid, he explained to Cole's mom, was just too much for him, plain and simple. Cole's mom told that to Cole, and he told it to me, and I thought, *It's plain and simple, all right.*

Even back then, I figure I loved Finn as much as Cole did, so I couldn't understand how her dad could up and leave like that—like that baby hamster didn't need him more than air itself. Then when my dad died a year later, three days after my thirteenth birthday, the way I saw it, girls like us—girls without fathers, like Nell Bannon and Finn Wilder—we needed to look out for each other.

Finn is five now and looks totally healthy on the outside, but she still has something wrong with her lungs, so from three to six on Mondays and Fridays it's my job to make sure she doesn't stop breathing. Most of the time, she's just fine, like a regular kid, but sometimes she isn't, and the not-breathing thing comes on fast. The doctors say that fresh air is good for her, so on the days I watch her, if it's not raining or icy cold, I take her to the park, where there's lots of fresh air, at least if you don't count all the thick exhaust from the semis that roll by on the interstate and the black puffs of smoke that billow from the stacks down by the river.

Mrs. Wilder keeps telling Cole that what Finn has is asthma, but he thinks she's lying and it's something way worse. I figure he's right, 'cause lots of kids have asthma and they didn't start out in life like Finn did, hooked up to machines and looking like newborn-hamster lab experiments.

But me and Cole go back to way before Finn was born. All the way back to the first day of kindergarten. He showed up wearing brand-new red sneakers that day, and when we were alone in the cubbies I told him that boys can't wear red shoes. And then I stole his snack. The thing is, he let me get away with it. He didn't even know me, and he said absolutely nothing as I ate his animal crackers. The next day, he brought two bags of animal crackers and handed me one of them. He leaned in close, looking all serious, pointing past the rain boots and lunch boxes to the other kids in our class, and whispered, "Remember, Nell, it's you and me against the rest of 'em." And he was so convincing that I nodded slowly.

The thing was, I had stolen snacks before—from lots of kids at preschool and the babysitter—and they all got mad and cried or told on me. But Cole, he was different. He brought me animal crackers and cut-up carrots and cheesy orange Goldfish every single day for the whole year, and then watched me eat them. Him saying stuff like, "It's us against them, Nell," and "Special things are coming for us."

Looking back, I figure that the wheels were turning in his head even then, 'cause Cole Wilder already knew that me and him would make a good team going forward.

I didn't know what was coming, but apparently the wheels were turning in my head too, 'cause I'd already figured out that I needed people I could count on. And Cole, he fit the bill.

+ + + + + + +

After I hit my locker, I'm heading out the front doors of Clawson High School, the ones that open onto the turnaround where all the buses pull in, when Stevie B chases me down, looking for a ride. I keep walking and swatting at him like he's a pesky horsefly on a hot summer day, but he bear-hugs me from behind and picks me up, twirls me around, then hands me a picture he drew of Cole looking like a badass dragon. Sort of like Fin Fang Foom but wearing a dress. I take a look and tell him he has a real special power to be able to draw like that and he should listen to the teachers who are telling him to apply to art school. But he ignores me outright and crumples the picture up, then changes the subject by promising to buy King Frosties for me and Finn at the Perky Queen up on Route 102 if I'll drop him off at Mason's Hardware, where his dad works.

Stevie B draws comics mostly. Not villains like Fin Fang Foom or superheroes like Captain America and Spidey, just regular everyday people without universes or metropolises to annihilate or save. Characters he makes up himself. They're pretty much normal, so they don't do much but they have special powers. Like they can shoot flames out of their fingertips, or teleport to far-off places, or blow shit up with their minds.

When Cole's not around, sometimes Stevie B draws pictures of him as a villainous antihero, with evil fire eyes and spools of drool and dragon spikes and heinous crab claws like he's a part dragon/part human mutant. And he draws me in this Wonder Woman outfit, with a winged helmet and cute little horns, and says he'd give me *all* of the superpowers, not just one—that is, if he was in charge of doling them out. Like I'd get a whole basketful of powers if I got radiated, or landed here from another planet, or the pencil-toting gods of comics were handing out ray-gun fingers and laser-light eyes willy-nilly, just for fun, and he could pick who got what.

I told Stevie B once there's only one superpower I'd want: a giant magnet to hold on to people to keep them from slipping away. He looked at me long and hard after that. You know, like he wanted to say something or do something but he didn't know what or how. So he just said, "Nell" in that way of his, and I turned away.

+ + + + + + +

When we're driving toward Finn's school, I ask Stevie B if he knows where Cole went.

He says, "Probably nowhere, Nell. It's just Cole sulkin', is all."

"Learn anything more about the new girl?" I try.

"I learned a ton," he says. "They handed out her bio in shop class, with pictures and everything. Mr. Heller spent a whole hour going over the details. Said there's gonna be a quiz on it tomorrow."

"So that would be a no, then."

He reaches over and squeezes my neck. "Yes, Nell. That would be a no on the new-girl intel." Then he asks me what's in the bag at his feet.

"Take a look," I say, smiling.

"A butterfly net?" he asks after he pulls it from the bag.

"That's right, but me and Finn are gonna use it to catch something way bigger."

"Something way bigger, like"—he raises his arms above his head and starts beastly growling and scary hooting—"a monster, maybe?"

"The moon," I tell him sternly. "It's a moon-catching net, Stevie B. Not a monster-catching net. Now, don't go scaring her. She's five."

"Finn'll actually believe that?"

"Damn straight she'll believe it," I tell him, and I think about the poem I read to Finn when she can't sleep—the one about making a moon-catchin' net. I don't normally read poems, but I swear, reading that one out loud is more like tasting words made of spun sugar than any normal poem I've ever read, and Finn just plain old loves it too.

+ + + + + + +

When we pull up in front of Westbrook Elementary, Finn's standing outside in the pickup area, wearing a pink ballerina tutu with cowboy boots and a silver tiara. Stevie B asks, "What the hell is that costume?" Then he pulls out a piece of paper and a pencil from his backpack and starts sketching, and I tell him to keep his mouth shut about her outfit. Before I hop out of my truck to fetch her, I grab the pink-and-purple moon catcher and tell him to keep his mouth shut about monsters too.

A few minutes later, when the three of us are sitting in front of the Perky Queen slurping our King Frosty shakes, Finn stands up on the bench and starts swooping her net, announcing that she's gonna try to catch the sun. It's not three minutes before she plops down on the ground complaining, "It's too high up, Nell."

"That's a good thing," I say, "'cause the sun is way too hot to hook on a day like this, and too big for a normal person to hold on to anyway."

Finn has a high ponytail that's slipped halfway down in a sloppy blond mess, and her lips are ringed in chocolate, making her look both ridiculous and adorable. But her expression is flat-out heart-crushingly disappointed, so I add, "But there are plenty of pixies worth catching."

"What kind of pixies?" she asks.

"The four-inch-tall invisible kind."

She glances around the parking lot. "So like fairies, then?"

"Exactly like fairies, just better, 'cause they're smaller and can fit in your pockets."

She checks her sweatshirt for pockets, and Stevie B rolls his eyes, so I smack him. But Finn apparently buys the whole thing, 'cause she sets off with her net on a pixie hunt, calling back over to me, "Where are they, Nell?"

"Over there and there . . ." I start random pointing, adding, "They're mostly in the shade under the picnic tables. And watch out, 'cause they're fast."

She bends down and swoops. "Got one!"

"Stick it in your pocket and find some more," I instruct. "And make sure you stay where I can see you."

Finn spends fifteen minutes or so scrunched down peering under the tables, swooping her net, and talking to herself before she climbs onto my lap all bright-eyed and flushed, and I ask, "How many did you get?"

"Fourteen."

"Fourteen? That's probably a Perky Queen record."

She then slowly takes all fourteen of her pretend pixies out of her pockets and lines them up on the table before announcing, "They're hungry, Nell."

I give her pretend pixie food, and Stevie B rolls his eyes again, and I elbow him. And it turns into a whole thing of flying elbows and silliness until I ask Finn, "How about I take you on a moon hunt this Saturday night before me and Cole go out?"

"For real?"

"Yes, for real."

"After it's dark?"

"Of course, after it's dark."

"With the net?"

"Absolutely with the net."

"Can the pixies come?"

"No way. We have to leave them here."

"How come?" she asks, looking disappointed again.

"This is where they live, Finn. So you leave the pixies here, and you and me, we'll go moon hunting in the dark on Saturday. Deal?"

"Deal."

Me and Finn do our special high-five, low-five, thumbs-up, fist-bump handshake, both of us getting most of it wrong. Then I show her the picture Stevie B drew earlier, with her wearing the pink tutu with angel wings and cowboy boots, and she practically has lightning bolts shooting out of her eyes when she sees it. I give Stevie B the elbow again and nod toward Finn, and he gets to see how happy he made her before she loses interest in the picture and starts blowing into her straw to make bubbles in her shake.

"Hey, don't do that," I warn. "It's too noisy." Me making up an excuse because I'm worried she'll run out of air and stop breathing.

Finn does as she's told and goes back to talking to her pretend pixies and feeding them invisible pixie food, and I ask Stevie B, "How is it that you can afford to buy three of these shakes?"

He looks at me all smiley, like he's got a secret. "I don't have to pay, Nell," he says, and then he glances over at the girl behind the counter at the Perky Queen, with this sweet look on his face. I think to myself, *Stevie B and me have life skills. We just didn't learn any of them in Ms. Daniels's class.*

"Should I be jealous?" I rib, poking him in his side.

"You have nothing to worry about, Nell. I'll always love you the most."

He says that and I know he means it.

Stevie B didn't take it too well when me and Cole made it official, so I feel bad and lean in close and kiss his cheek, and it happens before I realize that wasn't the best idea under the circumstances.

"Any chance I can get a second serving of that, Nell?" he asks, and he looks downright adorable when he says it.

So I try to change the subject by jabbing him in the side again and asking, "Can you keep a secret?"

"What kind of secret are we talking about?"

I think about everything that happened today. About how weird Cole acted about knowing the new girl and about that necklace she was wearing—how I've seen it before. Then I feel her cell phone pressing against my calf when I say, "I don't know just yet, but I suspect not the good kind."

4

That's when I show Stevie B Charlotte's phone. Me saying, "Now, don't judge me," as I pull it out of my boot, and him saying, "Aw, come on, Nell!" as soon as he sees it. "Now why'd you go and do that?"

He sighs and acts all annoyed and uncomfortable before I even get the screen open—but not annoyed enough to not look, 'cause he's staring over my shoulder the whole time. "How'd you get the passcode?" he asks.

"I grabbed it when I watched her send a text in Ms. Daniels's class."

I was expecting to get a glimpse into her past life by reading her messages and looking at pictures of her friends, but that's not what we find. Me and Stevie B, we kind of just scroll through—me not saying anything more than "Huh," and Stevie B making noises and fidgeting and looking around the whole time, like Charlotte might show up at the Perky Queen and catch us.

Then the phone pings with a text message, and we both jump.

Stevie B blurts out, "It's from Cole, Nell." Like I don't see his

26

name sitting right there on Charlotte's phone. Me and Stevie B keep staring at that message like reading it a thousand times might change something about what it says or who it's from. We don't say anything more for the longest time, until the quiet gets too hard to listen to and he mumbles, "Why do you think he's meeting her tonight by the quarry?"

I say, "I have no idea," then I sketch out a whole detailed plan for what me and Stevie B are gonna do about it.

When I put Charlotte's phone away a few minutes later, neither one of us says anything more about it one way or the other. But then when Stevie B hops out of the truck in front of Mason's Hardware, he says, "Ask him, Nell. Ask Cole. There has to be an explanation."

I'm thinking, *There's always an explanation. It's just not always one you're gonna like.* But I don't say that; I nod. And then he turns to Finn and does this whole moose-antler thing with his fingers wagging on top of his head and his tongue sticking out.

After he walks off, I see his sketchbook sittin' on the floor of the truck, and I call out the window, "Hold on," as the door to the store closes behind him. Finn asking, "What's wrong, Nellie?" Me saying, "It's nothing. He forgot his sketchbook. I can give it to him later." And then I toss it on the back seat and put the radio on, and Finn starts singing along with Taylor Swift as we drive toward the park.

Halfway through the song, Finn stops singing and calls out, "He drew every picture the same, Nell," and I glance in the rearview mirror. She's holding Stevie B's sketchbook, flipping through the pages, getting chalk all over her fingers, so I say, "Put that down, Finn. He doesn't like people looking at his stuff," but I'm mostly thinking about how she's breathing in all that chalk dust and that can't be good. Then she announces, "He drew a hundred million trillion pictures of you, Nell."

I peek at her again, and she nods, with her little red face busting out a Christmas morning smile, as I try to convince myself that Stevie B drawing a hundred million trillion pictures of me doesn't mean anything.

Finn puts the sketchbook down like I told her to and goes back to singing along with the radio as I turn left on Bellmont.

Not two minutes later, I spot Cole's truck in my rearview mirror. He's right up behind me in no time, waving and riding my bumper, leaning on his horn, trying to get me to pull over. I ease onto the side of the road, and he pulls up behind me, kicking up sand, as I put the old truck my daddy left me in neutral and shut the engine down.

Cole shows up on the passenger side and hops into the front, all breathless and sweaty, and then he kisses me in a way he never kisses me in front of Finn—or anyone else, for that matter.

Him slowly running his fingers over the rose-colored heart-shaped birthmark sitting just under my collarbone when the kiss ends and whispering, "You're my one in a million, Nell."

My eyes scream, *What's going on, Cole?*

But he doesn't offer an explanation; he just says, "Give it back."

My head is still spinnin' dizzy from that kiss as I try to figure out what he wants me to give back, 'cause it doesn't seem possible that he could know about me jacking that girl's phone already.

"It's not yours, Nell," he whispers in my ear. "Please give it to me."

When I don't say anything or make a move to give him something, Cole starts to frisk me, searching the pockets of my sweatshirt and jeans so slowly that it feels . . . Well, I don't know *what* it feels like, but I lift my hands up like I'm saying *What the hell?* Or maybe *Please don't stop.* I'm not sure which, because the whole thing is weird and confusing, and honestly, it's kind of pissing me off and kind of hot too.

Then *he* starts smiling and *I* start smiling, and he says, "I guess we have to keep doing this my way." He dumps my backpack out on the floor and forages through the keys and pencils and coins. I yell, "Hey, hold on! Watch the food!" And I realize that he surely knows about the phone I lifted, which doesn't seem possible but somehow is.

"I'll trade you for it," I whisper, with my face close to his.

Normally, I would have made a move to kiss him right about now, but Finn is here watching us, and besides, I'm pretty sure we're smack in the middle of something that's shaping up to be a fight. And then he says, "This isn't a game, Nellie."

So I inch away and lean against the truck door to buy some time to think. "Sure feels like one, Cole."

Finn starts kicking the seat and whining, "Hey, Cole! Look what I have!" and I'm afraid she's gonna hold up Stevie B's sketchbook with all those drawings of me and open up a whole new snake pit full of trouble. Cole knows how Stevie B feels about me, so I figure those pictures won't land well. But Finn ignores the sketchbook and picks up her doll in one hand and the moon-catchin' net in the other, then tells Cole that the Perky Queen has a hundred million trillion pixies living under the picnic tables.

I figure Cole's gonna ask me what a pixie is, but he doesn't. Instead, he asks, "What do you want to trade for it?" Like maybe he's reconsidered and thinking that trading's not such a bad idea after all.

I say, "Information."

He traces his fingers over my lips, and his face gets dark. "I can't do that," he says all hushed and quiet-like, and he looks real sad about sayin' it.

"Yes, you can, Cole. You just don't want to."

When he doesn't comment one way or the other, I ask, "What's going on here, Cole?" and there's this shift in his eyes.

All of a sudden I feel fear creep in like a swamp fog that leaves you so blind you can't see the very ground you're standing on. Then I have a flash of what me and Stevie B found on that girl's phone and it messes with my head and heart, and I'm sitting here wondering how a person—a normal person like me—can be both angry and not angry with another person at the same exact time. Me wondering how that can possibly be. It's like somehow love got mixed with hurt, and in a way that threatens to implode, like a building collapse in an earthquake.

So I have this fear all coiled up, and it's not the good kind of fear that comes with a hefty dose of excitement—like the time I was about to jump off the ledge at the quarry but then full-on chickened out in front of everyone. That time I was scared, but excited too. But the kind of scared I'm feeling right now has no excitement attached to it. It's just raw fear, stripped down to nothing else.

5

That quarry jump was just over two years ago—the summer before tenth grade. Most of the other kids were older, but still, I was the only one who didn't jump that day, so I got taunted real bad. When Cole caught up with me as I headed for home, me feeling embarrassed and bad about myself, he told me to meet him later that night so he could teach me how to jump. So I snuck out after lights-out and met him on the dirt path that runs behind our houses. He grabbed my hand, and we pounded down the path with the moon shining bright overhead, lighting our way. When we got to the edge of the rocks above the quarry, the water looked even farther down than I'd remembered. It was black with little slips of silver dancing on the top, and Cole confided that his whole life he'd had nightmares about drowning but he'd managed to muster the courage to jump, so somehow that meant that I could too. Then he promised it was safe and he would hold me tight the whole way down, if I was brave enough to let him.

"What about that kid who died jumping?" I asked him, and he

said, "That's not real, Nell. It's just some old story kids made up to scare other kids."

I knew he was lying, 'cause my parents went to school with that dead kid and so did Cole's. I'd seen his picture and knew his name—Levi Tanner—but Cole was so convincing and I figured he meant well, so I let it go. Then we both kicked off our sneakers and ditched our phones, and he told me we would jump together and it would be okay and he would keep me safe. He said, "I will hold you and keep you safe forever," and I believed him so fiercely that I wrapped my arms around his back and hitched my legs up around his waist and squished my eyes closed tight. And Levi Tanner, that dead kid my parents knew, was the last thing on my mind, because when Cole jumped off that ledge holding me like that, I felt the safest I'd ever felt in my entire life.

When we crashed through the surface of the water, we were surrounded by pitch black and icy cold and my lungs burned like they were gonna bust wide open—but I still felt safe as we fired down deep. And I felt full of excitement as we swam back up to the surface in a pool of murky water and rising bubbles. After we broke through to the night air and took a few breaths, we circled around each other as the water licked at our skin and those slips of silver moonlight danced on the surface like minnows, and Cole kissed me for the first time. My lips were shivering, his soft and warm, and my heart, it took me places I'd never been before. That kiss made me start to think that maybe I'd been wrong, that maybe there was magic and fizz and sparkly glitter in this life after all. And that shimmering and glitter just might be Cole.

But right now, he's sittin' here in my truck, asking me about Charlotte's phone, and he's not the least bit sparkly, and he's not promising me anything, and he's not making me feel safe. He's confusing me. I reach down with my hand trembling and pull that phone out from the inside of my left boot, where I'd stashed it again after me and Stevie B went through it.

"When you take stuff, Cole, you don't hide it in an obvious place like your pockets or backpack. *You* taught me that. Those are the first places the cops'll look. And you checked my pockets and bag, so what's going on here?"

He doesn't answer; he just takes the phone from me, looks at it for a minute, then hands me a big folded envelope. "I was going to give you this on Saturday, Nellie. But here. You should have it now."

I hesitate, then take it. "So this is the trade? The new girl's phone for what's in this envelope?"

He kind of shrugs.

"Will it explain anything?"

When he doesn't answer, I say, "I guess that's a no, then," and pull open the envelope.

Inside is a passport, with a smooth blue cover. "How much?" I ask, my voice so soft it's almost inaudible.

"Five bucks," he says. "On eBay."

I start flipping through the pages. "How many countries?"

"Twenty-seven."

"Any good ones?"

"They're all good ones, Nell."

Before I stick the passport into my knapsack, I think about all the places me and Cole have fantasized about traveling to after we graduate—both of us knowing full well we're not going anywhere. Then I mumble, "Thanks," not really meaning it under the circumstances, and in a flash, there are hot flames licking at the moment, pushing me to fight back.

Now, I know I shouldn't yell and curse in front of Finn, but I do it anyway. "What the hell, Cole! You can't kiss me like that and look at me like that, and then give me some stranger's expired passport you bought on eBay as a trade for that girl's phone like everything is normal! Tell me something, anything, about what's going on with you and her!"

He leans over and hugs me so tight I think I might break. Then he whispers, "I love you, Nell. I've loved you forever. You know that. But I can't tell you anything right now. I want to, real bad, but I can't." Then Cole Wilder says, "It'll be over in a few days," and I damn near lose the breath in my lungs.

I manage to ask, "What'll be over in a few days, Cole?"

But he doesn't answer; he just kisses me again. And we're right back to confusing and messed up, 'cause I'm hot-piss mad at him and hot-piss mad in love with him at the same time, and he's not explaining a damn thing.

6

After Cole takes off, I drive Finn straight to the park. And when we get there, I look through Stevie B's sketchbook. Finn's standing next to me in the parking lot, holding on to my leg and whining the whole time about how I just told her Stevie B doesn't like people looking at his pictures, so I tell her that didn't mean me.

I flip through the book, and she's right about him drawing a hundred million trillion pictures of me—they're mesmerizing too. Every last one of them. I mean, I can't explain it, but it's *me* on those pages, just different. Better, I suppose, and it sends my heart thumping. I look beautiful and vulnerable, and something else . . . Strong, I guess. Or . . . brave, maybe? They look private too—like he sees my thoughts or caught me when no one was supposed to be looking.

I'm thinking, *He shouldn't be able to see me that way.* And I'm thinking, *I'm glad he sees me that way.* It's like he drew the outside of me but captured what's inside.

I know that as much as I love Cole—have *always* loved Cole— sometimes I look at Stevie B looking at me, *seeing* me like he does, and I think I love him so much too. Then I get mad at myself, 'cause that's messed up.

But Finn's here stretching my name out thin, like a piece of putty. "Nelllll . . ."

So I say, "Whaaaaat?" feeling guilty that I was thinking about Stevie B like that even for a second.

"The swings," she reminds me.

So I put the sketchbook down and lock up the truck, but I'm still thinking about those pictures the whole time I'm pushing her on the swing, wondering if me and Cole and Stevie B are gonna end up in some kind of lifelong love triangle—'cause I don't see me and Cole ever breaking up and I don't see Stevie B ever not being in love with me, so that seems like the only option. And the entire time I'm imagining how heartbreaking and awkward that whole thing would be, I'm trying to teach Finn how to pump her legs, and she's making it entirely clear that she straight-up prefers my arms doing the work.

But then I hear her wheeze and see her color turn from rosy to a pale white that I fear is headed toward slate blue, "Like Vermont patio stone," I heard Cole's mom describe it once when Finn stopped breathing altogether. So I start slowing the swing down, heart racing toward panic, trying to hold on to the hope that nothing bad is happening.

"Finn, how you doing?" I ask. "'Cause I spy a pixie."

But she doesn't answer; she just looks scared—like she knows what's coming—her one hand clutching the swing, her other reaching out to me, her skirt a cloud of pink tulle floating around her waist.

When I lift her from the swing, she burrows in tight to my chest, and I feel her cold face against my warm neck and hear the wheeze in her lungs rattling and growing deeper, and I know we're in trouble.

"Sisters aren't supposed to do that," Cole said to me that first time he saw it happen.

"Do what?" I'd asked him.

"Stop breathing."

At the time, Finn was only a few months old, and even though I was just a kid, I knew that most stuff didn't work the way it was supposed to. I'd seen so much messed-up stuff by that age—kids going hungry and people overdosing and livin' on the streets, and women dressed up fancy visiting men living out their lives at the prison—that I couldn't imagine a world where everything worked the way it was supposed to instead of being all fucked-up and broke. So babies not breathing right kind of made sense to me even back then.

I'm already fumbling to get my phone out when Finn's breathing gets even worse, so I go ahead and dial 911, asking for an ambulance to be sent to the kids' playground at the corner of Elm and Washington, just like Mrs. Wilder instructed me to. "Don't wait," she always says. "Call for help the moment Finn has trouble breathing." Me telling the operator as calmly as I can, so as not to scare Finn, "I have a five-year-old who's having trouble breathing. Meet us by the blue pickup in the main parking lot." Then I start to run toward my truck, leaving the line open, Finn clutched tight in my arms.

I lay her down on the grass, race over to get her inhaler, then struggle to unzip her backpack, saying, "Come on! Come on!" as the dispatcher's asking me questions I'm not answering. I'm scared out of my mind that I can't do this. That Finn Wilder is one more thing I can't fix.

"Okay," I say, holding her head up and handing her the inhaler. When she puts it in her mouth, I say, "Good girl. Inhale on the puff," my heart thump-thumping, my voice screaming inside my head, *Do not do this, Finn! Do not die! Breathe!*

Two puffs, and she's lying there on the grass with her eyes closed, breathing a little better—maybe. I can't tell for sure.

When the ambulance finally pulls in, siren screaming, everything happens so fast. The EMTs firing off questions and hooking Finn up to all sorts of equipment.

I text Cole and his mom while Finn gets loaded into the ambulance. Her with an IV in her arm and a mask over her face, machines beeping away as I climb into the back and we hightail it toward Clawson General.

When we pull in, I see Cole pacing back and forth on the sidewalk at the entrance to the ER. Then the hospital doors come flying open and doctors and nurses rush outside as the EMTs unload the gurney. I catch Cole's eye as I climb out of the ambulance, and he holds his hands up close to his heart in a prayer position, like he's thanking me, then he runs alongside Finn as they rush her through the doors.

When I enter the ER, the EMTs are still yelling out stuff as they push the gurney into an exam room, and Cole's holding on to Finn's hand firing off questions I figure no one's ready to answer.

One of the nurses takes his arm and pulls him back as I hurry over in time to hear her say, "Please step aside and let them work."

Then Cole stops to hug me hard, him whispering, "Nell, no. This can't be happening! Not now. Not like this."

The nurse tries to calm him down, saying, "Let's have you two wait over here, out of the way." Her guiding us toward the waiting area as she adds, "I'll get you an update as soon as we know what's going on." Then she studies Cole carefully. "You've been here with Finn before. You're family?"

"Brother," he confirms as he sinks down into a seat.

She turns to me. "Friend," I report, which feels somehow wrong and not enough.

"And your mom? Mrs. Wilder, right?" she asks Cole.

"She's still thirty minutes out."

"Okay, no problem. We'll take good care of Finn. I promise. Now, you two wait here and let me see what I can find out for you."

After she leaves, Cole asks, "How bad was it, Nell?"

I look at my boots caked in playground mud. "Same as last time."

"So she didn't lose consciousness?"

"No. She was awake the whole time."

"You sure?"

"Yeah. I'm sure."

"That's good, then."

"Yeah. That's good."

"You must have been so scared, Nell. I'm sorry. Real sorry about—"

I stop him right there. "Cole, look at me. I was okay. Honest. And I'm okay now. Finn's okay now too." I add, "She was real brave. Put on her bossy pants and took charge and got me through the whole thing."

I tell him that, and I'm full-on lying, but it's worth it because I see it: the little creep of the almost smile on Cole's face that sets the world right.

One of the doctors comes over, and Cole jumps up. "Finn's stable now and breathing on her own, so that's good," he tells us. "But we're still doing tests and we'll be admitting her."

Cole looks relieved. And I feel relief too. Like maybe if they keep her here, she won't die tonight. And maybe if they do enough tests, they'll figure something out. But then Cole says, "This keeps happening, and you keep saving her but not fixing her. Why can't you just fix her lungs for good?"

The doctor looks like he wants to help and say more but knows he can't do either. "Look, since you're not Finn's legal guardian, I can't tell you anything else. But I promise we are doing everything we can for your sister."

When the doctor leaves, I hold out my empty hand for Cole saying, "Here. Take this," explaining, "It's an invisible pixie I stole for Finn from the Perky Queen. She'll know what that means." Then I whisper, "One lung from me . . ."

And Cole, his eyes well up and he scoops that invisible pixie from the thin air above my hand and puts it into his shirt pocket before he hugs me and says, "And one lung from me."

+ + + + + + + +

As I watch him walk over to the nurses' station, I have a whole bunch of messed-up feelings. I'm flooded with love and fear, then guilt rushes in when I think about Stevie B being in love with me and what I was thinking about earlier. Then Cole leans over the desk as he talks to those nurses and I feel a warm rush as I have a flashback to the first day of English this past September when Ms. Ellison closed the door and took her place in front of the class. How everyone settled down waiting for her speech explaining that somehow *this* year and *this* class were gonna be special, but Cole kept standing in front of my desk like class hadn't even started.

I whispered, "Cole, you have to sit down," and he said, "No." Him standing there with a hint of that I-don't-play-by-the-rules smile of his when I asked, "Why not?" And he said, "I like the view from here."

I didn't know that words could have heat and swagger until Cole Wilder showed me that they could. And I didn't know that they could spark and catch, then burn a girl to the ground, either. But the way I figure it, Cole's been burning me to the ground since we were in middle school like I was a highly combustible, timber-frame barn.

"Mr. Wilder, take your seat, please," Ms. Ellison called out that day like she meant it, but Cole still didn't move. He just put his hands down and leaned over my desk, his back still facing the front of the room.

"Do you have something you'd like to share with the rest of the class before we begin today, Mr. Wilder?" Ms. Ellison asked, but Cole stood his ground, statue still, and said nothing.

I whispered, "Cole, don't. We can talk later." Me, feeling all the eyes on us like they had the grip of fingers and the certainty of fists, but Cole never cares who's watching or what they think, he just speaks his heart and lives in the treasure box of the seconds he pulls out of nowhere and claims for himself. "Say it," he whispered, and I breathed, "Say what?" even though I knew *what* 'cause he'd been asking me to "say it" over and over again ever since he spoke those words to me at the quarry two nights earlier. Then Cole dropped down and leaned his forearms on my desk and said, "It is . . ."

"We are . . .," I uttered back, all breathy and warm like the two of us were the only people left in the whole world.

"Mr. Wilder? Loop us in, why don't you?" Ms. Ellison said as me and Cole stared into each other's eyes and the earth stopped spinning and those seconds ticked silently by.

Cole straightened up, then shifted to face Ms. Ellison partway, but he kept his eyes on mine the whole time, pinning me with his gaze, and I surrendered without a fight. I couldn't have broken free if I'd wanted to. And I didn't want to. Not when I found myself lightheaded and dizzy and not when he finally blinked and his hair fell in front of his eyes and I had my only real chance to turn away. I was done in; pinned shoulders to the mat by the full force of Cole's eyes that stole my breath and made my heart beat entirely too fast, then skip a few measures altogether.

"Cole, don't," I eventually managed to say. But inside I wanted him to.

And he did. He declared it for the whole class to hear. "It is, we are, seventeen . . ."

Then Cole paused.

Ellison prodded, "Go on . . ."

And Cole started over again, then he kept going as heat rose from my heart to my cheeks as he recited those words. "It is, we are, seventeen, like a song; musical notes and lyrics that go so perfectly together they should never be played if not side by side, or one on top of the other."

When Cole finished, he just stood there and dead silence filled the empty space, followed by a hoot and a whistle from somewhere in the back of the room before Ellison asked, "Who wrote that?" her arms now folded across her chest and a confused look plastered on her face. Her staring down the boy with the fearless heart and the fancy words, the too long hair, ripped jeans, and beat-up work boots.

"I did," Cole informed her as he finally took his seat. "I wrote those words for Nell."

So that's what I'm thinking about as I watch Cole talking to those nurses. I'm thinking about how he can pin me with his eyes then burn me to the ground with the heat and swagger of his words. I'm thinking about how he always says that the two of us fit together so perfectly that he can't imagine life without me. Him sayin' we're some law of nature not even God'll mess with— that what we have is love, or energy maybe, or hope or promise or loyalty or time, or all of that, somehow stitched together as one featherlight enormous thing. I'm thinking about how Cole Wilder told me that whatever it is that we have between us, it can't be contained with letters or words or a universe such as this, and it's something that can never be explained. And as I watch one of the nurses take him in to see Finn a few minutes later, that nurse holding up her hand saying, "Family only," and bruising my heart when I hop up and try to go in with them, I'm thinking real hard about the fact that I can't bear the thought of losing one more person I love.

Not Finn Wilder.

Not my mom.

Not Stevie B.

And never, ever, Cole.

7

I get a ride back to the park to pick up my truck, and Stevie B is in my room, sitting on my bed, when I get home.

"What are you doing here?" I ask, wondering why he didn't show up at the hospital, 'cause he usually does.

"Just hanging out and rifling through your stuff, Nell. Looking for something I can steal."

"Like my prize rock collection?" I tease as I pull my sweatshirt off.

"Something like that," he says, leaning back on the bed, watching me.

"I brought you these." He hands me a little bakery box from Bag of Buns.

I light up. "Ginger snickerdoodles?"

"Always," he says, and he's watching me with that face of his that breaks my heart.

"How many?" I ask, peeking into the box.

"How many did I buy? Or how many are left?"

I smile and bite into a cookie.

"How's Finn?" he asks.

"Better. But they're keeping her in the hospital overnight."

"How bad was it?"

"Scary shit show. EMTs took forever to get there." I almost say, *I thought Finn was gonna die.* But I don't. I see his face and go with, "They say she's gonna be okay. Cole's with her. So's Mrs. Wilder."

Stevie B looks relieved.

"Thought you'd show up to check on us after I texted you."

"Got stuck at the store. My dad had me doing inventory."

I plop down next to him on the bed. Then I blurt out, "I have your sketchbook. You left it in my truck."

He freezes. I feel weird.

"I tried to tell you. I called your name when you were headed into the store, but you didn't hear me."

He acts all embarrassed. "Did you look inside?"

"What? No. Why would I . . . ? It's still in my truck. You can grab it on your way out."

"Okay . . . But you didn't look, right?" he asks again, studying my face.

And I flat-out lie. "Nope . . . I told you. I didn't look." Then I walk over, pick up a photo from my desk, and hand it to him.

He studies it carefully. It's an enlarged close-up of a man's face. "Name?"

"Don't know."

"Crime?"

"Triple homicide."

The man looks like a hardened killer. Big set jaw. Teardrop tattoo slipping down under his right eye. White skin, tanned like leather. Nose broken more than once. But his eyes look soft, almond-shaped and sad.

"Your mom got it for you?" he asks.

"Yep. She still thinks it's creepy that I want them, but she got it from work."

He inhales sharp and quick, then looks up at the photos I've glued on the wall, starting near my bedroom door and snaking around my room at waist height. Old pictures of inmates my mom gets from Manville Correctional Facility. All of them alone. In their cells. Peering out from behind bars. Or standing against the peeling cinder-block walls, or out in the yard beneath barbed-wire fences. I enlarge some of their faces on the copier at school to make their eyes extra-big—so big that after I cut those eyes out and paste them onto the wall they seem to follow me as I walk around my bedroom.

I started doing it last year, and when Stevie B first saw it, he said, "You're designing a wallpaper border out of prisoners' eyeballs." It wasn't a question.

I told him it was eyeballs *and* whole prisoners, and he said, "No, it's mostly eyeballs."

He had a point. The whole-person pictures are bigger, but the eyeballs are what devour you. They shred your soul, then gobble you up like they have teeth.

He says, "You do know that this inmate-eyeball decorating theme is super weird and super creepy and super freaking me out, right?"

I nod. "Duly noted. Creeps me out too."

"So why are you doing it, Nell?" He hands the picture back.

I think about what Cole said when he saw it—that I was building myself a prison. But I say, "No clue. No apologies." Then I ask, "Did she give you a hard time?"

He seems to think about that for a bit. Like maybe he's not sure we're done with the previous topic, but he eventually says, "I used Cole's entrance, to avoid her."

Cole's entrance being the window, and *her* being my mom. She's not a big fan of me having friends over, always saying something like *Working at the prison is no picnic, Nell. I've got stuff on my mind, and I need peace and quiet.* So I stopped asking.

I know a big part of that stuff on her mind is my daddy dying and her needing to take care of me and her alone, so I try to give her what she wants, by staying out of her hair. But she pretty much killed any chance we had at making it when she got addicted to the painkillers her doc gave her. I've been real worried about that, because lately, like most of the other things in my life, I don't figure it's gonna end well.

"You and your mom," Stevie B says, "you okay?"

"Okay enough, I guess."

"She gonna make it, Nell?" he asks softly.

"Is who gonna make it? Finn or my mom? 'Cause I'm a tiny bit confused right now, what with the fact that everyone who's ever loved me is dead or dying."

He whispers, "Not everyone, Nell," and I feel bad for being mean. So I toss in, "I know that, Stevie B," even though I want to tell him what I just said *is* true. Everyone who loves me, everyone *I* love, is dead or seems to be headed there on the express train. Maybe not Stevie B and Cole, but my grandma, my dad, and now my mom . . . Finn maybe.

"I couldn't save my dad," I say. "My grandma either. But my mom . . ."

"You can't blame yourself for your mom's drug—"

"I know that," I say.

"Sounds like you saved Finn today. That's something, Nell."

What I don't tell him is that I almost *didn't* save her . . . And that little kids shouldn't need saving in the first place. And that family is supposed to be forever. Family *promises* to be forever. But forever isn't real. And my family is . . . Well, there's a whole bunch of words that would work.

Fucked up . . .

Going . . .

Gone.

And definitely not forever.

"Cole knows," I say, desperate to change the subject.

"About you being afraid of your mom dying?" he asks. "Or about you stealing the new girl's phone?" Then his voice gets as soft as a hum when he adds, "Or about me still being in love with you?"

I smile. "The second one."

"So the phone, then?"

I shrug, then smile a little wider. "And the first one." I catch his eye. "And the third one too."

"Is he mad?"

"Practically ran me off the road chasing it down."

"Did you tell him what we found on it?"

"Nope. He wasn't in the mood for talking, just for getting it back. He gave me this, though." I pull the envelope out of my bag and hand it to him.

Stevie B peers inside, and his shoulders fall. "You sure this is legal?"

"Like I keep saying, it's a gray area. But people buy and sell them all the time."

He looks up, worried. I shrug, then give him the same spiel I've given him all the other times he's asked if it was legal. "If a passport's been expired for more than fifteen years, then selling them and buying them is kind of okay."

"Kind of okay?"

"Yeah. That's the general consensus. Kind of okay."

"What's her name?"

"It's right there. Henrietta something."

He runs his fingers over her picture, then flips through to the back. "How many stamps?'

"Twenty-seven."

"What do you figure she was doing, going to all those places?"

"Based on the countries, I'd say international spy or private eye."

He smiles a little, and I feel lighter, lifted off the ground.

We've done this before—*a lot*. I buy expired passports online and show him. He gets nervous I'm gonna go to jail, because if I get caught the cops'll think that I'm stealing identities. I remind him that I'm not a criminal, and we make up fake stories about the passport holders.

"Why are you doing this, Nell?"

"Because people like her, they're everything I'm not."

"Old and wrinkly and dead?"

I smack him. "No. Brave and fearless. They *do* stuff."

"Nell . . . can you *please* stop hitting me?"

"I'll work on it."

"How many passports do you have now, anyway?"

"A bunch. I have a bunch of passports."

"Maybe you should stop collecting passports and *get* a passport and—"

"And what?" I snap.

"Go somewhere, and do something."

For a moment, my heart flutters like it grew wings. But before it has a chance to crack through my rib cage and take off for some exotic location, I feel something heavy pulling me back down. "Maybe I like it here in Clawson."

"Maybe you don't," he counters.

I give him my don't-mess-with-me look, then add, "Maybe I don't want to go anywhere."

"Face it, Nell. These passports say otherwise. They say there's a big world out there and you'd like to see some of it."

"How 'bout you?" I ask. "Any chance you'll reconsider applying to art school?"

"That's different."

"No it isn't. That's *going somewhere*," I say before I take Henrietta's passport from him, stuff it back into my bag, then add her name to the growing list I have on my phone—what Stevie B calls my Brave Bitches List. Then, to change the subject, I say, "Speaking of badass bitches like Henrietta, what do you make of what we found on Charlotte's phone?"

"Dunno. But, trust me, Nell. A girl like Charlotte has a passport."

"Way to make me feel worse."

"Nell . . . that's not what—"

"What I want to know, Stevie B, is if you moved to a new town, even if you changed your name, 'cause you were hiding out or running from something, wouldn't you keep the stuff on your phone like music and pictures and texts? Even if you got a new number. Even if you got a new phone. Just to remember who you were before?"

"Definitely."

"So it's weird that she wiped the phone, right?"

"Very weird."

"But what's even weirder is—"

"That you collect expired passports and have pictures of prisoners serving life decorating your wall?"

"No. That it's a cheap burner phone and she's only got one number on it, and it's Cole's. And that she's sent only *one* text message and it was to *him*. How does she know Cole, Stevie B? And why is he planning on meeting her tonight at the quarry?"

"Don't know, Nell."

"And how does she even know about the quarry, being that she just moved here?"

He doesn't answer. He sits up and runs his fingers through

his hair, then asks, "Do you think that meetup will still happen tonight? With Finn in the hospital?"

"Unlikely. I mean, Cole's not gonna leave Finn."

"But you're still going to the quarry to spy on them? Just in case."

"Yep. And so are you."

"I know that's what we talked about, Nell. But maybe it's a bad idea. What if he does show up? And what if they're, you know, hooking up? What if Cole's seeing her behind your back?"

"He can't be! It's Cole! Cole and me, we're . . . Well, he's mine, is all," I say.

"Jeez, Nell. I know it hurts, but you gotta admit, with what we found on the phone and all, that's what it's looking like. Maybe he met her somewhere and now she moved here, and . . ."

I put my hands over my ears. "Just wear black and keep your mouth shut, Stevie B. And get out of here. I'll meet you on the path at nine."

"Can we talk about this some more?"

"Go! And whatever you do, wear black, like I said. Not that bright-orange hunters-gone-wild safety-vest thing you have."

"How come?"

"Because it makes you glow in the dark and easy to spot—like you're a practice target for visually impaired hunters."

"Just to be clear. Is that a hard no on the orange vest or a maybe?" he asks, smiling.

"A hard no." I smile back.

When we're standing by the window, there's this moment. It's part sad and part electric, and I want to hug him, but I know that I shouldn't. "Hey, thanks for the cookies."

"No problem," he says, his voice soft.

"And thanks for coming over."

"Nell . . . I . . ." He doesn't finish, and I don't respond. We stay like that, with our faces close, for longer than we should before I turn away.

Some people say Cole and Stevie B look alike, just that Cole is taller and more muscly. They both have dark, straight hair that starts to curl at the bottom if it gets too long, a strong jaw, and a cute smile. But Cole's smile is slower to show up and quicker to exit, which makes him look serious, like he's mad all the time or he's got something important on his mind, maybe inflation or melting ice caps, or an outbreak of flesh-eating bacteria. Stevie B's got more of an easy-to-show-up smile and a freewheeling party-boy dumb-fuck vibe going on, like he thinks mostly about doughnuts and comic books and weekends.

Stevie B brushes a strand of hair off my face. "That thing I said earlier today, about how you might have reason to be jealous of the new girl? I didn't mean it. You're straight-up fire, Nell. Blinding, fucking hot. So hot it's like looking at the sun sometimes."

Then he whispers, "What would you do if I tried to kiss you right now?"

I give him a little smile. "I'd call the police."

"And report what, exactly?"

"A Four Twenty-Eight."

"What the hell is that?"

"Possible unlawful kissing and felony heartbreak in progress."

That gets him to smile. Then he plants an actual kiss on my cheek, and mumbles, "Guilty as charged," before he swings his feet over the window ledge and slips down to the ground from my second-floor bedroom. I call after him, "Don't be late tonight, and don't forget to grab your sketchbook out of the truck."

I hear my mom yell, "Nell, what's going on up there?"

And under my breath I mumble, "I have absolutely no idea."

8

The kitchen's dark. Dim's actually a better word. So dim that when I stand in the doorway I almost don't see her at first.

"We got a new inmate today, Nellie," she calls out after I flip the lights on. "Lifer. A skinhead hellboy. Real monkey mouth," she adds, as she leans back in her chair. "He went on and on about this and that. Took forever to get him through intake."

My mom's still wearing her guard uniform. She's a CO—correction officer—at Manville Correctional Facility. More than half the town of Clawson works at Manville. "The pen," as the guards call it. My mom started working there when my dad got sick, then she took a second job on the loading dock at Walmart. But that ended when she injured her back hauling fifty-pound bags of rock salt onto shelves.

Mrs. Wilder pays me to watch Finn, and she pays me in actual cash too—like paper bills. Says she doesn't like electronic money zooming around on the internet making like it's a bunch of numbers and not real.

I drop this week's pay onto the table right next to my mom's gun. She glances at the cash and nods.

Her gun's lying in the middle of the kitchen table like it's nothing. Just a bottle of ketchup or a set of house keys, or a stack of bills she's supposed to pay. I glance down at it to make sure the safety's on. I know it's loaded. It's not supposed to be, but it is.

She pulls two pill bottles out of her shirt pocket and pours the contents onto the place mat in front of her, then starts counting out the pills with her head down low, close to the table, like they're hard to see. The pills and her addiction come courtesy of a real doctor—her back doctor—or at least they did in the beginning.

"What are you taking?" I ask, as she pops a white one and then a pale-green one into her mouth, sweeping them back with her tongue and swallowing them without water.

"Something for the pain, Nell. You eat?" she asks, her words a little slow and mushy already, which makes me wonder how much and what else she might have taken.

I nod. But I don't say, *Not a real dinner, Mom. Just two mini coffee cakes and a Jell-O I jacked from the lunchroom at school.*

"Where'd you get those?" I ask, pointing to the pills, knowing that the back doctor stopped writing her scripts a while ago so she must have found another dealer. If they're street drugs, I worry they might be laced with fentanyl and she might be buying from an inmate.

She doesn't answer; instead she busies herself with the pills, looking like a little kid with her Halloween candy, her face all scrunched up, like counting to fifteen twice suddenly got too hard.

I glance at the three twenties I tossed onto the table. They could buy food, but they won't. I looked it up and at a dollar a milligram on the street, sixty bucks'll pay for two green pills. 'Cause street dealers and prison inmates don't take insurance.

"You got anyone upstairs?" she says.

I shake my head, and she scrutinizes me for a minute to see if I'm lying.

I pull a chair out and sit down across from her, watching as she counts.

You can tell she was pretty once, but now she looks worn-down and beat-to-shit, crow's feet spiking out from the corners of her eyes, her hair graying in spots, pulled up in a messy bun, her skin sallow and her face like a porcelain platter that's finely cracked all over.

Mrs. Berringer, the art teacher in middle school, told our class that it's called "crazing" when the glaze on a piece of pottery gets covered in fine lines like that. Then she said it's called "smoking" when that kind of cracking happens to a person's face. She was trying to get us not to start smoking. Figured we probably cared more about how we looked than if we lived.

My mom pulls a cigarette out of the top pocket of her shirt and lights up, then takes a long drag and exhales loud and slow, closing her eyes like she's drifting off to sleep as the smoke hovers around her face and head like a cloud.

"Remember when Grandma used to visit and she'd make that roast chicken with garlic and lemon?" I ask, thinking back to a happier time when my dad and grandma were alive, and my mom didn't work at the prison and didn't take pills. "She served it with those mashed potatoes with the skin still on and gobs of butter," I add.

When she opens her eyes, I catch a flash of recognition on her face. "Your daddy loved that chicken," she says, leaning back and closing her eyes again, her lids fluttering at lightning speed. "It sure did smell good when it was cooking too."

"You know, we could make it sometime," I offer, my stomach rumbling. "We could make the chicken. I could help. You could teach me how, maybe. I mean, if you know how."

Her eyes open, and she gets this glazed look that tells me the pills are kicking in and she's headed out of the conversation.

I reach over, thinking I'll pat her arm, but then pull back instead to swipe at a tear that spilled onto my cheek. "You eat anything?" I ask. "I could heat up some lasagna for you."

She kind of shrugs, like eating doesn't matter when you're addicted to opioids like she is. "I'm gonna lie down, Nell. I gotta rest." When she stands up, I notice that her uniform is hanging off of her like it's sized for someone else. Someone who roasts chickens and eats dinner with her family.

"I caught an early shift tomorrow," she warns. "So you make sure I'm up by six."

She puts her pills back in their bottles, then drifts to the room behind the kitchen, stumbling a bit, then stopping by the doorway to turn around. "You doing okay, sweetie?" she asks.

The question takes me by surprise. I nod, and that seems to satisfy her, because she turns and keeps walking.

It's not a bedroom, really, where she sleeps. It's more of an alcove near the back door, where she dragged her mattress after my daddy died. We used to keep winter boots and the trash can there. It's hers now. She won't go back into their room. Not to get her clothes, and not to get rid of his either. I sit in there sometimes, in their old room, on the bare box spring, smoothing the quilted cover folded on the foot of the bed, staring at my dad's shirts hanging in the closet.

I hear the creak and sigh of her mattress as she lies down, and I figure she'll be out cold by the time I get up the stairs, and that'll mean I won't have to worry about getting caught when I sneak out tonight.

But then the tears start coming.

Slow at first and then in earnest when I think about how I won't have to learn how to roast a chicken or how to make my grandma's mashed potatoes with the skin on, and I won't have to worry about my mom embarrassing me at prom either. Her taking too many pictures on that Saturday night in June when me and Cole get all dressed up, her fussing over my dress and hair, running here and there, making sure my corsage is pinned on right, kissing Cole's cheek after he promises to bring me home safe. Those worries are for other girls.

I run my hands over my face to wipe away the wet, then pick up my mom's gun, flip open the cylinder, rotate it, and dump the bullets out. As I watch them fall onto the kitchen table, I'm thinking that I won't have to worry about a single thing. At least not any of the normal stuff kids worry about. I only have to worry about who her dealer is, and if she'll overdose, get arrested, lose her job . . . die.

As I walk around cleaning up the kitchen a bit, putting a plate into the sink, then locking the back door, I'm wishing that I could talk to her—that I could have told my mom about the new girl, and about Finn too, that I could have told her that I'm worried about Cole. But her back hurts and she's tired.

I hear music coming from the room where she sleeps. She's got it on low, but I recognize the song immediately. It's an old one by Blake Shelton that Daddy used to play all the time. I don't remember the name of it, but I know the words by heart and I start to sing along. We used to rib Daddy 'cause he never got tired of that song and he'd play it over and over again.

I keep humming and singing to myself as the song plays, thinking about the family dinners we used to have when my dad was alive and my grandma came to visit. We'd have that roast chicken and hot corn bread, and wood fires in the living room. And a couple of times we went apple pickin' in the fall and cored Granny Smiths and Galas and Honeycrisps, then stuffed them with brown sugar and cinnamon butter and baked them in the oven with a little water until they turned a tawny color and collapsed into themselves all soft and sweet. I remember how we poured heavy cream we bought up at Murphy's Dairy Farm over the top of those baked apples when they were still hot and ate them out of cereal bowls in front of the TV. Me sitting in between my mom and dad, my grandma in the big chair by the fire, watching the leaves spin outside the window when they got caught in a whirlwind of orange and red, the four of us laughing over this or that, living our lives like nothing bad—like my grandma dying or my dad's lung cancer or my mom's opioid addiction—was lurking just around the corner.

When I'm done picking up the kitchen, I open the cookie jar sitting on the counter right next to the sink and peer inside.

It's empty, except for the Narcan I stashed in there a few months ago.

I jacked it from the shelf under the register in the Coffee Klatch when me and Cole were there getting coffee to go. One spritz in a nostril after your heart stops when you overdose, and you pop back to life like a character in a kid's cartoon.

I turn toward the back room and whisper, "I love you, Mom."

I can still hear Blake Shelton playing on repeat as I head to my room, and I sing along as I slowly climb the stairs.

When you love someone, they say you set 'em free
But that ain't gonna work for me . . .

Tuesday

FOUR DAYS BEFORE

9

In the morning, when I park my truck at school, I see Cole's usual spot sitting there empty. Then I see Stevie B waiting for me by the front steps. I'm beat-to-shit tired, being that me and him sat at the quarry until after two in the morning. "Cole texted me early," I report after I catch up with him by the door. "He slept at the hospital with Finn, like we thought. So he must have told Charlotte. Canceled their meeting, like we said."

"So that's good news, then," Stevie B suggests as we walk into the building.

"How do you figure?"

"If I had a chance to go hook up with Hannah Hottie at the quarry, I would have showed up."

"No matter what?"

"Shit, Nell, yeah. No matter what."

He pulls me in close to the lockers to let other kids get by us and says, "I've been thinking, and there's only one reason she could be here with a wiped phone and a fake name."

"Which is?"

"The prison."

"Meaning?"

"Meaning maybe her rich dad got arrested and convicted of some white-collar crime like insider trading or fraud, and she wants to be near him."

"Trust me. There are no rich guys incarcerated in Manville. Only murderers and drug dealers and child molesters," I tell him. "The rich guys go to country-club prisons. Besides, that wouldn't explain how she knows Cole or why he was planning on meeting her at the quarry last night."

"There are no country-club prisons, Nell. Someone made that up."

"Are too," I insist. "They have satellite TV and air-conditioning and conjugal visits."

"I don't have satellite TV or air-conditioning or conjugal visits."

"Then it looks like you need to commit a felony, Stevie B. Some high-level white-collar crime involving paperwork."

He smiles, looking all proud of himself. "Already did."

"Did what?"

"The white-collar-paperwork-felony thing. I stole her file from the front office a few minutes ago."

"How'd you find it? We don't even know if her real name is Anna or Charlotte."

"They had a hard copy just sitting there on the desk, with a Post-it note that said 'New Student.' So I took it."

"What does it say?" I ask.

"That's the thing. It's *blank*."

"What do you mean?"

"Last name: 'Unknown.' Previous school: 'Unknown.' Address: 'Unknown.' They actually typed 'Unknown' three times."

"She's gotta have a last name. And she's gotta live somewhere," I tell him.

He stares back at me. "No kidding, Nell."

Then the bell rings, and we have to head to homeroom—and that's when I see the new girl, who has no last name, no previous school, and no current address, sitting there right next to Cole's empty seat.

"Hi, Charlotte," I say when I walk past her. But she doesn't respond.

Midmorning, Cole texts to tell me he's ditching school to stay at the hospital with Finn, and then he texts again around lunchtime to say that they are sending her home.

Charlotte doesn't talk to me all day—not after I say "Hi, Charlotte" when I pass her in the hall. And not when I say "Hi, Charlotte" when I sit behind her in Life Skills. Then when I text Stevie B, complaining that she has no manners, he slaps me down by texting back, **Maybe it has something to do with the fact that you stole her phone yesterday.**

After school, I drive over to Cole's to check on Finn. I let myself in, and when I get to the top of the stairs, it's dead quiet. The bathroom door in the hall is half-open, and I can see Cole on his knees, fully dressed, leaning over the tub. Something in my gut turns to sour mash. I knock, then push the door the rest of the way open, not sure what I'll find. Not wanting to know what he's doing and needing to know at the same time.

The tub is full of water, and he has his face submerged. "What the hell, Cole!" I say as I try to pull him up by his shoulders, but he swats me away.

His phone is sitting on the side of the tub, with the stopwatch running, and I watch the minutes and seconds, the *hundredths* of seconds, tick by until he finally pulls his face up from the water, gasping for air. He grabs his phone and stops the clock. "One minute, forty-seven seconds," he says as he drips water everywhere, scribbling the time on a piece of paper.

I sit on the edge of the tub. "Cole, talk to me!"

He sinks onto the floor. "I can't."

"Why not?" I hand him a towel, and he starts drying his hair. "I just can't," he says, and then he hugs me tight. "Look, can you stay with Finn? She'll be asleep the whole time. Just till my mom gets home?"

"Cole, no."

"Please? I have to go somewhere. Just for a few hours." His eyes are pleading. The muscles in his chest and neck tight.

"Where do you have to go?"

"Don't ask me that," he says as he sweeps his hair back.

"So you're meeting her?"

"Don't ask me that either."

"Why the hell not?"

"Because I won't lie to you, Nell. And I can't tell you the truth either." Then he looks at me with his eyes full of real honest-to-God fear.

I've only seen eyes like that once before. Me and Stevie B were eleven years old, and we cornered a coyote inside one of the barns on Cole's granddaddy's property. The coyote was gaunt and mangy, with patches of fur missing, his ears slung back slick and tight against his skull, his eyes as cold as steel in the dead of winter. And he was holding his head low, just like Cole is now, like he knew something bad was coming.

Cole's daddy shot that coyote with a thirty-aught-six later that night. He told us he found him cowering by the side of the barn, growling and foaming from the mouth. He said an animal like that can't be trusted once it gets that look in its eyes.

The problem is, Cole has that look right now. Like he's cornered, with nowhere to run.

So I cave. "Yeah," I say. "Of course I'll stay with Finn."

He kisses me. And it's tender and soft and it feels like the saddest kiss in the history of the universe.

Like it's not Cole at all.

And it's not forever.

It's goodbye.

10

Later that night, I wake up with a start when I hear something—or someone—on the ground beneath my bedroom window. A crunch and a rattle, then leaves bristling and a snap.

My heart starts jackhammering in my chest as I lie in my bed listening, my eyes adjusting to the dark, me knowing my mom is downstairs, out cold, on the other side of the house, and won't hear a thing.

I glance at my phone. It's 11:27 p.m.

I look around my room and take stock. My lamp's off, but moonlight's pouring in. My bedroom door is shut. The prisoners' eyes shine in the light. There's stuff scattered all over the floor. My window's closed but not locked—the latch is broken, has been for years.

I sit up, put my feet on the floor. Shiver in the cold.

It seems quiet again.

I wait, thoughts running fast through my head. *Maybe it's nothing—just the wind, or an animal walking along the outside of the house.*

Or maybe it's Cole.

Cole's been climbing in through my bedroom window since we were kids—just not without texting me first. And not likely tonight. Not with what's been going on between us, and not with Finn as sick as she is. I quickly open my phone to check if he sent a message.

He didn't.

There's another snap.

I stand, then edge over toward the wall to get a better angle to see outside. The wind is blowing and shadows are dancing on the lawn, but I can't make out anything or anyone down on the ground. Then there's a clear thud and a rustle, and I lean flat against the wall like paint.

It stays quiet until I hear a distinct creak of the gutter pipe—then another. That's a sound I know.

Someone's climbing up the side of the house.

My heart leaps. My breath catches in my chest, fear thumping as hard as fists. I look around for something to hit an intruder with, but I see nothing. Just clothes and papers. Books. A phone charger. Useless as weapons.

I'm clutching my hairbrush when the window is pushed open a few inches. Then it slides higher, and I raise my arm, ready to swing . . .

I see fingers, then a hand. It's all a blur . . .

A blue shirt. A flash of red. My heart dips then races.

More red. I exhale, drop my arm, then make a sound like a whimper.

Those are red Converse sneakers coming in through my window.

"Jesus! Cole!" I whisper, pushing the window open wider for him.

He climbs and stumbles, practically pouring into my room. Then he stands there, sweaty and out of breath and disheveled, as he holds his finger to his lips, telling me to shush.

And he points at the bed.

Even with him lying about knowing the new girl, and his number being in her phone, and him texting her about meeting at the quarry, and the weird bathtub stuff, and him not talking, and him going to see her this afternoon—even with all that, when the corner of his mouth turns up in a smile, my insides still get warm and melty, and turn as soft as cookie dough slipped into a hot oven.

"Good thing I don't have my mom's gun, Cole. Or a dad," I say, hiding my own hint of a smile as I crawl back under the covers, shivering in my T-shirt, glad he's okay and that it was him coming in through my window and not some drug-crazed, porch-climbing felon.

He lies down on the bed and wraps his arms and legs around me. We stay like this for a few minutes, with him holding me tight. But then I feel his muscles start to relax, and his chest heaves and he starts to cry.

"Is Finn okay?" I ask, alarmed.

"Same," he mumbles. "And I can't stay. I just wanted to see you for a few minutes. Sorry I didn't text—forgot my phone in the truck. And sorry about earlier, and sorry about everything."

"Is this crying about Finn, or the bathtub thing, or the new-girl thing?" I ask, hoping he's gonna say the bathtub thing is just him being weird, and there is no new-girl thing, and Finn will be okay.

But he doesn't. He says, "Yes." And then I feel him nod his head against my back and neck.

I sit up a little. "Which thing is it, Cole? Finn or the bathtub or the new girl?"

When he doesn't answer, I lie back down. "Can I help? Remember it's you and me against the rest of them. That's what you've always said. I want to help, Cole. Honest."

"Nobody can help, Nell."

I freeze.

But then he adds, "I can't do Friday at the diner or Saturday at my house."

I smile into my pillow. "I thought you weren't listening to me."

"I'm always listening to you, Nell. I just got stuff on my mind."

"Stuff you won't tell me about."

"Stuff I *can't* tell you about," he says.

It gets quiet again as I think about that. "Can we just talk about normal stuff, Cole? Not Finn and not Charlotte, and this whole thing. Just for a few minutes?"

"Normal *normal* stuff?" he asks. "Or normal *pretend* stuff?"

"Normal pretend stuff," I confirm.

"Like what, Nell?"

He knows "like what," because we play this game all the time, but I tell him anyway. "Let's talk about that trip we want to take."

"The one where we travel on trains and boats and airplanes?" he asks.

"Say that again."

"How come?"

"I love your voice."

"We'll travel on lots of trains and boats and airplanes, Nell."

"And we won't plan anything," I add.

"We'll just wander, and find beautiful hotels for no money."

"And we'll eat food we've never had before."

"And we'll look at the stars and the moon every night," Cole says, his voice all warm and soft and hypnotic.

"To make sure they aren't in the wrong places."

"And haven't fallen out of the sky," he adds.

"Exactly," I say.

"And we'll sleep all day."

"And stay up all night."

"And we'll meet new people. *Exciting* people, Nell."

"People who drink champagne and chocolate milk and eat exotic pastries."

"And sleep on beaches," he adds.

"And we'll call home every day."

"And everyone'll be fine," he promises.

"And they'll tell us we don't have to hurry back."

"We'll float around the world," he says.

"Like big clouds made out of whipped cream," I suggest. "And then?"

"And then we'll come home," he tells me. "Because coming home is the best part." Cole always says, *Coming home is the best part.*

"How come?" I ask—I always ask, *How come?*

"We'd miss the doughnuts," he informs me this time.

I elbow him. "You don't even like doughnuts, Cole. And I'm guessing that we can get doughnuts anywhere in the world."

"Not the stale ones you love from the Gas 'n Go," he teases.

"Okay, fine. We'll come home for the doughnuts."

"And for Finn," he adds.

"Of course for Finn . . . And for Stevie B."

"And our moms," he says. "But mostly for the doughnuts." And then Cole squeezes me tight, and for a few minutes it gets quiet again. Nice quiet, safe quiet, quiet that feels like home. Quiet you could live in.

Then I ask, "Are we gonna be okay, Cole? You and me?"

He doesn't answer, and for a breath or two or three, I think he might have drifted off to sleep. But then he kisses my neck, and I feel tears hit my skin—*his* tears—warm and telling.

"Cole? Are we gonna be okay? You and me? Forever?" I ask again, whispering as the fear that keeps climbing into my head and heart spills out into my voice and sits there all mixed up with the rest of it: sadness, anger, confusion.

Cole takes a while to respond. "I don't know what 'forever' means anymore, Nell," he finally says, and I see that flash of bright light. That intense, blinding light that paralyzes you when you realize that everything you've ever feared is coming true—that you know something, *really* know something, you don't want to know.

"How about tomorrow?" I try, my words bruised and aching with want. "Are we gonna be okay tomorrow? If you can't promise me forever, can you promise me tomorrow?"

Cole doesn't answer. He just says, "I have to go." Then he sits up and puts his feet on the floor. "Nell?"

I slide up onto my elbow. "Yeah?"

"I would never hurt you on purpose. You know that, right?"

"Yeah, I know that."

"So you're just gonna have to trust me."

I freeze. "For how long?"

And Cole says, "Maybe forever."

He stands up and moves silently in the shadows of my room.

As I watch him climb out the window, that thing my mom says about feeling things and knowing things runs through my head. 'Cause I'm feeling things and knowing things I don't want to feel and I don't want to know, and it doesn't feel right. Not one bit. Not for tomorrow. Not for forever. Not for me. And not for Cole.

After he's gone, I get up to close the window, then watch him run silently across the lawn toward his truck. When I can't see him anymore, I climb back into bed, pull my covers up, shut my eyes, and think back to a less scary time.

Back to when me and Cole were fifteen and jumped into the quarry together for the second time, then the third and the fourth . . . I think about how, each and every time, Cole promised that whenever we jumped together it would be okay, and how I believed him. How I would wrap my arms around his back and hitch my legs around his waist and squish my eyes closed tight and bury my face in his neck, just like I'd done the first time we jumped. I remember how thrilling it was to trust someone so completely. To believe with all my heart that Cole would keep me safe and that there would always be a tomorrow with him in it.

+ + + + + + + +

That first summer, we rarely talked when we met up on the path and walked toward the quarry. We held hands, our eyes skittery in the dark, our ears listening to the breath of the night: the sounds of the insects and the wind in the branches and the crackle and break of the leaves beneath our feet. Sometimes, when it was real quiet, I'd listen to Cole breathing, and sometimes he'd sing softly—songs by George Strait and Lee Brice, mostly. Not whole songs either, just catchy little lyric runs floating on those melodies he had stuck in his head.

We never told Stevie B what we were doing. Jumping was something me and Cole did without him knowing—some nights really late, after the three of us had hung out. Cole started bringing a blanket, and I started bringing a change of clothes and wearing strawberry-flavored lip gloss and lavender perfume I shoplifted from Henley's Drugstore.

In the beginning, we were nervous about being alone together since up until that first jump it had always been the three of us, me and Cole and Stevie B, and now it was just me and Cole sneaking off together, which felt wholly wrong and wholly right and wholly different at the same time.

Then we'd sit on the blanket and kiss. And sometimes, when the kissing got past kissing and what was done was done, we'd lie on our backs and Cole'd point to the stars in the night sky, telling me stories about how big the universe is and how special we are, with me not believing one drop of what he was saying but lapping it up anyway.

I'd be the one to pull away and climb up high on the rocks, and Cole would follow me, and we'd stand together at the highest point and we'd face the fear of jumping together. Him being the bravest, me latching on to that like it was something we could share, like being brave was no different than a snack bag full of cookies. Then he'd scoop me up and he'd jump off the rocks into the quarry, holding on to me so tight that it was like we were molded into one.

At first, we jumped mostly because it was an excuse to hold each other, but it became something else, and that wasn't quite the whole of it anymore. It was more about the thrill, because in an instant we'd be falling fast, clinging to each other as that rush of adrenaline filled us up to the brim.

But there was something more than that, even.

Every time we stepped off those rocks, life felt bursting with possibility, like we were jumping off the earth or jumping away from our lives here in Clawson. Or maybe it was the thought that we might be jumping *toward* something better that made it feel so special. But each and every time, it felt like we were flying. And soaring like that, falling away from this place, felt like we were sneaking some thrill we weren't meant to have. Then, when we'd pierce the surface, feet first in a rush of cold, we'd feel the sharp knife cut of the water against our skin. And right before our faces went under, we'd gulp a final, frantic breath of air into our lungs, and in that moment we'd know we were alive.

+ + + + + + +

As I'm lying here in the dark, trying to make sense of the world, I keep thinking about the rush I got every time we stepped off those rocks together. How it felt to fall with abandon. How the brace of the icy cold shocked me each time we hit the water. How even though we were submerged in the cold and dark, I felt more exhilaration than fear, even when it seemed that my lungs might bust wide open.

Then as I drift closer to sleep, I remember that first kiss. And the second. And the third.

How we circled around each other each time we resurfaced and caught our breath, and life licked at our skin and hearts, and those slips of silver moonlight danced on the water. How each time Cole's lips were pressed against mine, how each time he promised he was my forever, I believed that there just might be magic in this life after all, and for me that magic was Cole.

Then I jolt wide awake. Eyes open, heart pounding, tears spilling onto my pillow as I'm thinking how badly I want that feeling back. Not only in memory, but for real.

I think about how badly I need to trust Cole even when we're falling fast and we don't know when or where we're gonna land, or how much it will hurt when we do. Then I have flashes of Cole at my side the whole time my dad was dying. How a year later we found my mom lying on the kitchen floor after she overdosed, her heart not pumping and her lungs not filling with air. How I stood there in the doorway, frozen as pond ice in the dead of winter, but Cole knew exactly what to do. And he did it.

I think about how many times he's been there for me—and me for him. How he defends me and holds me up, acting the whole time like that's what's meant to be. Then there's all the normal everyday stuff of Nell and Cole—the ordinary things that are *everything*, even though they're nothing. But that's not the whole of it either. There's something about me and Cole that makes us fated and destined and inseparable. It's something I can't explain with normal words—even words like those.

I try my hardest to hold on to that, but then I start thinking about the time me and Cole jumped into the quarry and got separated and I almost lost him. How I searched for him, like I was searching for myself. How I dove down again and again, resurfacing each time, exhausted and spent, flailing about in the water, calling his name, thinking he'd surely drowned—thinking I'd surely drowned too, at least halfway. Then I think about how that night, in the end, I didn't do the right thing by him, and I know what I have to do now.

I sit up. Grab my phone and send Cole a text: **If you're too scared to jump, I will hold you and keep you safe forever.**

I wait an eternity for a response, staring at the blank screen as the wind gusts and the trees sway, sending shadows to dance around my room like ghosts.

Then, three dots and he's typing.

My pulse quickens, and my breath catches in my throat.

Four words pop onto the screen.

When I read them, I tell myself it's going to be okay.

I tell myself we'll figure it out tomorrow.

I tell myself that it's only four words.

I tell myself all those things you're supposed to tell yourself when you feel like you're cornered with your back against a wall with no way out, but I don't believe any of it.

Then I slump back down in my bed, pull the covers up, and read what he wrote one more time.

Those four words, they break me.

Not this time Nellie.

Wednesday

THREE DAYS BEFORE

11

I don't sleep much for the whole rest of the night, and I show up at school with a bruised heart and my head filled with a tangled mess of confusing thoughts. But Cole doesn't show up at all. He cuts again to stay home with Finn, and I don't see Stevie B until sixth period.

We grab tacos and pretzels and fruit cups, and when the lunch ladies aren't looking, I lift a whole slew of stuff to bring home—coffee cakes and fruit and sandwiches. As me and Stevie B make our way through the line, I tell him about the bathtub incident and the weird way Cole acted when he climbed in through my window—leaving off the scary part about what he said at the end.

After we pay, we take our trays and head for the tables, and we see Charlotte sitting with a whole welcoming committee of senior boys.

Stevie B asks, "Did you see her bag?"

I glance over. "Yeah? What about it?"

"It's not a regular knapsack. It's called a dry bag."

"Which is what, exactly?"

"Something scuba divers use to keep their stuff from getting wet." He takes another bite of his taco as he starts eyeing my tray.

"Nobody scuba dives in Clawson. We're hundreds of miles from any ocean."

"I know," he says, wiping sauce from his chin. "Which is why it's weird."

I glance back at the large black bag sitting on the floor.

"Think about it, Nell. Who brings a dry bag to school?"

"Maybe she uses it to keep all of her stuff dry. You know, in case it rains."

He leans in close to me. "Or maybe she's here to bust her dad out of Manville and they're planning to escape by boat."

"The prison's not near any water, Stevie B."

He takes out his phone and pulls up a map of Manville Correctional Facility.

"See!"

"See what?"

He points. "Water."

"That?" I ask, staring at the small area of blue.

He nods.

"That's nowhere near the prison, and it's practically a puddle!"

"Lake."

"Fine. Where's he gonna go once he gets *in* the lake?"

"I don't know. Maybe he'll escape by just—"

"Stevie B, stop. No one has ever escaped from Manville."

"Got anything I can eat?" he asks.

I toss him a coffee cake. "We should steal it."

"Steal what?" he asks.

"Her bag."

"*Steal it* steal it?"

"More like borrow it for a few minutes, then give it back," I tell him. "Just to, you know, see what she has in there that she doesn't want getting wet."

"You know what I'm wondering?" he asks. "I'm wondering why Cole is sticking his face underwater in the bathtub and the new girl with no last name and no past—who he clearly knows—is carrying a dry bag around like she's planning a boat trip with her convict dad."

"What else you got?" I ask.

"Where?"

"Inside that small idea factory of yours," I say, pointing at his head.

"You mean, if the prison thing doesn't pan out?"

I nod.

"You don't want to know."

"Yes, I do. Throw out anything. Spitball."

"I gotta plead the Fifth here," he says, licking the coffee cake crumbs from his fingers as I sit back and watch the new girl for a few seconds.

"Tell me you aren't thinking she's a mermaid, Stevie B."

He turns red. "Shit, Nell!"

I lean in close again, like I actually think he's onto something. "The only question is: Are you thinking real girl grows a tail and turns into a fish, or cute animated cartoon mermaid like Ariel?"

He eyes her and shrugs. "Gotta be real hot girl turns into a fish, Nell."

I reach across the table and smack him. "Jesus, Stevie B! You're serious?"

"Darn it, Nell! Stop hitting me!"

"Then stop saying sexist things about girls morphing into beautiful aquatic wingless water harpies for senseless narrow-minded guys to fantasize about."

"Jesus, Nell! Ratchet down the overreaction."

"I'll work on it!"

"Just so you know, harpies are ugly bird people, and mermaids are beautiful half—"

I glare at him, and he stops talking.

We sit in quiet for a few minutes: Him rubbing his arm and acting all put-out and injured. Me thinking about a sketch he drew last summer of me, as a mermaid, crawling out of the quarry, dripping wet. It looked like it took every ounce of strength I'd had just to swim to the edge, and I was gasping for air like my lungs were busted. It was twilight; the sky was a deep blue black with a few streaks of light. I was draped across the rocks with my head lifted—swept up in the cold, looking so beautiful.

I never told Stevie B that I saw it. Or how that picture haunted me, how exotic and magical he made me seem.

"Hey, we're still stealing the bag, right?" he asks.

"What?" I ask, distracted.

"Charlotte's dry bag? We're still stealing it like you said, right?"

"Yeah. Definitely."

"What's the plan, then?"

"Simple. You distract her. I'll swipe the bag and go through it. Then I'll just put it back."

He seems skeptical. "How the hell are you going to do that?"

"Classic pickpocket. What we call 'a bump-and-run with mustard.' We work as a team. I'll cause a distraction—drop my tray and spill food on her." I hold up a plastic cup of mustard. "You rush in to clean her up." I hand him a bunch of napkins. "Use these."

Stevie B looks at me wide-eyed.

"She gets upset 'cause you're being all handsy, wiping at the mustard on her shirt. In the commotion, I lift the bag, run with it to the bathroom—presumably to get some water and more towels.

I rifle through the bag, check what she's got, then slip it back by her feet before she notices that it's gone."

"Won't someone see you take it?"

"Nope. They'll all be too busy noticing that you're molesting her."

"So I'm gonna get arrested and get those conjugal visits, then?"

"Not this time. This time, you're gonna get away with it. Think of it like *Ocean's Eleven*. Just on a smaller scale."

He leans back on the bench. "Who *are* you, Nell?"

"Right now I'm George Clooney."

"I like this Nell way better than prisoner-eyeball Nell."

"Me too," I say. "You ready?"

"Shouldn't we at least practice first?"

"Don't be ridiculous!" I tell him. "I've been practicing for this my whole life." Then I pick up my tray and start walking.

12

"You okay?" I ask, my voice and hands shaking when I return to the lunch table, blood drained from my face, Charlotte's dry bag back at her feet.

Stevie B's all red and flushed. Not like he's upset like me, more like he had a good time. "I think it's safe to say Charlotte won't be attending the prom with me," he whispers. "Please tell me it was worth it, Nell."

I'm staring straight ahead past him to the far wall. "It was worth it."

"So? What's in the bag?" he asks, trying to make eye contact. "A prison pic of her dad? An expired passport with her full name and address, maybe?"

"No prison pic. No passport," I state, my eyes still drilling a hole through the cafeteria wall. "Just clothes and books and . . ." I don't finish.

"And what? You just said it was worth it, and now you're saying you found normal stuff like clothes and books. Plus, you're acting weird, Nell." He looks around to make sure no one is listening. "What else did you find?"

I hesitate. "Some gadgets."

"What kind of gadgets?"

"I don't know exactly. I had to rush. Techy things I didn't recognize."

"Techy things like a phone charger or an Xbox, or techy things like a bomb?"

"Neither. Just weird, expensive-looking electronic things."

He sits back and smiles. "No mermaid paraphernalia?"

"Stevie B, don't."

"No clip-on fins or gills? No fish food? No clamshell bikini tops or underwater spears?"

I slowly shake my head.

"Weird-looking harpy wings, maybe? Or, I know," he continues. "Maybe some my-dad-is-a-convict paraphernalia?"

I don't answer, and Stevie B stares out over the cafeteria. "This is fun, Nell. I like being a criminal with you."

I take out one of the pieces of paper I found in Charlotte's bag and pass it to him under the table.

He looks down. "You said it was gadgets. This is a piece of paper."

"No shit, Sherlock. Just read it!"

Before he can glance down at it again, he says, "Uh-oh. Don't look. She's walking over."

When Charlotte stops in front of us, I snatch the paper back.

"Sorry about before, Charlotte," Stevie B tells her, all sweet and smiley and turning red again. "I was just trying to help. Nell here can be a klutz."

She watches him for a minute, her shirt wet and smeared yellow. "If it makes you feel any better, Nell, I don't plan on staying here long," she says. Then she walks away.

"That's good news," Stevie B says after she leaves. "Whoever she is, she's just passing through. Which means two things."

I wait for him to explain.

"One," he announces, "you get to keep Cole."

That stops my heart. "And two?" I manage to ask.

"It's probably the prison thing."

I watch Charlotte head toward the cafeteria door. "Not so sure about that," I say. "Read this." I hand the paper back to him.

"This is just medical mumbo jumbo," he says after glancing at it.

"That's not the important part. Check the date."

He looks down again to read. "Nell, that has to be a mistake."

"Yeah, that's what I thought too. Now look at this." I slip one of the small gadgets I found in her bag under the table. "Ever see anything like this?"

Stevie B appears panicked when he sees it. "I thought you were going to put everything back!"

"Well, it looks like I didn't!"

He takes it from me and turns it over slowly, shaking his head. "What the hell! What does it do?"

"No clue, but she had a couple of them. Now, put the date on that piece of paper together with the high-tech-looking carbon-nanotube superhero gadget, and what do you get?"

He's quiet for a minute and then whispers, "I get 2101."

"That's what I got too."

"So you're saying . . ."

"I'm not *saying* anything," I snap.

"What do we do?"

"Let's go." I stand up.

"Where are we going?"

"To talk to Cole."

13

We fly over to Cole's, my truck's transmission making straining and groaning sounds as I shift, like it might officially die as we head up the hill to his house. Cole's mom's still at work, so we don't knock; we walk right in, pushing through the screen door, and head up the stairs toward Finn's room.

From the landing, I can see that Finn is sleeping, the bathroom door in the hall is half-open, and Cole is on his knees next to the tub again. He's bent over at the waist, fully dressed, with his face in the water, exactly like yesterday.

Stevie B sees Cole, then whispers, "Jesus, Nell." Then he adds, "Let me talk to him. I have to take a leak anyway."

He pushes past me and opens the bathroom door the rest of the way saying, "Hey, Cole. What's going on?" But Cole's still submerged, and he doesn't respond.

I stand outside the door and call out, "Right now, he's inducing a hypoxic episode."

"Speak English, Nell."

"I googled it. It's a fancy way of saying he's holding his breath."

"Why would he—"

"No idea."

Stevie B pops his head back out into the hall and whispers, "Is he trying to drown himself?"

"I don't think so."

"How do you know?"

"For one, he's petrified of drowning. So if he's trying to kill himself, he'd probably go another route. For two, he's timing it." I point at the stopwatch sitting on the side of the tub.

"So can I take a leak, then?"

"Have at it," I say. Then I slide down onto the hallway floor to google *breath holding* and *boyfriend doing weird stuff* and *prison breaks* and anything else I can think of, but I get nowhere.

Cole comes out of the bathroom as I hear Finn coughing and the tub draining. "Just over two minutes," he announces, and then he slips down onto the floor next to me and kisses my cheek as he drips water everywhere.

"And that's good? The just-over-two-minutes thing?" I force myself to ask.

"It sucks, actually. But it's better."

"Better than what?"

"Yesterday's record."

Stevie B comes out of the bathroom zipping up his jeans. "So you're either trying to set a world record for bathtub breath holding, or you're trying to drown yourself, or . . ."

Cole looks at him like *Or what?*

"Or you're going to help someone escape from prison underwater."

"*What?*" Cole asks, turning from Stevie B to me, eyes wide, mouth hanging open.

"Or . . . ," Stevie B continues.

Cole looks back at him, annoyed.

"Or you're . . . you know, having some kind of a breakdown," Stevie B says.

"It's the first one," Cole says.

"Trying to set a world record?" Stevie B asks.

"Yep."

"Are you sure?"

"Positive."

"What's the record?" Stevie B asks.

"Twenty-four minutes and thirty-seven seconds. Set by a Croatian free diver in a pool."

When Cole says that, my uh-oh meter ticks up into the red zone.

Stevie B asks, "What's a free diver?"

"It's basically someone who scuba dives without oxygen tanks," Cole tells him.

"What's the point of that?"

"No clue."

"Your record?" Stevie B asks.

"Two minutes, six seconds."

I stand up and step into the bathroom.

"What are you doing, Nell?" Cole calls after me.

"I'm refilling the tub, because it seems like you need to practice more." Back in the hallway, I ask, "Can you tell me one thing, though?" I have to defy every instinct, every feeling in my head and heart, just to keep my voice strong and sound brave.

I lock eyes with Cole so I can read his face, and say, "Tell me what you know about the year 2101."

14

I hand Cole the paper I found in Charlotte's dry bag, with the date February 9, 2101, printed on the top, and Stevie B pulls the electronic gadget out from the waistband of his pants and hands it to me.

The blood leaves Cole's face as he turns from me to Stevie B, then back again. "So . . . you didn't just take her phone."

Stevie B says, "Nope."

"Look, Cole," I say, "we're gonna help, but you gotta fill us in."

"I can't."

"Why not?"

"You won't believe me. You'll try to talk me out of it. You'll tell someone."

I glance at Stevie B, then back at Cole. "We won't. We promise."

"You can't promise that until you know what it is," he says sharply.

"Okay, so what *is* it, exactly?"

"I can't tell you that."

Stevie B gets frustrated and punches the wall, saying, "Cole, you're my best friend, and I'm watching you do something that's tipping toward fucked-up and full-on off-the-wall. See this," Stevie B whisper-yells, pointing to a long white scar on his forearm. "You saved my ass when I fell off the rocks up on Hill Creek Road and shattered my arm. And this?" he says, grabbing Cole's head. "This here skull of yours? I saved it when you cracked it open on the ice on Wagner Pond and I dragged you home unconscious through the snow. So you and me? We save each other. And it sounds like you need saving, Cole. It sounds like you cracked your head wide open." Stevie B takes a breath before adding, "Plus, you can't get weird, Cole. Nell's weird, with the eyeballs and the passports. You have to . . . you know . . . be *normal*. Or maybe not *normal* normal, but, I don't know, *Cole* normal. Not drowning yourself, at least."

Cole looks guilty as hell, and he's teary-eyed when he reaches for Stevie B and hugs him.

I let them hug it out for a bit before I say as softly as I can, "Let's back up a little and start slow. Maybe Cole'll be willing to answer some easy questions."

Cole sort of nods like *Okay, maybe,* and he's still got his arm around Stevie B's shoulder when I hold up the device I found in Charlotte's bag and say, "Let's start with this. What is it, Cole?"

He stares at it for a long minute but doesn't answer.

"Okay," I continue. "Where'd you meet Charlotte, then?"

He hesitates. "She kind of . . . found me."

"Found you? Where?"

He doesn't answer.

"It's a really easy question, Cole. Where'd you meet her?" Stevie B tries.

Cole blurts out, "The dark web."

"The dark web?" I ask, shocked. "You don't even go on the regular web!"

"What the hell is the dark web?" Stevie B asks.

"It's where criminals and drug dealers and perverts hang out," I tell him. "It's encrypted, and your IP address is untraceable, and bad shit goes down."

Stevie B flat-out stares at me. "How the hell do you know that, Nell?"

"My mom works as a guard in a prison, remember? I know all sorts of criminal stuff."

"So it *is* the prison, then," he says.

I ignore him and ask Cole, "Why were you on the dark web?"

"I can't tell you that."

"But that's where you met her? On the dark web. Like a criminal. For real?"

He gives a reluctant nod.

"Damn it, Cole! I was expecting you to say that you met her up on Lafayette when you were picking up groceries, or over on Barnesville at the Quicky Mart, or something reasonable and normal like *at work*."

"I quit work."

"You quit your job?" Stevie B asks. "Jeez, Cole! Does your mom know?"

He shakes his head.

"Why?"

"I need time to practice."

"Practice?" I ask, glancing at the bathtub.

Stevie B mumbles, "Oh shit."

"Okay, hold on. Let's backtrack," I say. "Why did you think her name was Anna?"

"That's the name she used."

"On the dark web?" Stevie B asks, like he still thinks this is bullshit.

Cole nods.

"Okay, so you meet Charlotte, who is using an alias on the dark web, where criminals hang out, because you were doing . . . *what*, exactly?" Stevie B asks.

"I told you guys—I can't tell you that!"

"Cole, come on!" I yell.

We hear Finn coughing. Cole goes to her, and me and Stevie B lean against the hallway wall, listening to the tub fill with water and staring at our feet.

"So," Stevie B whispers, "Hannah Hottie is . . . what? . . . A con artist? A criminal? Or she's . . ."

He doesn't finish. We exchange a look, but I don't say anything. I go and turn the water off so the tub doesn't overflow.

"So we're talking . . . *what*, exactly?" Stevie B asks when I return. "Either she's a sophisticated criminal running some scam with fake documents and high-tech gadgets, or she's . . . from the *future*, Nell? That's what you're thinking? That's where we are with this? *Time travel?*"

"No one has actually said that!" I snap.

"Well? I kind of *did* say that, 'cause that's what we're both kind of sort of maybe thinking, isn't it? I mean she has a news article dated 2101, so . . ."

I sigh. Because he's right. We are kind of sort of maybe thinking it. Plus, there's the other stuff I didn't tell him yet.

"Nell! Come on! There has to be another explanation besides some sci-fi beam-me-up-Scotty wormhole time-travel bullshit!"

I don't respond this time either. Because he's right about that too. This can't be time travel. It has to be a con.

Then he asks, "What would the breath holding in the tub have to do with her supposedly coming here from the future, anyway?"

I still don't answer. I start reading things on my phone. Things about con artists and scams and time travel and the dark web.

Another few minutes pass, and then Stevie B asks, "Nell, why *Cole*? And why *here*? If she can freakin' time-travel, why would she waste her time coming to Clawson, the crown jewel of nowhere?" Then he adds, "Just for the record, I'm goin' with she's some kind of con artist. Or maybe she's just a normal girl and this is blown out of proportion. You know, a ridiculous misunderstanding."

"That would be a pretty elaborate con, don't you think? I mean, what? She saw Cole, thought he was cute, and said, 'I know, I'll have some fancy electronic devices made and print up some documents with fake dates from the future to see if I can trick him into . . . ' what?"

He shrugs.

"Thinking she can time-travel?" I ask.

He gives me a dead-eyed stare.

"Taking her on a date?" I try.

"Nell!"

"What?"

"I was thinking a bigger con than, you know . . . getting a date."

"What possible con could she be playing? Cole doesn't have anything *to* con."

"I don't know!" Stevie B says, still whispering so Cole won't hear us. "Maybe blackmail. Maybe it's like I said and it really is about the prison. Maybe she wants to break someone out of Manville, and she thinks she can trick Cole and get his mom to help by concocting some fantastical mumbo-jumbo bullshit story. I'm serious, Nell!"

"Cole's mom does paperwork. She's not in a tactical unit! And she's not some criminal mastermind. And Cole . . . he's . . . not *gullible*. He's pretty levelheaded."

"Yeah, but, Nell, why would anyone have an article dated 2101? Come on!"

I go back to my Google search.

"Look," Stevie B continues, "I was reading on the way over here that at Sing Sing, during a prison football game, three prisoners escaped, and they—"

"Stop." I glance up from my phone.

"The quarterback and two other players," he continues.

I sigh. "I don't think Manville Prison has a football team. Besides, what year was that?"

"1935."

"I think prison security's been beefed up a bit since then."

"Okay, in another famous prison break," he whispers, "some guy painted nectarines to look like hand grenades, then used them to make his way onto the roof."

"Onto the roof? Of the prison?"

"Yeah. The prison roof."

"What good did that do?"

"His wife picked him up in a helicopter."

"Seriously?" I ask. "His wife picked him up in a chopper on the roof of the prison?"

Stevie B nods. "She took lessons."

"Chopper lessons?"

He nods again.

"What else you got?" I ask. "I mean other than painted nectarines, chopper lessons, and merpeople?"

"There's the guy in Korea who went on a hunger strike, then squeezed through the food slot—"

"*What?*"

"And El—"

"Do not tell me the El Chapo story," I warn.

"Why not?" He grabs my shoulder. "He had a mile-long underground tunnel built with air-conditioning so he could walk out of prison. In comfort."

I sigh again. "So what's your point?"

"These stories make my underwater escape from Manville by some elaborate I'm-from-the-future con seem, you know, *feasible*."

I look him dead in the eyes. "No. They. Don't."

"Okay. Then maybe it's to steal money."

"Cole's family has no money."

"Prison money, then. Maybe she's planning to scam Mrs. Wilder to steal—"

"You know I can hear you guys, right?" Cole calls to us from Finn's room.

Me and Stevie B exchange a look.

"I'm meeting Charlotte tonight at ten, up at the quarry," Cole says, "if you guys wanna come."

I call back, "Definitely."

Then Stevie B pushes me into the bathroom and whispers, "What do you make of that?"

I shrug. "At least he invited us."

He whispers, "Nell, I have to go. My mom's been texting me. School called because I cut three classes today, and she's pissed. But tell Cole to pick me up tonight. Our only hope is to catch Charlotte sounding like a con artist or a snake oil salesman or, you know, the daughter of an inmate in need of a shiv or a shovel."

"Might be smarter to ask for a security code or a freakin' ray gun than a shiv or a shovel, don't you think?"

"That's not the point, Nell!"

"Hold on," I say, grabbing his arm. "You can't leave. There's something I didn't tell you."

"Shit, Nell! *What?*"

"You know how I went through her bag and I said there were clothes in it?"

"Yeah . . ."

"Well, the clothes were pretty much . . ." I don't finish.

"Pretty much *what?*"

"Pretty much a wet suit."

Stevie B's eyes get wide, and he gets a glazed-over look. "A wet suit?" He studies my face. "Jesus, Nell! What else didn't you tell me!" Then his phone pings. "It's my mom again, and she's monster pissed."

"Still thinking this is some kind of prison break?" I ask, trying to keep my voice down.

He shakes his head, then says, "I don't know, maybe. Maybe there is a way to get from the prison to the quarry underwater, El Chapo–style. This can't be time travel!"

"Well," I offer, "I don't know what to think."

Stevie B whispers, "Does Cole know about the wet suit?"

I shake my head. "I have no idea."

"Should we tell him?"

We step back into the hallway, and I hear Finn coughing. I shake my head again and say, "I don't know that either."

15

Around eight thirty, I start watching for Cole's truck from my front window. I'm picking at the peeling paint on the window-sill, craning my neck as I peer out toward the back of the house, my eyes scanning the woods, remembering when me and Cole didn't want the nights to end after we'd jumped. We'd sit there, up high on the ridge above River Bend Road, the two of us looking down at the silhouette of my house against the sky, watching the lights on the front porch and in the living room, catching the amber glow from the kitchen and the blue haze of the television if it wasn't too late. It looked so pretty from far away. No details, just the cast of shadow and the glow of people, warm and living. We'd sit there side by side on that hill, shoulders touching, not wanting to close the distance or let the magic of the quarry jump fade.

Then Cole got his driver's license, and we hardly ever took the path anymore. We still jumped, but we didn't walk; we drove. We'd ride home with the radio on, holding hands and not talking, me thinking about how much things change and how much they don't.

I see Cole's headlights round the bend as he pulls up my driveway. Then I watch them bounce along the trees as he heads to the back. I don't bother calling out to my mom that I'm going out, 'cause she won't hear me, won't care, won't remember. I grab my jacket and hurry outside, letting the cold air wash over me as my daddy's favorite song plays in the background.

As soon as I see Cole's truck up close, I stop dead in my tracks. The driver's-side window is taped up with cardboard, making it so he can't see out, and I can't see in.

"What happened there?" I ask after I climb in, and he holds up his bandaged left hand. "Giant hole. Installed it myself this afternoon."

"As in, you punched in the glass with your fist, Cole?"

"Mostly used a brick," he admits, in an aw-shucks ashamed-of-himself way.

"Any special reason?" I ask, hoping that this might nudge him to tell me something about what's going on.

But he gives me a look like *You've got to be kidding.*

I know I shouldn't say it, not now with everything that's going on, but I do. "Your mom doesn't need any more medical bills, Cole."

I say it softly, because it's coming from a place of wanting to help, but then I wish I could take it back when he says, "That's why I bandaged my hand up myself."

"You need stitches?" I ask as he backs the truck up, working both the gearshift and the steering wheel with his good hand when he says, "Probably."

"I can do it for you, you know."

He smiles. "No, thanks, Nell. I've seen your sewing skills."

And I smile back, 'cause for a minute me and Cole feel normal, even though his hand's all cut up and we're about to go meet some girl who might be here from the future.

Cole's got the heat blasting, because it's chilly out, and now there's a draft coming from his side window. We ride with the radio on, set to Country 94.7, not talking much, just listening to Luke Combs singing "Beautiful Crazy":

She can't help but amaze me . . .

Then Lee Brice comes on, singin' "One of Them Girls":

Well, I'm one of them boys . . .

And I'm listening to those lyrics and thinking how normal this would have felt only a few days ago, before Charlotte showed up in Clawson. Me and Cole riding over to pick up Stevie B, then heading over to hang out in front of Henderson's Ice Cream. Or, if Cole just got paid, grabbing burgers at the diner, him ordering extra fries and a chocolate shake, and flirting with the waitress trying to get me a teeny bit jealous.

When we pull up in front of Stevie B's house, Cole turns the headlights off and shuts the engine down, and texts Stevie B to come out. Then he stares out the front and says, "I'm scared, Nell. Real scared." And that's the first time he's admitted that outright—at least about the whole Charlotte thing—and the way he says it feels all soft and honest.

I reach for his hand and turn it over, palm up, then trace his lifeline with my finger, saying, "Me too, Cole."

I'm waiting for him to say more, *willing* him to say more, but he doesn't. So I ask, "Who is she, Cole? And what kind of hold does she have over you?" Then I'm thinking about kissing him—not because I want to kiss him, but because these last couple of days it feels like everything has changed.

But he doesn't answer and I don't ask him again, and I don't kiss him either. I just keep holding his hand and tracing his lifeline over and over, wondering about things I've never wondered about before—breath- and soul-crushing things.

"What are you most scared of?" he asks, and it's the old Cole. Sweet Cole. Soft Cole. Kind Cole. My Cole. Not the Cole of late, who's fighting something so big that neither one of us can see past it.

"Yesterday I would have said, 'Losing you to some hussy who was moving in on my man.'"

And that gets him to smile, and it's that smile I love so much, the one where one side of his mouth turns up and his eyes get crinkly.

"That sounds like the lyrics to a country song full of other people's problems," he says, and I lean in and kiss him after all. "And today?" he asks when the kissing ends and he's got me tucked in against his shoulder.

"Charlotte mostly," I admit. "And people dying, I guess. Finn dying. My mom dying . . ." I hesitate before I add, "You dying . . ." Then I try to nudge something out of him by asking, "How 'bout you, Cole? What are you most scared of?"

"Finn dying, mostly," he says right off. "And me dying, I suppose. A little."

I want to ask, *Why do you think you're gonna die, Cole?* But I don't. I say, "Don't forget my mom."

And he pulls me closer and squeezes me tighter before he says, "Your mom's not gonna die, Nell. God's too scared of her."

"I thought you broke up with God," I tease, 'cause he tells me that a lot.

"I did," he says. "But we still talk from time to time."

"What about me? Aren't you afraid of me dying?"

"Nah," Cole says, like he really means it. "You can't die, Nell. You were made to last forever."

I jab him with my elbow, then tuck into his shoulder even tighter, swiping at the beginning of a tear and thinking about how lucky I am that I found him in the cubbies in kindergarten and how lucky I am that he was brave enough back then to take me on.

"What else are you afraid of?" I try, still hoping to shake something out of him as I wipe a whole storm's worth of tears off my cheeks.

"The world not being what I thought it was," he offers, and then he looks through the windshield at the night sky studded with stars. "It's bigger than we thought, Nell. Way bigger."

"What do you mean?" I ask, not entirely sure I want to hear his answer.

"You think we're stuck here in Clawson with only *this*," he says. "You're wrong, Nellie."

"You aren't thinking about going somewhere without me, are you?" I ask, sick with the thoughts spinning in my head.

Cole doesn't answer that directly; he says, "It's gonna be okay, Nell."

And I kiss his hand and look up at him, wishing that was true and wishing I could roll back time and we could be alone tonight. Just me and him lying on a blanket under the night sky. Cole dreaming like he does, talking about the bigness and the promise of the universe. Him pointing up at one of the constellations— Cassiopeia or Orion, Jupiter shining beneath Leo, or the bright stars of the Northern Cross—as he traces his finger through the air like he's touching the sky, me peeking through the pine boughs with my head on his chest, not seeing what he's pointing at but pretending that I do. Then Cole slowly running his fingers over mine like he's in no hurry, touching for no reason but the closeness of it, as I blink away a stray tear that makes no sense, since I am nowhere near sad. Because it's not now—it's before—and Charlotte's not here—never was here—and it's just an ordinary night, strung with stars like party lights, and time has stopped and morning is a million miles away. Then Cole whispering, or humming a song, touching my skin like he's tracing stars, telling me good things are coming. Then kissing, or maybe more. Softly at first, and then with more urgency, until everything is blurred and entangled, then frenzied, and then over and calm. Us damp with sweat, like the dew on the leaves at night or the grass in morning or the forest floor beneath us.

But I can't manage to hang on to those thoughts, because I catch Cole's eye and he pulls me back to this truck, to here and now, when there is so much I could say—about tonight and about the future, about us, about Charlotte and about tomorrow. But I say nothing. Because you can't fit a lifetime of words into a hurry of a moment.

Then Cole leans in, and his breath is on my neck and then my cheek, and I get a chill when he whispers, "Nell," then, "Nellie," soft as a breeze through flowers in summer as he kisses the heart-shaped birthmark sitting just beneath my collarbone and whispers, "You're my one in a million." And I whisper, "Cole," as he sweeps both of his arms around me in a hug.

Then the two of us sit there, not talking, just holding each other, until the moment is shattered when we hear a door slam and muffled voices, and we turn to watch as a light pops on and Stevie B steps outside onto his front porch, hurries down the steps, and full-on runs toward Cole's truck.

16

After Cole parks under the pines off the dirt road up by the quarry, we hop out of the truck and he tosses us flashlights, then pulls out a duffel bag he's got stashed in the bed, doing all of that with his one good hand. The three of us then hike the last two hundred yards, taking in the crisp fall air and the black of night, letting our flashlights hop and dance along the forest floor. We're walking single file, and we're not talking. Cole's out front. Me next. Stevie B bringin' up the rear. I'm listening to the crickets chirping, and the trills and warbles of a thrush, and the raspy croak of the night herons as the leaves shuffle underfoot. And I'm thinking bad thoughts, mostly. But if this was any other night, if we were here for any other reason—a normal reason—we'd be breathing in the smoke from some distant fire or taking in the butterscotchy perfume of the pines and the earthy scent of the leaves decaying on the ground, musky and dank with rot. Stevie B'd be cracking jokes, or complaining about this or that, and Cole'd be holding my hand maybe, or singing that Lauren Daigle song he loves: *"I will send out an army to find you in the middle of the darkest night . . ."* Him adding my name at the end or maybe messing up the lyrics, his voice strummin' my heart like it has strings, and I'd be thinking about nothing at all, or plain old normal stuff.

Cole stops when he gets to the gray stones that surround the jumping-off place where we sit sometimes after we climb back up to collect our things, the two of us wrapped in a blanket, all charged up—fiery-hot and shivering-cold at the same time. I watch as he sets his duffel bag down and looks around, me wondering what he's thinking and what he's got in the bag, but I don't ask about either. I walk over to the edge of the cliff face and shine my light down the thirty feet or so to the inky black water of the quarry as Stevie B sits on a flat rock off by himself, head down, hands shoved into his sweatshirt pockets.

I start thinking again about me and Cole, back to when we jumped together that first time, and the night after that, when we jumped again, and then a few nights later, when we jumped the third time. It became a regular thing after that, me and him jumping a couple of times a week that first summer and the two summers that followed. The two of us jumping from early June, when the air was giddy and sweet with honeysuckle and wild rose, until spring leaned into summer, then tumbled into fall when the leaves blazed scarlet and amber and burnt orange, and the nights stretched out dark and cold. By the time fall tipped into winter, the two of us were wholly missing the sheer thrill of the summer quarry. Not just the jumping, but all it entailed—the sneaking out and sneaking back in; the fact that me and Cole had carved out something we had together that no one else knew about.

I get all warm and tingly thinking about those feelings now: that rush and swoop of fear and excitement that were wrapped up in those summer nights when dusk and dawn were separated by such promise and possibility. But then all those good feelings fall away when I look over at Cole, his shoulders slumped and his head down, as we wait for Charlotte to show up, and for the truth to land, cold and bracing.

"How long would it take to freeze to death down there this time of year?" I call out to the two of them.

Cole answers real quick, saying, "Head up and breathin', but in the water? Fifteen to thirty minutes, give or take." And those words cut with a razor-sharp edge.

"Sounds like you've given that some thought already," I challenge.

"Quarry water's way colder than seawater, is all," Cole says, and I'm wondering if that's true, and how it is that he knows it. "Inflow of groundwater keeps it colder than you'd expect," he continues, like he heard my thoughts and he's now an expert on quarry temperature.

I'm thinking about how, by the time we climbed back out onto the rocks after we jumped, me and Cole would sometimes be so cold, even in the heart of the hottest summer, that our lips would be as pale blue as robin eggs in May, or the chicory flowers that bloom along the side of the road in July.

"How about in a wet suit?" I ask, thinking about the one I found in Charlotte's bag. "How long you figure it would take then?"

When Cole doesn't answer, Stevie B asks, "We gonna talk about this, guys? *Really* talk about this being-from-the-future thing and what Cole's doing? Or are we just gonna sit here in the dark discussing the temperature of the water?"

"Charlotte's gonna be here any minute," Cole offers, "and she'll explain everything."

"So you told her we'd be here?" I ask, and it comes out fast and harsh. Way harsher than I meant it to. I figured Cole was gonna surprise Charlotte with us being here. Ambush her, so she couldn't say no. But I guess that's not the case, 'cause even in the dark, I can see Cole nod.

"I wanna hear it from you first," I tell him.

And finally, he starts to talk.

Slow and low and serious at first. Then the words start pouring out of him, like a squall that sprang up from a dark place. And those words, they sting, then soak us to the bone.

17

Charlotte says the bottom of the quarry is a place where you can enter."

"Enter *what*, exactly?" I ask Cole, my heart thump-thumping and my breath coming in hungry, shallow gulps.

He hesitates, then says it outright. "She says there's a time portal."

Stevie B lets out a moan, then shoots up onto his feet, steaming-mad. "Seriously, Cole? *A time portal?* Like that's a *thing?*"

"Let Cole talk," I say sharply.

"This is bullshit!" Stevie B yells. "Listen to yourself, Cole!"

"I heard you two talking at my house," Cole yells back at him. "You knew where this was going."

"It's different when you say it out loud like that, Cole," I tell him, feeling just *how* different it is as I try to defend Stevie B.

"Were you expecting a time machine?" Cole asks him, ignoring me.

Stevie B's ignoring me now too, and the two of them are standing nose to nose.

"Like something from an old movie? An H. G. Wellsian steampunk contraption? Or Donnie Darko and a giant rabbit?" Cole continues. "A velvet chair, a giant spinning wheel, and flashing lights? Or something *Back to the Future*–esque. A DeLorean?"

"A DeLorean would be way cooler than drowning yourself," Stevie B shouts back.

But before Cole can answer, there's movement somewhere—on the path or in the underbrush—a rustle and a crack, and all three of us freeze. I expect to see Charlotte appear, or a deer maybe, but there's nothing.

"It's right here. Like I said, at the bottom of the quarry," Cole continues after it quiets again. "You go in. You climb out. Same place, different time."

"So let me get this straight," Stevie B starts, anger still steady in his voice. "You're saying Charlotte time-traveled here from the future by jumping into *this* quarry? *That's* what we're supposed to believe."

Cole nods. Stevie B turns to me, then back to Cole. "So she lives in the future? That's what you're saying?"

"It's complicated, but yeah. She lives right here in Clawson, in the future."

Stevie B keeps staring right at him, fed up and pissed off like he can't believe any of it, then says, "Bullshit, Cole!" before he turns to me again. "Nell, I'm sticking with Cole's having some kind of breakdown. Or maybe Charlotte *is* some kind of con artist, aiming to steal money or break someone out of prison underwater El Chapo–style. Maybe she's duped Cole here into helping her. I don't know. But either way, I'm not buying this."

I just stand there, broken down, not saying a word, not agreeing or disagreeing—not *anything*—and Cole says, "Look at me, Nell."

And I do.

"Is that what you think too? That I would do this, leave you, leave Finn and my mom, risk everything, for a prison break or blackmail or some kind of con?"

I freeze.

Stevie B freezes.

I take a step back. Glance toward the quarry. "So you're going, Cole? With Charlotte. To the future," I ask, my voice barely louder than a heartbeat.

He looks at his feet, and I have my answer. "Tell me *why*. Why are you doing this?" I beg. When he doesn't answer, I ask, "How come we never time-traveled, Cole? You and me jumped off these rocks into this quarry a hundred times. Where was the time portal then?"

Stevie B tenses up even more, his eyes moving back and forth between me and Cole, probably wondering when we were jumping off anything without him. But he doesn't utter a word.

"It's not that simple," Cole defends, his voice soft now too. "We never stayed under long enough. We never went deep enough. We came close, though. Right, Nell? Tell him! Tell Stevie B about that time we went too far and stayed down too long. Go ahead! Tell him what happened!"

I don't say anything. And Cole doesn't push me.

Stevie B asks, "What is Cole talking about?"

When I still don't answer, can't answer—fear's fingers in a stranglehold around my throat—Stevie B whispers, "One of you has gotta tell me what happened!"

I manage to say, "I don't know what happened," the words blunt and true.

Stevie B sighs, then turns to Cole. But Cole doesn't say a thing.

"Well," Stevie B adds after a long moment, "at least Cole's breath holding and Charlotte's wet suit make sense now." Then there's another creak and shudder as a gust of wind courses through the treetops.

When it quiets, I ask, "What does she want from you, Cole? If it's not a prison break or a con or blackmail, why's Charlotte here? Where is she taking you, and what does she want?"

Cole shakes his head like he's not gonna tell us.

"Cole, come on!" Stevie B presses. "If she *can* time-travel, why Clawson? And why you? Tell us why *you're* doing this!"

When he doesn't answer, Stevie B starts shoving Cole's shoulder, trying to start a fight. I know he's just pissed off and wants to stop Cole from doing something dangerous, so I say, "Stevie B, don't!" But he shoves Cole again. Harder this time.

Cole ducks a blow and whispers, "Stop," begging for this part of whatever this is to end.

"What are you doing, believing this?" Stevie B yells. He grabs Cole's shoulder again and then hits him for real, harder this time. "You promised you'd never hurt her!"

Cole freezes. "This isn't hurting her," he yells back. "I have no choice."

"What are you two talking about?" I ask.

Cole gives Stevie B a look of warning.

"Tell me what the hell you're talking about!"

"*You*, Nell," Stevie B, says. "We're talking about *you*. Cole promised to never hurt you. And this is hurting you, Nell."

"Cole would never hurt me!"

"This is hurting you, Nell!"

"Stop," Cole says, near tears. "Both of you stop!"

But I can't stop. I love them both so much, and we're all hurting, and it feels like the whole world might explode. Then Cole steps forward and hugs Stevie B.

He hugs him hard. *Real* hard. Scoops him into his arms in a bear hug Stevie B can't wrestle and pound his way out of. So he leans into the hug, into Cole's shoulder, and starts to cry big heaving sobs.

I join in, wrapping my arms around the two of them, and it still feels like the world is ending. But for a single breath, I get my bearings and I tell myself, *Remember what's important, and fix this.*

Then I start thinking about what Stevie B just said about Cole promising he'd never hurt me, and what he said about this being a con. The stuff about this being related to the prison. I think about Charlotte's empty phone, and her not having a last name or a place to live. I think about her looking like she's not from around here, and the dry bag she hauls to school with a wet suit in it, and those electronic gadgets she has. Then there's Cole and the bathtub and the breath holding, and him asking me to trust him.

Then I think about what Cole said about how he wouldn't leave me and wouldn't leave Finn and his mom. And I get this feeling— this feeling of knowing something with a degree of gut-crushing certainty—and it's like my mom always says, *We know stuff, Nell. Listen to it!*

I pull away from the hug and say, "I know why Charlotte's here," my words cold and heavy as river stones.

Cole turns to me expectantly. Stevie B lifts his head from Cole's shoulder, his face red and wet with tears.

I watch them both standing there, clutching each other, all of us afraid of what's coming, me knowing I have no right knowing this thing I know. And yet *I know.*

"Charlotte's not here for Cole, Stevie B," I say. "And she's not here for some prison break. And Cole would never hurt me. Not on purpose anyway."

I lock eyes with Cole and nod. "Tell him, Cole. Go ahead and tell him. Tell Stevie B why Charlotte's here."

And Cole says it for me: that thing I know, that realization that sucked my breath away.

Cole says, "Nell's right. Charlotte's not here for me, at least not really. And she's not here for money or some prisoner up in Manville either."

Me and Cole exchange a look of knowing, our hearts on the edge of breaking wide open.

And then his heart does. It bursts and pours out right here onto the forest floor.

Cole says, "You can't be mad, Stevie B. I'm not hurting Nell. I'm saving someone."

Stevie B looks from me to Cole, then back again.

And I say it for him. "Charlotte came here for Finn."

18

Cole unzips his duffel bag, removes a folded piece of paper, and hands it to me. It's a copy of a newspaper clipping from the *Clawson Gazette* with a grainy photo of Finn. Her hair's in pigtails, and her front teeth are missing. It looks so much like Finn right now that it could have been taken yesterday. I glance up at Cole, and he nods like he's saying *Go ahead, Nell. See what it says.*

I hesitate, not wanting to. But when he nods again, I start to read.

The loving daughter of Emmett and Cindy Wilder . . .

Pulse quickening, breath short, heart shattering like candy glass, not sure what to do or think or say, I look up at Cole again. But he's turned away from me, like the truth of this is just too hard to face. I glance over at Stevie B, and his face is open and blank, like fear is the only thing he knows right now.

I force myself to read the rest of it.

*. . . and the adored sister of Cole Wilder, Finnegan Shay
Wilder, died on October 19, from complications due to an
unknown respiratory illness.*

My eyes travel back up to Cole, my hands shaking, my skin
cold as quarry water, my eyes big and wet. He meets my gaze
this time, reeling from the truth of this, and it's me who turns
away.

I keep reading. Not wanting to but *needing* to. Flashlight in one
hand, newspaper clipping visibly trembling in the other.

*Finnegan Shay Wilder was pronounced dead at Clawson
Hospital Center at 5 p.m. last Saturday. A service will be
held . . .*

I don't finish.

Cole says, "Check the date, Nell."

"Already did," I whisper. Then I try to hand the article to
Stevie B, but he swats my hand away.

"Just tell me what it says, Nell."

I don't tell him. I don't say anything.

If I can believe what the piece of paper in my hand is saying,
what Cole is saying, Finn is gonna die in three days. *This Saturday.*
And I don't know how any of us will be able to climb over that
much pain.

Then Cole speaks. "It's an article from the *Clawson Gazette* that
says Finn's gonna die, Stevie B." His voice comes out as a coarse
whisper, those words pallbearers of a weighty truth. "In three days,
Finn's gonna die."

Stevie B whimpers, like some fatally wounded creature.

Cole says, "And Charlotte came here to save her."

19

I manage to ask, "How?" but it comes out closer to a moan than a word, so I clear my throat and try again. "How will Charlotte save her, Cole?"

"I saw Finn's chart, Nell. A month ago, when she was in the hospital. They don't know what she has, but it's not asthma. It's just like I thought all these years. It's something way worse, and my mom's been lying to me about that. So I started searching on the internet for what Finn might have, or a treatment for kids who stop breathing, and there was nothing that made sense.

"Then I stumbled onto the dark web and started looking for a miracle—any way to help Finn. Like a drug that's not approved yet. Or some kind of experimental treatment in another country. And all I found was other families who had little kids die from respiratory failure the doctors couldn't explain.

"Then Charlotte found me. She saw my posts and she said she knew exactly what Finn has. I didn't trust her at first, but she said some things that made me think she was for real—science things, and things about Clawson that I could check out. And she convinced me that if I do what she says, she can save her."

Cole looks directly at Stevie B, his eyes pleading. "You've been a brother to me my entire life, and I know how this sounds. And I know you're still thinking this is some kind of scam and you're just trying to protect me and protect Nell—I get that. But . . . Finn . . . she's gonna die. This Saturday, Stevie B!"

"But you found Charlotte on the dark web, Cole!" he protests.

"He's right, Cole," I say. "The dark web's for drug dealers and crypto criminals and child traffickers and con men and weirdos."

"And time travelers," Cole says before he reaches into the duffel bag and pulls out a wet suit. And that's when we know for sure that his mind is made up.

A twig breaks in the woods nearby, and Cole spins around.

There's another snap. And another.

Stevie B looks alarmed, but Cole heads off down the path, shining his flashlight as he goes.

Then we hear muffled voices.

"Must be Charlotte," I say, peering into the dark.

"What do we do now, Nell?" Stevie B asks.

"Only one thing we can do."

"What's that?"

"Figure out if what Charlotte's saying is true."

"How?"

"By listening to her, I guess."

"And if it is?"

I hear Cole's voice on the day Finn was born:

I'd give Finn my lungs if I could.

Followed by my words that day:

One lung from you and one lung from me is a way better plan.

"Then we have to help them," I tell Stevie B.

"So that's it?" he asks. "That's what we do?"

"That's it," I confirm. "That's what we do."

Then I grab his hand and hold it as tight as I can, because it feels like the earth is spinning so damn fast right now that I might go flying off into the dark and lose everything.

20

When Cole returns with Charlotte, he doesn't say anything.
And she doesn't say anything either. She just sets her dry bag down on the rocks, then acts like she's not thrilled that we're here but maybe not shocked either. The four of us stand there all awkward— Cole and Charlotte close to the quarry, me and Stevie B a couple of yards away, by the tree line.

"How far in the future are you from?" I call over, breaking the ice with a sledgehammer.

"Seventy-seven years," she says.

"So that would be . . . ," Stevie B starts.

"The year 2101," Charlotte answers.

It's a lot to process, her saying it like that. Like it's nothing. "And you're here because . . . ?" I ask, wanting to hear her say it.

"Because Finn's going to die."

"When?" I ask.

"This Saturday at five p.m."

"From what?" Stevie B asks as my heart misses one beat, then another.

"A genetic mutation that causes degenerative lung disease and usually ends in death before the age of ten. Mostly in children of European descent who also carry a gene for . . ."

She keeps talking about medical stuff I don't understand. Stevie B flashes me a look like *Nell, do something or say something!*

"It didn't say that in her obituary," I interrupt.

"Which part?" she asks.

"The whole thing," I snap.

"They didn't know what she had back then."

"'Back then' being now?"

"Yes."

I'm trying to understand. Trying to process all of this information. "And you can save her?" I ask, glancing at Cole. "Because in 2101 there's a cure?"

"Exactly."

"What kind of cure?" Stevie B demands.

"It's a single pill. A form of therapy that delivers healthy copies of the gene," Charlotte offers.

My eyes dart from Charlotte to Stevie B to Cole. Charlotte looks confident. Stevie B seems pissed off and skeptical. But Cole appears so hopeful.

"And if she takes the pill, Finn won't die on Saturday?" Stevie B asks.

"That's correct."

"Just like that?" I ask.

"Just like that," she confirms.

"If all of this is true, why didn't you bring the medicine here yourself, Charlotte?" Stevie B presses. "And save Cole the trip."

"Cole has to see it for himself. All of it. The future. The lab . . . Otherwise, he wouldn't believe me, or risk it. Would you give Finn some pill I handed you now, with this story I'm telling you? Or would you want to go with me to check it out?"

Stevie B stands there looking at her. We all know the answer. "So why Finn? Why save her?" he continues. "Millions of little girls die, Charlotte. Why save Finn?"

"Stevie B, stop!" Cole yells. "I don't care why! I only care that she does it!"

"Have you done this before, Charlotte?" I ask. "Come to Clawson from the future to save someone?"

She stares me down, not answering one way or the other.

I'm desperate and grasping at straws. "What about Levi Tanner?"

Charlotte appears surprised. Snaps, "He doesn't matter."

Cole seems alarmed, like he figured this would unspool differently. "Who is Levi Tanner?"

"The kid in our parents' class who supposedly drowned after jumping in the quarry twenty-three years ago," I tell him. "You told me they never found his body and it was a made-up story. But it's true, Cole. Levi Tanner disappeared after he jumped into this quarry. I don't know if he drowned, but I do know he never came back."

Cole keeps staring at me, then nods like he remembers before he settles his eyes back on Charlotte. "Do you know anything about him?" Cole asks. "Did Levi Tanner drown in this quarry like everyone thinks, or did he time-travel?"

"That's not important," she says.

"Did he drown?" I press, my eyes riveted to Charlotte. "Levi Tanner."

"I told you," she says, "we don't have time for this, and he doesn't matter."

Cole says, "She's right, Nell. Finn matters now. Nothing, and no one, else."

"No. Nell's right," Stevie B insists. "*You* matter, Cole. And that kid Levi Tanner? He mattered too. And we have no real hard proof that *any* of what Charlotte's saying about a time portal or saving Finn is actually true."

"She's the proof," Cole tells him. "Her being here with those articles . . . Finn's obituary! And those futuristic gadgets she has."

"Listen to yourself," Stevie B yells. "It sounds like you've been brainwashed! And you've been sucked into some ridiculous, made-up bullshit story."

Cole walks over and puts his arm around Stevie B's shoulder. "Hey, it's gonna be okay," he whispers, like Stevie B's a little kid who's scared of something there's no reason to fear.

And I'm torn. I know what's at risk in both directions: If we believe her, and if we don't. If Cole goes with her, and if he doesn't. It's Finn's life and Cole's life, but I need more information.

"So assuming what you are saying is actually true, how does it work, exactly?" I ask. "The time-travel part."

Stevie B grabs my hand.

Cole looks down at the ground.

And we wait for Charlotte to answer.

21

The north and south sides of the quarry have access points to a portal," Charlotte begins. "Something called a CTC loop. It's a closed timelike curve that connects to a gravity tunnel. The portal on the north wall brings you to the future. The portal on the south wall takes you to the past."

Stevie B whispers something under his breath. Cole squeezes his shoulder.

"You guys know anything about quantum physics or how gravity tunnels work?"

I shake my head. "No clue."

"If you drilled a tunnel through the center of the earth and traveled through it, because of certain characteristics of both gravitational force and the density of the planet, you would travel much faster than you'd be able to on the earth's surface. In fact, you could travel straight through the earth to the other side in thirty-eight minutes. That's over seventeen thousand miles per hour for part of the trip, and close to eight thousand miles. In *thirty-eight minutes*."

"Yeah? Who figured that out?" Stevie B asks, still spitting mad.

Charlotte turns to him, cool and dismissive. "Hooke, Sir Isaac Newton, Galileo, Voltaire, Hawking. And those are only the early thinkers. Basically everyone who is anyone in the world of future science or quantum physics."

"But what you said—that's covering *distance* fast," I challenge. "It's not time travel."

"They're connected," Charlotte says.

"Yeah? Who fucking connected them?" Stevie B asks.

Charlotte looks at him long and hard before she says, "Hermann Minkowski."

Stevie B stares at her like he can't believe she had an answer. "Hermann Minkowski?"

She nods. "And Albert Einstein. In 1906. The space-time continuum."

I google it on my phone. "She's right, Stevie B. About Minkowski and Einstein."

He mumbles, "Fuck me."

Charlotte asks, "What do any of you know about cosmic strings? Or wormholes? Quantum tunnels? Larmor clocks? Or how particles reaching or exceeding the speed of light allow for time travel? Or—"

"Nothing," I yell, my voice trembling. "We know nothing about any of it!"

She looks defiant. "Well, think of it this way, Nell. If you're wanting to get somewhere you have no business going, like the future, you've got to go really, really fast."

"Enough, Charlotte," Cole says. "You've made your point."

Stevie B asks, "Is there a flux capacitor involved? Any bright flashing lights? Plutonium? Magic cupboards, maybe?"

"Stevie B, *stop*," Cole begs. "Everybody, stop!"

"No. I won't stop," Stevie B tells him. "I don't want to go to the cemetery for you, Cole."

"And I don't want to go for Finn," Cole shoots back. "So give Charlotte a chance."

"Look," I say to her. "Instead of the science-y parts, can you explain what Cole has to do to get the medicine to save Finn?"

"He has to hold his breath and swim down as far as he can . . ."

"How long?" I ask.

"Longer than he thinks he can."

"*Not* okay, Nell," Stevie B mumbles.

"He's going to have to watch the clock very carefully, push past the pain, then swim up at exactly the right time," Charlotte continues.

"How long?" I ask again, strength building in my voice.

"Longer than you'd think possible."

"You said that already! How long?"

She doesn't answer.

"Three minutes? Four? Five?" I press.

"Longer."

"But he'll be dead!" Stevie B yells. "What if he blacks out? Drowns? Gets hypothermia?"

"You need less oxygen because it's cold," Cole chimes in.

I pull out my phone and start googling stuff. "Okay," I say. "One minute without oxygen, and brain cells begin to die. Three minutes? Serious brain damage begins to occur. Ten minutes?" I look up. "Lots of brain cells destroyed." I pause to make the point. Then say, "Recovery? Unlikely. At *ten minutes*!"

Cole just stands there. I keep reading from my phone. "Fifteen minutes? Recovery all but impossible. *Impossible*, Cole."

"What about the world record, Nell?" Cole asks. "The free diver in Croatia. I told you guys. It was over twenty-four minutes. That's longer than fifteen minutes. Want to know why those divers don't die?"

I shake my head. "You don't have special training. You won't be monitored or in a pool with medical experts and lifeguards standing by. This is different, Cole!"

"What about her?" Stevie B interrupts. "Is it hard for you, Charlotte? Or do you have some special futuristic gills or underwater—"

"I have nothing special," she says harshly. "It's just as hard for me. My lungs are the same as Cole's and yours. So it's as risky for me to time-travel as it is for him. The only difference is, I've done it more."

"Why not use oxygen tanks?" he asks. "Or some high-tech underwater breathing—"

"We tried that," Charlotte snaps. "It doesn't work. We need to be oxygen depleted for it to work."

Stevie B stares her down.

"Look," she says, "there was a climber I read about. A couple of years ago, your time, in the state of Washington. Research it if you want. He was in the snow, lost for a week, then frozen for days. They found him, and he was presumed dead. No heartbeat—which means no oxygen. They warmed him up with saline anyway. A shot in the dark. And they brought him back, and he was fine. He was dead. And then he wasn't. That was in the snow, but it's the same in the water. Cold is cold."

"She's right," Cole says. "All of your organs are protected by the cold."

"Charlotte, tell us how long Cole has to hold his breath," Stevie B demands.

She still won't answer.

I step forward. "Just tell us!"

"Sixteen minutes," she finally says. "Cole will have to hold his breath for exactly sixteen minutes."

22

Sixteen minutes, and he'll be there. In the future. In the year 2101," Charlotte continues as she sits down on the rocks, her legs crossed in front of her, the dry bag sitting at her side, her hair up in a tight bun, prepped for swimming. But what really catches my attention is the necklace hanging around her neck. The gold necklace with the turquoise stone as luminous and transparent as her eyes. The same gold necklace with the tiny pearls she was wearing when she showed up at school two days ago.

"How'd you come up with sixteen minutes?" I ask, watching the necklace catch the light from our flashlights.

"There's a formula. It's a fraction under twelve and a half seconds for each year."

"So sixteen minutes is . . . what?" I ask.

"If we hold our breath for exactly sixteen minutes—nine hundred sixty seconds—it will bring us seventy-seven years into the future," Charlotte confirms.

Stevie B has a dazed-and-confused look. "So anyone can time-travel?"

"Yes. Assuming they have access to a portal and know how it works."

"And you're saying you can go anywhere in time just by holding your breath long enough and jumping into this quarry? So someone could go a thousand years into the future or back to the Ice Age?"

"No," Charlotte says. "The longest anyone has traveled in either direction—so far, at least—is just under eighty years."

"How come?" Stevie B demands.

"The limits of holding one's breath."

"So you admit there are limits, then?" he presses.

"I never said there weren't," she snaps.

"Both of you, stop!" Cole begs.

"And this medicine that will cure Finn, it was invented when, exactly?" I ask, trying to redirect the conversation.

"A few months ago. My time," Charlotte says. "June of 2101. That's why I'm here now."

"How will Cole know when nine hundred sixty seconds are up?" I ask.

She pulls out a small electronic gadget half the size of a cell phone—it's identical to the one I took from her bag. "This device computes exactly how long you have to hold your breath, and where along the wall you have to be to enter, based on the exact date and time you want to travel to."

She unfolds it and opens two screens: one a timer, the other a map. Then she starts the timer counting down from 960 seconds.

959, 958, 957, 956 . . .

"When the countdown hits four hundred eighty, we have to have reached the right entry point along the quarry wall, which corresponds with this location on the map," she says, pointing.

"So it's both time *and* depth?"

"Exactly. Cole and I will then enter the gravity tunnel by

pressing up against the wall at exactly four hundred eighty seconds in this exact location."

"Then what?" I ask.

Her eyes get big. "Whoosh!"

Stevie B mutters, "Shit!"

"When we reach the other side," Charlotte continues, "the device will pick up again at four hundred eighty seconds. We'll then immediately begin a controlled ascent, back up to the surface, timing it so we stick our heads out of the water when the timer hits zero."

I turn to Cole, and he seems determined. Stevie B is wide-eyed.

"Eight minutes down. Enter the tunnel. Eight minutes back up," she says.

"What about the transit time in the tunnel?" Stevie B challenges.

"Light speed, or close to it," she reports. "So, negligible."

"Then what?" I ask.

"Then I take him to 225 Decatur Street so he'll see this is legit."

I google the address on my phone.

"Then that night, he goes back alone, I'll give him the security codes, he breaks in, goes to the third-floor lab, and steals a pill from the vial labeled 'LR-009.'"

"The third floor? The third floor of 225 Decatur Street?"

"Yes."

"That's the Dunkin' Donuts," I say.

"That's a Dunkin' Donuts *now*," she says. "In 2101, it's a biotech company owned by my family."

"So he'll go to the Dunkin' Donuts that's now a biotech company in his wet clothes?"

"He'll have dry clothes," she says as she points to her bag.

"Hold on," Stevie B says. "Why does he have to break in and steal it?"

"My family doesn't know what I'm doing. They *can't* know what

I am doing. *I* can't get caught. There are a lot of people in my time who don't want us doing this."

"So why are you doing it, then?" Stevie B asks.

"That's easy. To save Finn."

"But why do you want to save Finn Wilder? You didn't answer that question," he says. "And who exactly is 'us'?"

"I can't answer either of those questions."

"But if Cole can successfully steal the pill and doesn't get arrested and he actually makes it back and gives it to Finn, you're saying she'll be cured?" I ask. "She won't die on Saturday?"

"Yes, Nell. That's why we have to hurry."

"So he'll be back when, exactly?" I ask.

"In one day. *Thursday.* Two days at the latest."

"So Friday?"

"Yes."

"What if it takes longer?"

"Then Finn will die."

"What if the medicine doesn't work?" I challenge.

"What if it does?" Cole says.

"It will," Charlotte says. "Or I wouldn't be here."

"One dose?" I question. "And she's cured. For life. Finn won't die?"

"As long as she gets it before five p.m. on Saturday," she confirms, "Finn won't die until she's old."

"How does Cole get back?" I ask.

"The same way he got there," she says.

"But without you."

"Correct."

"If he's off by just a few seconds or a few feet in either direction, he won't be here to save her!" Stevie B comments.

"Then I guess I'll have to get it right," Cole says.

"What if he can't?" I ask.

"Can't what?"

"Hold his breath for sixteen minutes on his way to 2101, or on the way back."

"Then he'll be dead or stuck there."

"Will *I* be there in the future? If Cole gets stuck in 2101?" I ask. "I'd be what?"

"Ninety-four," she says. "Assuming you're not already dead."

"Well? *Am* I dead, Charlotte?"

"I don't think she can tell us that, Nell," Cole says softly.

"Why not? Because I'd kind of like to know."

"He's right," Charlotte says. "I can't."

"Because?"

"Because of something called a causal loop."

"Which is what?" I ask.

"If I tell you something like that, like what you're asking, you might do something to change things. And that can change history, so I can't tell you."

"You're already changing history by saving Finn!" I challenge.

"That's because Finn's not supposed to die," she shoots back.

"Why not?" I press. "And how do you know?"

I'm standing nose to nose with Charlotte when she says, "I'm sorry, but I can't tell you that either."

23

"Look," Charlotte says, "I can't answer all your questions, and you have to stop trying to understand everything. Just know that there are reasons—good reasons—for all of this, and it's important that Cole comes with me and that Finn doesn't die. And there's no time. So we have to go tonight. *Now*, in fact."

Cole picks up his wet suit and starts putting it on. He won't look at me.

Charlotte hits a few buttons on one of her devices, and it produces a super-high-tech hologram display with colorful laser lights, diagramming the quarry.

Stevie B mumbles, "What the . . ."

When Cole's dressed, Charlotte looks him over. Her eyes settling on his bandaged hand. She says, "That's going to slow you down."

"No, it won't."

She seems to consider that, but then lets it go and turns back to the hologram. "Remember the outcroppings, here and here," she says, pointing. "The stone ladder we'll climb down is located under this ridge on the north wall. Remember the handholds, on this side. Use your good hand. You're going to feel pain—ignore it. And count the whole time, like we practiced. One, one thousand, two, one thousand, three . . . There will be a warm current on the eastern side, about halfway down. And we want to reach *this* spot, right here, at three hundred forty-five seconds. We'll be using the map feature to track our descent as well. And remember what I've explained about the free fall at fifty feet or so."

Cole nods.

Charlotte holds up her timer. "Then, one hundred ten seconds later, assuming all goes well, we'll hit the icy pool. That'll send pain shooting through our limbs. We talked about this. Push past it. Grab hold here and here," she adds as she points out different places on the hologram. "You'll become numb. It's okay. Just keep watching the clock as we descend. And count. One, one thousand, two, one thousand . . ."

She keeps talking. I memorize every word she is saying. I think about being determined and strong. I think about how brave Cole will have to be to do this.

I think about Finn dying.

And I think about Finn not dying.

Then I tell myself I can be brave. And I concentrate on counting in my head, like Charlotte's telling Cole to do. Counting the seconds. *One, one thousand, two, one thousand, three, one thousand . . .* I get to ten, then start again. I hear her voice saying, *Repeat that pattern ninety-six times.*

"How can he possibly follow this," I say, when she's done talking, "and time it right?"

Charlotte looks over at me. Her necklace catches the light again. It distracts me, until she confirms what I already knew.

"It's simple," she says. "He has no choice."

24

Then I say the thing I've been afraid to say. "I think we can trust her."

Cole instantly looks grateful, but Stevie B stares at me like I just betrayed him.

I go out on a limb. "Look at the necklace she's wearing."

I catch Charlotte's eye for a flash. She seems surprised at first, then something else. Relieved, maybe.

I look at the turquoise stone, the tiny pearls that surround it, the glint from the chain. "Cole, read the engraving."

He looks at me, questioning.

"Go ahead. The engraving on her necklace. Read it."

Charlotte removes the chain from around her neck, then hands it to Cole.

I ask him, "Does it say 'To AW from LMW'?"

He looks down and finds the engraving. Shock and confusion register on his face before he stammers, "How did you know that?"

Charlotte steps back looking concerned.

I was right. I wasn't certain. But now I am. And I'm guessing that she didn't think anyone would recognize it.

"Cole's grandma had the same necklace. Not one *like* it," I say. "She had *exactly* the same one." I reach down and pull out the necklace I have stashed in my boot. I hold it up. It catches in the light too.

Hers and mine. The gold chain, the turquoise stone, the tiny pearls, the engraving—the prophecy and the legacy—they are identical.

"Cole," Stevie B presses, "is that true? Is that your grandma's necklace?"

Cole is still visibly rattled as he hands the necklace back to Charlotte. "I don't know. I don't pay attention to jewelry. But the engraving, the initials . . . It says 'To AW.' Alice Wilder. My grandma. 'From LMW.' Lawrence Mercer Wilder. My grandpa."

Stevie B turns to me. "You knew that, Nell, about the engraving, this whole time?"

"No. Definitely not. Not until Cole read it just now. But I thought I recognized the necklace when Charlotte wore it to school on Monday. Here." I hand him the necklace I'm holding. "I took this from Finn's room when Cole asked me to babysit yesterday. I saw the engraving and . . ."

Charlotte hands her necklace to Stevie B, and he compares them. "So if this is Cole's grandma's, then how are there *two* of them?"

"Double occupancy," Charlotte says.

Stevie B mutters, "Fuck me."

She shrugs. "A single object can exist as two objects simultaneously if one of them was transported from a different time period."

"How?" I ask, feeling both validated and untethered.

"Because of the laws of quantum physics and the space-time continuum, and the fact that there are continuous sets of spatiotemporal locations—something known as the Cheshire Cat effect."

"What does that all mean? In simple English!"

"It means, Nell, that you can have the necklace and I can too."

I take both necklaces from Stevie B and look at mine, then at hers. I feel overwhelmed . . . "So these are actually the same necklace?" I ask. "There's only one?"

She confirms. "It's a fourth-dimension thing."

"Because you brought it here from the future."

"Exactly."

"And if Charlotte has Cole's grandma's necklace," Stevie B continues, "that means Charlotte must be Cole's—"

"So you must be my . . . ," Cole says, voice shaking, and it's clear Charlotte hasn't told him everything. He has no idea who she is. And neither do I. I didn't think this necklace thing all the way through.

Stevie B jumps in with, "Not his wife . . ."

Charlotte takes her necklace back from me before she says, "Let it go. It's better if you don't know."

I'm thinking, *Okay, so I'm right. She didn't think that the necklace would be recognized. And she doesn't want us to know who she is.*

Cole keeps staring at her. Then he turns from Charlotte to me and back again.

I look at Cole. Then at her. I search her face for clues.

And then I see it.

And I know.

I take a step back. "You're Cole's . . ."

"Great-granddaughter," Charlotte whispers, her words closing one scary door but opening another. "I'm Cole Wilder's great-granddaughter."

25

Cole keeps staring at Charlotte.

I stare too, trying to think about what this means, and what else she knows, and what to ask, and what to do, and how this changes things.

Stevie B asks Cole, "So you didn't know?"

He shakes his head. "No."

"Did you know, Nell?"

"Absolutely not."

Then Stevie B says, "Fuck me," again.

It's so clear now. The resemblance.

The lips that turn up slightly on one side. The shape of her shoulders. The hunter's eyes.

I see something else too. Her lighter hair color: amber to Cole's ebony. The shape of her nose: softer, less angular. Her skin: light to his dark.

"So . . . ," I start, my heart pounding, the words catching in my throat. No, that's not where they're caught—it's my heart that has tangled them up. "If you're Cole's great-granddaughter, then who's . . . ?"

I don't finish. I glance at Cole again, then at Charlotte.

I feel panicked. I want to run, need to stay. Can't feel my fingers or toes. I just feel my heart. It's enormous and pounding. She looks like Cole, but does she also look like . . . me?

I want to ask *Who am I? To you, Charlotte. Am I your great-grandmother? Or did Cole have a baby with . . .*

. . . someone . . . who's . . .

. . . not me?

Cole sees that question all over my face.

He turns away.

He doesn't know either.

Stevie B's eyes jump from me to Cole to Charlotte, then back to me, before he blurts out "Fuck me" one more time.

"I know what you're asking, Nell. And I can't tell you," Charlotte says softly. "Remember what I said about the risks of you knowing things that might create a causal loop? The less you know, the better. So that thing you want to ask me? Please don't ask it."

I lower myself onto a rock, because my legs can't support the weight of this. I exchange another look with Cole; it's as quick and as charged as a lightning strike.

The new girl? The one who says she's here from the future? The girl who says that Finn is going to die and she can save her? The girl who says she's Cole's great-granddaughter? The girl who may—or may not—be related to me? The girl with all the answers?

She just stands there and doesn't say another thing.

26

Cole sits down next to me, a few yards away from Charlotte and Stevie B. "Where's the necklace?" he asks, brushing his hand against mine, entwining our fingers. Then his hand is on my shoulder; he traces the birthmark beneath my collarbone, plants a kiss on my cheek, whispers, "You're my one in a million, Nell." And he pulls me into a hug, and my lips are on his neck, then his cheek . . .

"The necklace?" he asks again. "Where is it?" His voice as soft as a breath.

I hold it up.

"I want you to wear it. Forever. No matter what happens, don't ever take it off."

I reach around my neck to secure the clasp.

He whispers, "It ties us to each other through generations."

"What if it doesn't?" I ask.

"Doesn't what?"

I nod toward Charlotte. "Tie us together through generations?"

"What if it does?"

That's me and Cole. The pessimist and the optimist. The dark and the bright.

"We leave in a few minutes," Charlotte calls over to us as she puts her necklace back on, shimmies out of her running pants and steps into a sleek black hooded wet suit. I'm thinking she looks like Catwoman or a sexy Navy SEAL or one of Stevie B's merpeople when Stevie B blurts out, "Tell us something that gonna happen tomorrow, Charlotte."

She stops what she's doing. "What do you mean?"

"Tell us something that's gonna happen in the world tomorrow. Anything. A climber dies on Everest. A hurricane hits Florida. Or, I know: The Knicks are playing the Lakers tomorrow night. What's the score gonna be?"

She dismisses his request. "I don't have access to that kind of information while I'm here." Her voice is softer. Kinder.

"So use one of your futuristic devices. Look it up!"

"It doesn't work that way," she tells him. "I can't get information from the future when I'm in the past." She stops. "Wait, hold on . . . There is something that caught my attention. Tomorrow there's going to be an attempted escape at the prison."

"At Manville?" he asks. "Manville Correctional Facility?"

"Yes. There's a guy named . . . Wozniak, I think. He makes an escape attempt during a medical escort to the hospital."

"What kind of hospital visit? Routine or emergency?" I ask, alarmed.

I'm thinking, *My mom is on the hospital transport team at the prison. She's on the day shift tomorrow.* The day shift handles routine hospital visits.

"Routine."

"You sure?" I ask.

"Routine. It said 'routine transport.'"

"What happens?" I ask, thinking, *If there's a prison break, a guard could get killed.*

"He gets shot," Charlotte says.

"Wozniak gets shot?" I confirm.

"Yes. He dies."

"So if Wozniak tries to escape, gets shot, and dies tomorrow," Stevie B continues, "then we'll know for sure that Charlotte's telling the truth. So we wait. Until tomorrow. Then you go with her. Tomorrow, Cole. If she's right about Wozniak."

"No," Charlotte says. "I've given you enough proof. We have to go tonight. *Now.* Finn can't wait."

"She's right," Cole says. "There's no time. Tomorrow's Thursday. If I leave tomorrow, I have almost no time to get back."

"Look," Charlotte says, "you guys can't tell anyone about any of this. Not about me or time travel or the quarry—or the necklace. Or the prisoner escape. Not anything."

"Anyone get hurt?" I ask. "I mean, other than Wozniak?"

Charlotte shakes her head. "Not that I remember."

Cole tries to clarify, "So no guards escorting the prisoner to the hospital get hurt?"

"No."

"You're sure?"

"What I read, and what I remember, is that the only person who gets hurt is the inmate, but I didn't know I was going to be drilled on the details. I just didn't want to stumble out of the woods with no ID on a day the town was swarming with cops."

I turn to Cole and whisper, "My mom . . ."

"I know, Nell."

"With only two guards on the escort team, it's fifty-fifty that she'll be the shooter, Cole. And they'll drug test. And it *will* come back positive."

"Nell . . ."

I keep my voice down so Charlotte won't hear. "And that means she'll go to prison."

"I'm going, Nell," Cole says. "I have to. We'll figure out your mom after. I promise." He kisses me. "I'll be back tomorrow or Friday. Two days at the latest."

"So do I wait here?" I ask. "Just sit here at the quarry and *wait until Friday?*"

"No. Go home. Act normal. Go to school." His voice is hushed. "Watch Finn. Don't bring attention to this place." He tries to hand me his phone. "Here. Take this. Send my mom texts once or twice a day. Pretend they're from me. Tell her I went for a ride to the mountains to clear my head."

"Cole, no!" I plead, pushing the phone away. "I can't do that!"

"You have to, Nell. It'll keep her calm, and she won't . . . report me missing."

"Jesus, Cole!" I take the phone from him.

He kisses my cheek and lips. "I love you," he says. "Before and after. Now and then. Always and forever . . . If something happens and I don't make it back in time . . ."

I whimper, "Cole, no."

"On Saturday, Nell . . . if Finn dies—"

"Cole! No!"

"Take care of my mom for me."

He doesn't wait for me to respond. He just walks away and hugs Stevie B.

Then I walk over to Charlotte and hug her.

I hug the girl who may or may not be here from the future.

The girl who may or may not save Finn.

The girl who may or may not be my great-granddaughter.

The girl who is taking Cole away from me.

I hug her tight and I hug her hard.

And then I let her go.

27

*When Stevie B shines his flashlight on the two of them stand-*ing together on the jumping-off place, Charlotte turns toward me. I nod ever so slightly, like I'm saying *Good luck.* Or *Take care of Cole.* Or *I trust you.* Or maybe *Goodbye.* Then her eyes do that thing again where they turn from a pale turquoise to deep sapphire to boiling black.

Cole doesn't look over at us. I know he can't. It would be too hard. He's made his decision.

I stare at them in silhouette.

They look like Cole and me.

Tall and short.

Ebony and amber.

Two people tied together, certain in one thing.

They are going to jump.

Me and Stevie B don't move.

Not when Charlotte takes Cole's hand. And not when she starts to count, "One, two . . ."

And not when they jump on three.

We just stand there and wait for the splash.

I cringe when it comes.

My body stiffens and jolts.

When they hit the water, it sounds violent. Like something breaking.

We listen as their wake laps the stone.

Then we wait until the water settles to still.

And then we wait some more: Listening to the silence. Waiting for another splash. A gasp for air. Our names being called out . . . The sound of someone climbing back up onto the rocks below us. Something. Anything at all.

I'm counting, in a hushed voice. I started as soon as I heard them hit the water. It's more breath than words. "One, one thousand, two, one thousand, three, one thousand . . ." It sounds like a prayer.

After a few minutes, Stevie B whispers, "Nell . . ."

That's it. Just my name.

I keep counting. "Six, one thousand, seven, one thousand, eight, one thousand . . ." I have to count out 960 seconds.

It will take sixteen minutes.

It takes forever to count out sixteen minutes.

Every time I get to *ten, one thousand*, I start over. Exactly like Charlotte taught Cole. *One, one thousand, two, one thousand, three, one thousand . . . Get to ten, then start again.* Forty-eight times to reach the tunnel. Forty-eight times to make it back to the surface.

"Nell . . .," Stevie B tries again.

"Three, one thousand, four, one thousand . . ."

He stops interrupting. I keep counting.

When I've completed the 960 seconds—when I've counted to ten ninety-six times and the sixteen minutes are up—I listen.

It's still. Painfully, heartbreakingly still.

There's a brush of wind in the trees. The last of the summer crickets and cicadas and katydids. A stray bird. A scuffle. Stevie B breathing. But no other sounds.

No gasp of air. No cry for help. No Cole.

"That's it. They're gone," I whisper. The words sound hollow.

I let go of Stevie B's hand and climb up over the rocks to peer down at the water.

I shine my flashlight to try to see better.

It's black and cold. No signs of Cole. No signs of Charlotte. No slips of moonlight dancing on the surface.

No signs of life.

No signs of death either.

Just the pure black and empty space of not knowing.

28

$Stevie$ B whispers, "What are we gonna tell the cops, Nell?"

"What do you mean?" I ask. Me thinking, *I watched my mom die when she overdosed. And then I watched Cole bring her back to life.*

Me thinking, *I watched my dad die too. I watched him die and not come back.*

And I don't know which this is. Living or dying. Leaving and coming back. Or leaving forever.

"Tomorrow, or the next day, when Cole's missing . . . what do we tell the cops?"

I don't respond.

"What do we tell his mom? And Finn?" he asks. The words come out of him like an ache.

"Cole told me to tell his mom that he went for a ride to the mountains for a couple of days, to cool off like he does. So that's what we'll tell anyone who asks."

"What do we say if he doesn't come back?"

"He's coming back, Stevie B. Cole's coming back."

"We don't know that, Nell. You just told us about a kid—Levi Tanner—who didn't come back."

"Cole's not Levi, Stevie B. Cole will come back."

"What if he can't? What if he gets . . . stuck there, Nell? What do we do about Finn on Saturday if he doesn't make it?"

I don't answer. I just think about what Cole said the day Finn was born: *I'd give Finn my lungs if I could.*

And I think about what it'd be like to not breathe for sixteen minutes.

To not breathe ever.

Thursday

TWO DAYS BEFORE

29

I wake with a start. Disoriented.

I sit up, gasping for air, like someone who's drowning.

It's dark. I'm in my room—in my bed. Dressed in the clothes I wore to the quarry. Even my boots are still on.

I barely remember coming home.

Then I have a flash of me and Stevie B leaving the quarry. Running on the path behind River Bend Road. Me out in front. Him two steps back. Feet pounding.

I pick up my phone, lying next to me, tangled in the sheets.

3:12. No messages. It's the middle of the night. Cole's been gone for just over five hours.

A countdown app is running in the background. Finn's death clock. A doomsday timer I set for Saturday at five.

I turn toward the window, half expecting Cole to show up. Climbing up the side of the house like he does, or tossing pebbles at the glass, texting me to come outside. Him telling me some story that would explain all of this. Something I can live with, forget about, then put behind me like it's nothing more than a nightmare or a fever dream.

But there is no Cole. No fever dream. No logical story to explain any of this.

One thought consumes me: *Go back to the quarry. Just to see. Just in case . . .*

I tell myself it's a bad idea. Then I tell myself it's a good idea. We argue. Me against me.

I win; the me who thinks it would be a good idea to go back to the quarry wins.

I convince myself that I might find something. Find someone. Find *Cole*. Maybe he needs me, changed his mind. Didn't quite make it but didn't drown either. Maybe he got partway . . . panicked . . . found an underground grotto with a pocket of breathable air, rested, then swam back up and now he needs my help.

Which means that I could still save him.

Then we could reset, me and him. Go back to before. Before Charlotte . . .

I get up, change my shoes. Double-knot my sneakers. Throw on a jacket. Open the window.

I sit on the sill.

Outside, the world appears huge and dark and empty. Like I'm the only person alive.

Inside my room, the prisoners stare back at me. The walls are closing in.

I swing my feet over the ledge, climb down the gutter pipe, half fall, half slide a few feet, then hit the ground with a thud.

Running across the lawn, across River Bend Road, and up the embankment to the path, I feel my limbs ache, pain in my joints and muscles. My right ankle twists; I get a stitch in my side; the earth gives beneath my feet. My lungs empty and fill, empty and fill. My heart beats.

It's hard to see in the dark on the path. Small branches reach out like fingers and grab me—snag my jacket, scrape my hands, clenched tight as fists. I count my breaths. *One, one thousand, two, one thousand, three, one thousand, four . . .*

I focus on breathing. I lengthen my stride, and I'm flying. Too fast, and I'm a tangle of limbs on the ground.

Then I'm back on my feet, and I trip again, catch myself, run past the sweep of pines. I hurry past Cole's truck.

I don't stop until I get to the jumping-off place and peer over the edge.

I see nothing. Then I stumble down the embankment all the way to the bottom, to the pool of water fifty yards below, where a body would be.

I sit down by the water's edge on a flat rock, afraid to look. I count. *One, one thousand, two, one thousand, three, one thousand, four . . .*

As I catch my breath, I startle every time I hear the wind in the trees or an animal in the underbrush. Fear pushes and pulls. But love does too.

In the end, love wins.

I stand up. It's only three steps to the quarry. I leave my sneakers and clothes on as I step into the water.

Life is warm, I think. *Death is cold.*

This feels like death.

It's cold. Colder than I expected.

It gets deep fast.

One, two steps, and the water's up to my shoulders.

I lean forward, and with a single sweep of my arms, I'm in over my head.

I circle and turn in the dark. Remember how it felt when Cole was here with me, in this pool of water, with our limbs entwined and one brave heart. Those nights when the stars lit the sky and love and life licked at our skin and anything seemed possible.

Now I feel the cold tongue of death lapping.

I spin and turn, again and again, searching.

I reach between the rocks, plunge my hands into the mud . . . Blind in the dark, I'm groping—hoping not to find anything. Hoping not to find a body. *His* body. Soft and bloated and cold. I search for ten, then fifteen, minutes.

And I see nothing. Find nothing.

I climb out, plant myself on a rock, and shiver and shake as the voice in my head screams, *Get home before you freeze to death.*

I breathe one word over and over again.

The only word left.

Cole.

30

"Well?" Stevie B asks after I sit down across from him in the lunchroom seven hours later.

I don't respond.

I feel like I've been running all night, running for my entire life. Everything hurts.

When I got home, I stripped off my wet clothes and climbed into bed, caked in mud. Didn't even shower. Too cold, too defeated.

I glance up at the clock. Twelve fifteen. And no Wozniak.

"Nell?"

I open the doomsday death clock on my phone. Fifty-two hours and forty-five minutes until Saturday at five.

That's 3,165 minutes until Finn's supposed to die.

I check messages and emails. I've done it ten thousand times since this morning.

One text from Cole's mom since I last looked. But nothing else that matters. "No alerts," I mumble. "No texts about a prison break from my mom." I feel cold and sweaty at the same time.

"So no Wozniak," Stevie B comments. "Anything from Cole?"

"Jesus, I would have mentioned that!" I snap.

"How do you think he'll let us know . . . I mean, assuming he gets back . . . How will he . . . ?"

"He'll just show up," I say. "He'll find us. He promised."

Stevie B looks me over closely. "What happened to your hair?"

The quarry happened, I think. *I promised to stay away.* But I don't say that. I don't say anything.

I'm waiting for the sirens to go off. School security. State police. Clawson patrol cars. SWAT teams. FBI agents. Principal Harris with a megaphone . . .

I touch the necklace around my neck. Even with all the proof we have, I still want more.

Stevie B leans in close. "You didn't tell her—your mom, I mean—about Wozniak, did you?"

"No. Of course not."

I'm not sure he believes me. "I had to wake her up. For work this morning . . . so . . ." I blink away a tear, then add, "I hugged her. Because . . . you know. It could be . . . I mean . . . I don't know what's gonna happen today, and . . ."

A flash of worry sparks on his face. "But you didn't—"

"I didn't say anything," I fire back. "But I don't hug her anymore, so . . ."

He's searching my face, looking for what I'm not saying. "You hugged her. That's it?"

"Yeah. I hugged my mom."

"Add your name," he says.

"What?"

"To that list you have on your phone. The Brave Bitches List. You should be on it, Nell."

I nod slightly. Then someone drops a tray, and we both jump.

"No lunch?" I ask, glancing down at the empty space in front of him when the commotion's over.

"Not hungry," he states.

"That's a first," I say, eyeing him carefully.

He looks a mess. His hair is sticking out everywhere, and he's in the same clothes he was wearing last night at the quarry. His fingers are now stained dark gray and cobalt blue from his drawing pencils. "Hey, did you sleep?"

"Hell no," he replies. "I was having a heart attack all night. Jumped through the ceiling when my dad knocked on my door this morning."

He's watching me, eyes glassy, his gaze traveling from my face to the necklace, then bouncing around the cafeteria. Then he reaches into his backpack and hands me a piece of paper.

"What's this?"

"Don't know. It's nothing. I drew it this morning."

I look at the picture. Then at him.

He shrugs. "It's a sexy aquatic wingless water harpy for senseless narrow-minded guys to fantasize about . . . Or . . ."

"Or what?" I ask, trembling.

"A prophecy," he responds.

I examine the drawing closely. "Well, it looks just like her," I comment. "Charlotte, I mean . . . She's crawling out of the quarry."

"Now, check this out." He hands me another picture from his bag.

My heart explodes in my chest. It's a picture of me, looking like Charlotte, like a mermaid, or a sexy water harpy. I'm standing on the rocks alone, perched high up above the quarry, arms over my head, ready to jump. There's moonlight streaming down. My eyes are fiery and fierce. I have a gold chain around my neck with a turquoise stone. Exactly like the one I'm wearing now. Exactly like the one Charlotte was wearing last night.

I touch the necklace again. I'm almost too afraid to ask, but I ask anyway: "When did you draw this?"

He turns the picture over. Points at the date.

"That's almost two years ago," I comment as my heart pounds in my chest. Too fast. Too hard. Break-my-ribs hard. I study the details of the drawing. I want to ask how it is he drew the necklace, *this* necklace with the turquoise stone, so long ago, but I don't. I want to ask how it is that I look exactly like Charlotte did last night when it's not Charlotte jumping. It's *me*. "What do you think this means? How did you . . . ?"

"Don't ask," he snaps, his gaze bouncing around the cafeteria again. "I don't know what I think. Or what any of this means. It's just . . . Stuff has gotten weird." He changes the subject. "Did Cole's mom call?"

"Yeah. She called this morning because he didn't come home. I said the three of us hung out, then he dropped us off. I said he told us he was gonna go for a drive, planned on cutting school. Be gone for a day or two. I just acted cool. Like nothing was wrong."

I almost sounded convincing. To Cole's mom then, and Stevie B now. Almost.

"And?"

"And nothing. That's it. She knows Cole. That's not exactly out-of-the-ordinary behavior for him. She's annoyed with him, is all."

Stevie B's eyes dart around again. He's antsy and twitchy.

I hand both of his drawings back. I want to tell him everything. But I can't. I clear my throat. "Then I sent her a text. From *his* phone."

He leans forward. "Shit, Nell! Cole gave you his phone?"

"He told me to text his mom. You know, so she wouldn't worry."

"What'd you say?"

"I stuck to what we talked about. 'Headed up to the mountains . . . Be back tonight or tomorrow. Don't be mad . . . '"

"What about his truck? We left it there. Someone's gonna find it."

"Let's hope Cole comes back before that happens," I tell him. "It's cold. No one goes up there this time of year. Here. Eat something," I say, pushing my tray toward him.

He ignores it. "Have you been back?" he asks, sizing me up, trying to see if I'm going to lie. His eyes settle on my hands: dirty fingernails. He scans my arms: scraped-up.

I put my hands in my lap, glance away. And he *knows*.

"Damn it, Nell!" He leans over the table again, his shoulders all hunched up. "We agreed to stay away!"

"Well? Sue me, Stevie B! I couldn't sleep either. I wanted to, you know, *check*." I'm barely holding it together. I have to hold it together.

"When?"

"This morning. Early. Four, five a.m. No one saw me."

"And?"

"And nothing. No evidence of anything. Truck like we left it." I pause. Glance at the clock again, then down at my hands. "No Cole." I reach into my bag. "Picked this up, though." I hand him the burner phone Charlotte was using. "She left it up top, next to the rocks, before she jumped." Somehow my voice is calmer.

Stevie B takes Charlotte's phone from me. I give him the passcode. He scrolls through. "Nine calls and lots of texts about meetup times to Cole's number. No one else." He slides it back across the table. "Good thing you went back, I guess. But we should ditch it."

I nod, then stick the phone back in my bag, thinking about what'll happen if Cole doesn't come back and the cops find his truck. I'm grateful that at least they won't find Charlotte's phone by the quarry now too.

"No bodies?" he asks, his voice cracking as his eyes go skittery again.

"No. Don't even ask that," I whisper-yell at him.

"You looked, though? In the water?"

"Jesus! Yes." But I don't tell him how I sat there next to the edge. Counting. How I waded in up to my waist in the pitch dark, then swam to the center, searched all the gullies and breaks. How I *expected* to find Cole. Dead. Face down. Spongy and bloated. Floating in the middle of the quarry or lodged between the rocks. How I climbed back up, all the way to the jumping-off place, trembling and wet, found Charlotte's phone, then ran home on the path. Sobbing. Broken in a way life's not supposed to break you.

"You sure no one saw you?"

"No one saw me! I took the path."

"And your mom? Did she notice you left early?"

I roll my eyes. "My mom . . . she wouldn't notice if I grew silver wings and horns." *Or arrived home at five thirty a.m. in wet clothes.*

"Nell . . ."

I glance at the clock. "If there was a prison break, we'd know it," I tell him, changing the subject—trying to move us in a forward direction. "The whole school'd be in lockdown."

"Did Charlotte say what time it would happen?"

"No. She just said it was during a routine medical transport on Thursday. *Today.* That's what she said. 'Routine.' Which means it isn't a health emergency."

Some movement catches my eye, and I watch as one of the janitors secures the back door. At first, I'm thinking maybe something is up, but he starts emptying the trash. I watch as he takes a large black garbage bag out of the can, then ties it in a double knot, taking his time, like nothing is wrong. I want to scream, *Everything is wrong!* But I say, "They only transport for routine hospital visits during the day shift, which ends at four."

"So that leaves . . ."

"A little over three hours," I say.

"And if it doesn't happen?" he asks. "If this Wozniak guy doesn't try to escape in the next three hours?"

"It means we blew it," I say, defeated. "And Cole is gone. And you were right. And we got conned, and Charlotte was lying, at least about some of this."

Stevie B's leg is bouncing up and down, his hands shaking. If I didn't know him better, I'd think he took something. He stands.

"Where you going?"

"Let's get out of here."

I grab my bag. "Where to?"

"Don't know. Just drive around," he suggests. "See if there's any activity. Drive by the hospital, maybe. Wait for Wozniak to show up."

I hand him the sandwich on my tray. "Eat this. You're scaring me. You look like a junkie." I worry he might pass out. He swats the sandwich away. I bus my tray. Tell myself, *Walk slow. Act normal.* No one should notice us leaving school. It's just a regular day. Nell and Stevie B going to sit in Nell's truck. Cut class. Maybe go for a ride.

No one pays attention to us.

No teachers ask where we're going.

The streets feel empty. Clawson feels dead. Deader than usual.

We barely talk. The radio in my truck is off. Heater's on high, but still I shiver and shake. Stevie B stares out the window for a while before he says, "I've been thinking, Nell . . . If Charlotte is Cole's great-granddaughter, like she said, then he can't be dead."

I swerve. Look over at him. Almost hit the curb.

"Think about it. In order for Cole's great-granddaughter to be born, he has to live long enough to have a kid. So he couldn't have died in the quarry last night."

"Okay . . . that's really smart. Unless she lied about them being related and faked the necklace somehow or—"

"Yeah, but there's something else too," Stevie B says. "Charlotte had to have been telling the truth, at least about some of this. If she lied about being related to Cole and if she lied about Wozniak, I won't be able to explain that. But think about it, Nell. She didn't concoct this elaborate time-travel Finn's-gonna-die backstory to convince Cole to jump into the quarry with her so she could *die*."

"What are you saying?"

"I'm saying, whatever this was—whatever it *is*—it wasn't Charlotte killing herself. *She* didn't come out of the water either. Which means Cole's alive, and the two of them are *somewhere*."

I reach over and squeeze his hand, saying, "Okay, that's really, really smart."

Then Stevie B says, "Now we just have to figure out where."

31

At four, me and Stevie B are in my room. Lying on my bed, me looking at my phone, him in a zombie daze, staring at the prisoners' faces and blown-up eyes lining my wall.

We saw nothing. No cop cars. *Nothing.* We just drove around and observed Clawson being what it is: Worn-down and tired. Normal. Gray. There were no text alerts. No sirens. No lockdown. No Wozniak.

So now that the day shift has ended with no prisoner escape attempt, we're *shredded.* We wait to see what's gonna happen next, the two of us doing boring time-killing things to distract ourselves as fear rolls through in waves.

"Who are the new guys?" Stevie B asks.

I watch him for a beat. "What do you mean?"

He points. "You have three new sets of prisoners' eyes on the wall."

I follow his gaze, surprised he noticed. Surprised he doesn't recognize them. I don't want to tell him, but I have no choice. "Us," I admit as something inside me shapeshifts to shame. "You, me, and Cole."

He flashes me a startled look, then turns back to study the eyes. *Our* eyes.

I feel like I violated his privacy or signed him up for something he wants nothing to do with. "I cut them from old photos I blew up a couple of weeks ago," I tell him, as if that justifies the violation somehow. "Then I glued them to the wall before I left for school this morning."

"Shit, Nell."

"I know."

His eyes move to the map of Europe taped to my wall. Me and Cole have countries circled. Spain. Italy. Greece . . .

"How's your passport collection coming?" he asks.

I shrug.

"You could get one, you know."

"Stop saying that."

"Then you could actually *go* somewhere." He glances at the map again.

"No, I couldn't."

"Why do you think that, Nell? That you can't go anywhere?" He points at the prisoners' eyes. "*They* can't go anywhere. But *you* can go anywhere you want."

"I'm up there on the prisoner wall too," I say. "All three of us are."

"That's a choice, Nell. You put us there. Go stand against the wall. The non-eyeball wall."

I walk over and stand flat against the wall. "Why?"

"I'm gonna take your picture."

"Mug shot?" I manage to ask.

"Passport photo," he says.

Then we switch places, and he stands against the white wall, and I take his picture. When we sit down on the bed, he asks for my social security number and starts filling out passport applications for both of us on his phone.

I ask, "What do you think happened to Cole? And who do you think Charlotte really is? And what is she doing, and why'd she take him? And why'd she bother to lie about Wozniak?"

"I don't know, Nell."

Then I ask, "What do you know about that kid Levi Tanner who supposedly drowned?"

He doesn't even look up. "Nothing, at all. It was twenty-three years ago."

"I don't know very much about Levi Tanner either," I say, "but I do know that he and Cole both went into the quarry and didn't come out." I hop up.

"Where you going?"

"My parents' old bedroom. To find my mom's high school yearbook."

32

She keeps it in the bottom drawer of her dresser, buried beneath her pajamas.

The cover is stiff.

Fake brown leather. The year embossed in gold.

I carry it back to my room. Stevie B watches as I run my fingers slowly over the letters. *Clawson High School.*

It makes a cracking sound when I open it. Under everyone's name there is a "Most likely" statement. We start reading them.

"Are we doing that?" he asks. "For our class?"

"Dunno," I say, adding, "I wonder what they'd put under my name," but not really wanting an answer.

Stevie B goes back to the passport applications, and I run through the options in my head. *Nell Bannon: Most likely to sit back and do nothing if you drown. Most likely to let her boyfriend die . . . Most likely to be serving prison time for the wanton disregard for human life.*

I find the memorial for Levi Tanner. "Check this out," I say. "He has a whole two-page spread in the middle of the yearbook."

Dying takes center stage. It's more important than football or field day or senior prom.

Stevie B stares at the photos of Levi for a long time, like he's memorizing them. Then he says, "Fuck me."

"You're sweating and breathing funny," I comment.

He grabs the yearbook and slowly traces his fingers over Levi's face. "Shit, Nell!"

"What?"

"Levi . . . He . . . looks . . ." He doesn't finish the thought.

"What? He looks *what?*"

"Forget it," he says as he starts rummaging through his bag. "It's nothing."

I study Levi's face. He's stern and serious, with olive skin and dark hair. He has a zigzag scar on his cheek and a half-moon-shaped scar above his right eye. *Car accident?* I wonder. "There were witnesses," I tell Stevie B. "Two kids were with him at the quarry that night."

"Did the cops suspect foul play?" he asks, his voice shaking.

"I don't think so. They tried to save him and called for help, so . . ."

"Can we go to jail for this?" he asks. "For being there when Cole and Charlotte jumped and not saving them? For not getting help when they didn't come back out of the water?"

"I don't know," I tell him. "But maybe."

"Who were they?" he asks.

"What?"

"The witnesses."

"Oh. I've been reading about them. Ben Wallace—he's a cop in Clawson now. And Margaret Campbell is one of the middle school English teachers. My mom used to talk about them sometimes. She told me Margaret and Ben weren't dating back then, but they married each other a few years after Levi disappeared."

I flip to Ben Wallace's page. "It says, most likely to become a cop." Then I turn to Margaret's. "Most likely to marry Levi Tanner."

"Hold on, Nell. Margaret was planning on marrying Levi, the kid who jumped? But he drowned, so . . . she married Ben? The other witness?"

"Looks like it," I say.

"That's messed up."

That could be us, I think. That could be my picture where Margaret's is, and underneath it could say *Most likely to marry Cole Wilder.* Then Cole doesn't come back, he gets a spread in the yearbook, and I marry Stevie B. The other witness.

"It's called trauma bonding," I mumble. "It's when two people experience something traumatic and confuse it for love. It happens a lot. I saw it in a movie once." I close the yearbook and put it down on the bed. "I can't look at this any longer."

"Me either," Stevie B says as he sits up, swinging his feet onto the floor. "Do you think that will happen to us?" he asks. "The trauma-bonding thing?"

"What do you mean?"

"You know what I mean," he whispers.

"I don't know," I whisper back. "Don't ask me that."

"Did he seem familiar to you?" His voice cracks.

"Who?"

"Levi. The kid who died."

"No. I mean, I've seen the yearbook before, but outside of that, no. Why?"

"Nothing. No reason. He just looks familiar."

We sit in silence for a few minutes, and then I ask, "Did you see her eyes?"

He appears startled. "Whose?"

"Charlotte's."

He stares at me for a beat, then says, "The color, right?"

So it's not my imagination, I think. *He sees it too.* "At first, I thought that blue-to-black thing was pretty," I say.

"And now?" he asks.

"Dunno."

"But it's something, right?" he asks.

I walk over to the window, pull the curtain back, and glance outside. "Yeah, it's something," I say, thinking, *All of it's something, Stevie B. We just don't know what.*

"I'll be back." I head into the hall, glancing at Stevie B before I close my bedroom door. He's hunched over, looking all serious, with his sketchbook out, flipping through the pages.

+ + + + + + + +

Ten minutes later, when I open my bedroom door again, I'm wet from the neck up.

Stevie B has the yearbook open, and he's staring at Levi Tanner. He looks at me, and his face falls—like totally collapses. "Oh shit, no, Nell!"

"Oh shit, maybe," I say as I start to towel-dry my hair.

"How long?" he whispers.

"Less than two minutes."

"That's a long way from sixteen," he says.

"I know."

"I'm applying for passports. For both of us," he reports.

There is so much I could say to that, but I say nothing. I think, *Maybe that's good.*

We might need to run.

33

There's the sound of gravel crunching and the hum of an engine as a car pulls into the driveway.

"It's my mom," I tell Stevie B as I peer out the window. "What time is it?"

"Five on the nose."

I run a comb through my hair, then walk down to the kitchen. "How was your day?" I ask, a little too eagerly.

She sets her gun on the table, then gives me a once-over. "The usual," she comments as she pulls her jacket off.

I watch as she goes over to the sink to get a glass of water. She walks slowly, like there are heavy stones in her pockets.

She'd say something if there was an incident. An attempted escape . . . If a prisoner died in a shoot-out. Plus, it would have been all over the news.

She pulls out a chair and takes a seat, then pours her pills onto the place mat. Hunched over, she counts the white ones and the green ones.

"So . . . nothing interesting happened?"

She doesn't look up. She just says, "Nope."

I slump against the wall and silently start to count. Not pills, but seconds. *One, one thousand, two, one thousand, three, one thousand . . .*

She pops a few too many pills into her mouth. Twenty or thirty milligrams, I figure, based on the color. Hopefully, none of them are eighties. I watch to see if she chews them or swallows them whole. Chewing spells trouble. It delivers the high faster.

She swipes them to the back of her mouth with her tongue and swallows.

I glance around the kitchen. It's dingy and quiet. Not like it used to be. *Not like home.* I wonder when this became normal for us.

"How was your day?" she asks.

I almost jump, but I don't answer.

She asks again, but she doesn't look up. She counts.

"Fine, I guess. I have an English essay to write, and Coach Langley made us do push-ups."

We're talking, but both of us are faking it. I'm too distracted, and she doesn't care. Too stuck in her own pain to see mine.

She says, "I'm gonna go lie down, Nell."

I stand there leaning against the wall until I hear Blake Shelton start to sing. Then I slowly head back upstairs. I have to tell Stevie B that he was right, that this was some kind of con. Because Wozniak didn't try to break out of prison, and there was no medical transport, so Charlotte lied about that.

My mom's got the song on real low, playing on repeat like my dad liked. It's a heartbreak of a song.

Tears fall down my cheeks. I start counting again, for something to hold on to. "One, one thousand, two, one thousand, three, one thousand . . ." Then I start to softly sing.

Looking in your eyes now, if I had to die now . . .

I jump back and forth between singing and counting. "Four, one thousand, five, one thousand . . ."

I don't wanna love nobody but you . . .

"Six, one thousand, seven, one thousand . . ."

I can't make up my mind. Sing. Count. Stay. Leave. Jump. Don't jump.

I feel like I'm drowning.

I need air.

Can't get enough.

There'll be even less if I jump.

None if I die.

I catch my reflection in the bathroom mirror when I pass by, run my hand through my wet hair. Who is that girl staring back at me? And what was she—*is* she—thinking?

I open the door to my room, hands trembling, heart aching.

Stevie B looks up. *He's always here for me.*

He sees my face, and he knows. I mean, he *knew* about Wozniak, but now he *knows*.

I turn away. It hurts to look at him. I think about the trauma-bonding thing, how tangled up and confusing my feelings are.

We're the same now. Me and him. Two pieces of a triangle that can't sit right when one side is missing. Joined forever by secrets and lies. Hiding a secret so awful, so tragic, we can't tell a soul. Petrified we'll be found out, we marry each other.

We're not quite dead, but we're not really living. Not in prison, but not out of prison either. We built the cell and put up the bars ourselves.

I glance at the eyes peering back at me from my wall. My eyes. Stevie B's eyes. Cole's eyes.

"Your mom's good?" he asks as I close the door. He looks petrified that I'll say yes.

I say, "Yes."

He props himself up on his elbow. "So . . . no prison break? Wozniak didn't—"

"No," I snap, the word sharp and weighty. It shuts down the conversation.

His face tumbles to a darker place. The darkest place there is.

I sit down on the bed. Looking over at him, feeling so grateful that he's here with me, I touch his cheek.

Then he kisses me.

He kisses me, and I don't pull way. I don't kiss him back, but I don't exactly *not* kiss him back either. He feels safe. And here. And wounded.

Just like me.

"I . . . ," he starts to say when the kiss ends.

"I know . . . Me too."

And then we hear a phone ring.

We both know the ringtone. It's Cole's.

Stevie B turns away. I'm flooded with guilt.

I take Cole's phone out of my bag and look at the screen.

It says MOM.

34

"How long till Saturday at five?" Stevie B asks.

"Just under forty-eight hours."

"Call her," he says when the phone stops ringing. "Cole's mom."

"What?"

"Call her. From *your* phone," he clarifies. "Not Cole's. Call her from your phone and check in. Don't say anything about his phone. Ask her about Finn. See if she's feeling okay—or if she needs you to babysit. Get an update. Find out her plans."

"Find out her plans for *what*, exactly?"

"Contacting the authorities. Reporting Cole missing. Check the temperature," he says. "Plus, I'm worried that you have his phone, Nell."

"What do you mean?"

"I saw this cop show once. This guy was missing. And they tracked his phone when it wasn't even turned on. Used the cell towers to, you know, triangulate or some shit like that. Then the cops showed up where the phone was."

I glance down at Cole's phone, sitting there on the bed between us. "What happened?"

"The guy with the phone became a person of interest."

"So, what are you saying?"

"That if Cole's mom reports him missing and the cops check if his cell phone has pinged a tower, then . . ."

"They find me," I say.

"Us," Stevie B says. "They find *us*, Nell. I'm sitting right here with you. I'm always sitting right here with you."

I'm thinking, *I know that! God, I know that!* But I don't say that. Instead I ask, "What happened? In the TV show, with the phone. What happened?"

"They arrested the guy who had the phone and charged him with murder."

"Jesus, Stevie B! Way to freak me out!"

"I didn't mean anything by it. It's just that Cole's not back yet, and you having his phone and texting his mom after he went missing is potentially . . . incriminating. That's all."

"So when they find Cole's phone . . ."

"That's the thing, Nell. They don't have to *find* his phone. They just subpoena the phone company and get the call records. And there don't even have to be any *actual* calls. Our phones ping towers all the time, even if we don't use them."

"What, are you in the FBI or something? Taking baby spy classes online? Joined PAW Patrol? The Police Explorers?"

He blank-faced stares at me. "You done?" he asks.

"Sorry. I'm scared, is all."

"I'm not trying to freak you out, Nell." His voice is soft. "But if Cole never comes back or if he's . . . you know, and his body shows up, it'll be obvious that he died before you sent those messages to his mom, and it'll look like you—it'll look like *we*—killed him, then covered it up."

"Why would it look like we killed him? Maybe it'll look like we were covering for Cole because he cut school and took off, like he always does, and he didn't want his mom to find out."

"Where do you take off for without your phone? And if he forgot his phone, he would have come back for it, Nell."

"So you're saying Cole'd pretty much take his phone unless . . ."

I don't say it.

He doesn't say it.

But it's there: *Unless something really, really bad happened.*

I let that settle in, then take my phone out.

"What are you doing?"

"Texting Cole's mom. From *my* phone. Checking on Finn, like you said. Maybe she'll tell me if she's gonna report Cole missing, and then we can . . . concoct a story. Or drop Cole's phone in the quarry along with Charlotte's. He could have texted her this morning and then . . ."

I don't finish. I don't say *drowned after.*

I type a completely boring text. **How is Finn? When do you need me?** Hit SEND.

"Nell?" he says.

"Yeah?"

"About before. About the kiss. I just want to say that—"

I freeze. "Don't."

"Don't what?" he asks.

"Don't say anything."

He nods. "Okay."

My phone pings.

I read the message. "She said she doesn't need me to babysit tomorrow. She's leaving work early Friday to take Finn to the doctor for a checkup."

"Did she ask about Cole?"

"No."

"So maybe she's not too worried. And maybe her taking Finn to the doctor's tomorrow is a good thing."

"How do you mean?"

"Maybe the doctor will find the thing that's gonna kill her and . . . fix it before Saturday."

I figure Stevie B's right about the Cole part—if Mrs. Wilder was worried for real or going to report him missing, she would have said something. But unless Charlotte *is* lying, the Finn part he got wrong. The doctor isn't gonna find anything tomorrow—or at least not anything he can fix—because Finn's gonna die the very next day.

But I don't get a chance to bust Stevie B's happy-this-might-work-out-fine bubble, because my phone pings again.

"It's Cole's mom."

I read the message once, then twice. "No, no, no . . ."

I read it a third time. *"No!"*

"What?" Stevie B asks, alarmed.

I hand him my phone. "Just read it."

"'Please remember to pick Finn up this Saturday at three,'" he says. It takes a second, but then it hits him like it hit me. "Oh shit, Nell, no!"

"I never babysit on Saturdays!" I'm practically yelling. "She asked me weeks ago. I . . . forgot."

"Tell her you're busy. Tell her . . ."

"I can't!"

"Why not?"

"Charlotte said we can't change things because we know something. That thing . . . What did she call it?"

"A causal loop," he says, defeated. "It's called a causal loop."

"I'll be taking care of Finn on Saturday at five o'clock."

When Finn dies—*if* she dies—it'll be on my watch.

Friday

ONE DAY BEFORE

35

Sometimes stuff hits you like machine-gun fire and you process it at lightning speed. Other times, it comes at you in slow motion. When the siren goes off in homeroom on Friday morning at 8:16, it's one of the slo-mo times.

I'm sitting here looking at Cole's and Charlotte's vacant seats. Just dead-eyed, staring at two empty chairs—thinking, *Cole said he'd be back by yesterday, today at the latest, and I know it's still early, but he's not here*—when Principal Harris's voice comes over the intercom, all clipped and staticky, announcing there's an emergency and to shelter in place.

My gaze shoots up, explosions of worry firing in my brain, as I'm thinking, *This isn't a drill—can't be a drill—if it was, they would have told us about it two hundred times and sent email and text reminders.* Then I tell myself to calm down.

The few kids who heard the announcement are looking around, but most everyone else is oblivious, still staring at their phones, or napping with their hoodies pulled up over their heads, or whispering to their friends in secretive deaf-to-the-world huddles.

Mrs. Stanwick, our homeroom teacher, doesn't say anything at first. She just pulls a laminated checklist from her top desk drawer, then locks the classroom door, turns the lights out, latches the windows, and pulls the blinds. Then she calls out in a half yell, half whisper that we should all get down on the floor, silence our phones, and keep quiet because of some unspecified safety concern.

The kids who weren't paying attention are now looking around, confused, as the rest of us gather our stuff then sit on the floor with our backpacks pulled in close as the words "lockdown" and "I don't know" travel from seat to seat.

I'm squeezed beneath my desk, still trying to process.

My phone is set to silent, and I'm shielding the light from the screen with my body as I fire off a string of texts, my fingers tripping over the keys. The first message is to my mom, saying **We're in lockdown. What's going on?** Then I send a couple to Stevie B—mostly curse words and question marks.

My mom doesn't answer—but Stevie B texts back, **Oh my God, Nell!** Which is basically my thought exactly.

I'm thinking that one way or another, this is *it* for us. Which could go in a whole bunch of scary-as-shit directions—including some I probably can't even imagine—and I'm not sure which one of them this is, or which one would be worse.

When a few minutes pass and my mom still hasn't answered, I text her again, saying **We're in lockdown. DO YOU KNOW WHY?** Me feeling like my world is coming to an end.

I'm worrying that this *could be* a prison break—just a day later than Charlotte thought—which means my mom could be the guard who shot Wozniak and she'll go to jail and I'll become a ward of the state. So I get mad and start thinking, *News flash, Mom: You can't shoot people when you're high! Didn't they teach you that in guard school?* And then I have to remind myself that it's premature to get mad at her for something that might not have even happened.

Next, I start thinking, *Maybe it's not a prisoner escape at all, and Charlotte just made that up—along with all the time-travel stuff. And maybe Cole did die and they found his body, and the police are looking for me and Stevie B.* Which reminds me that we never made it back to the quarry, so I still have Cole's phone *and* Charlotte's phone in my bag. And that gets me thinking that we're in lockdown because the SWAT teams are closing in. That they triangulated Cole's cell-tower pings and they know his phone is currently located in B wing, room 227, at the high school.

Then I start wondering if they'd even put the school in lockdown for that, and I have no idea. So I go from *probably* to *definitely, of course they would,* because they'd want to keep whoever has his phone locked up until they get here.

At which point I start thinking maybe both of those things happened, and I'm gonna be arrested and my mom is gonna be arrested, because Wozniak is dead *and* Cole is dead, I have Cole's phone, and, to top it off, someone has figured out that the new girl, Charlotte, appears to be missing too. And guess what? Her phone is in Mrs. Stanwick's homeroom at the high school in Nell Bannon's backpack too.

Then this thought dances through my head: *Maybe me and my mom can share a cell.*

I start feeling sick. *Really* sick. Mostly because I can't decide which is worse:

Wozniak escaping from prison and my mom getting arrested for being strung out on oxy when she shot and killed him.

Or me and Stevie B getting arrested because the cops found the bodies of Cole and Charlotte and traced their phones to me.

Or they didn't find any bodies, but they found Cole's truck and reported it to his mom, who told them something is *terribly* wrong, because she'd been getting texts from him saying he drove to the mountains while the cops say his truck is at the quarry and his phone is pinging from the high school.

Then there's Cole *not dying* and living in 2101 with Charlotte.

Or me not knowing what the fuck happened and Finn dying.

I stay looped in this monkey-brain doom-and-gloom thinking for over five hours, until Mrs. Stanwick reads an announcement. "CNN just reported that a prisoner named Carl Wozniak, incarcerated at Manville Correctional Facility in Clawson, New York, attempted to escape during a routine hospital transport. He was shot and killed by an unnamed correction officer."

At which point my phone lights up and I jump, hitting my head on the desk.

It's a text from Stevie B. **OH SHIT NELL! CHARLOTTE GOT THE DATE WRONG!**

36

Just after two o'clock, when the lockdown finally ends, me and Stevie B meet up in the parking lot next to my truck. Both of us are freaking out in our own ways—I'm still super charged up and wired, riding my roller-coaster thought spiral, and he's more stunned and confused. When we hug, the first thing he asks is, "Have you heard from your mom?"

I shake my head.

"So you don't know if she . . ."

"No."

He squeezes me real tight. "But this means time travel is real, Nell."

"And that means Cole might be alive and he can still make it back. And maybe Finn will be okay tomorrow," I say. Adding as I wipe tears off my face, "It also means that there's no way Levi Tanner plain old regular drowned twenty-three years ago."

Stevie B freezes, then pulls back a little. "We don't actually know that, Nell."

"Yeah, we kind of do," I tell him. "They didn't find Levi's body. Charlotte was weird when we asked about him. And the quarry happens to be a time portal, so . . . I don't think he just regular drowned."

"What are you saying?"

"I'm saying I think we should go see those two witnesses. The two kids who were with Levi when he jumped—Margaret Campbell and Ben Wallace."

"Right now? That's what you want to do *right now?*"

When I hold up my phone showing him Finn's death clock ticking down, he looks like he wants to run into the woods and hide.

"Yeah, that's what I wanna do right now. It's already Friday afternoon and Cole's not back, so we have what . . . ?"

He stares at the timer. "Twenty-six hours, forty-two minutes."

"That's just over a day until Finn's supposed to die. So even if there's only a *chance* they know something, maybe that something will help us figure out how to help Cole or save Finn, or . . . I don't know . . . *something*! Besides, you have a better idea? 'Cause if you do, I'll listen . . ."

"I've got nothing," he says.

"So come on, then. Into the truck. Let's go."

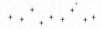

I pull up Margaret Campbell and Ben Wallace's address on my phone, and we head over to their house. We have to creep along slowly, because there are Clawson cops and state troopers everywhere—standing around on the side of the road, looking scary, drinking coffee, or taking down barricades. The state troopers have their Smokey Bear hats on, and some of them still have their long guns in hand and the berries and cherries still flashing red and blue on top of their cruisers. Most of them are still examining every car that passes with tight faces and cop eyes.

"You sure about this?" Stevie B asks after we pull into Campbell and Wallace's driveway.

"Nope," I say as I peer out at the peeling paint and sagging front porch. "Not sure at all."

I still haven't heard from my mom, so I don't actually know for sure if she shot Wozniak, which adds a whole other layer of worry for me. I've been checking my phone constantly, and I check it again before we get out of the truck. Then I check it again as we walk up the path to the front door.

"Anything?" Stevie B asks.

"No. Nothing at all."

He looks at me like he's worried. Not about my mom, or Cole and Charlotte and Finn, or time travel and the mess we're in—just worried about *me*. "Maybe she wasn't the shooter, Nell."

"Maybe she was. There are only two guards on a transport team, so . . ."

"Well, either way, you don't have to keep checking your phone. If you get a text from your mom, it'll ping."

"Yeah, I know that," I tell him. And then my phone doesn't ping, and I check it again anyway, and he doesn't say anything.

After we knock, a few minutes pass before I see the lacy curtains on the side of the door move. Stevie B jumps when Ms. Campbell's face appears in the little window, peeking out at us all pale and bug-eyed, before she opens the door a crack and announces, "My husband's not home."

"That's okay," I tell her. "We were hoping to talk to you."

"About what?"

Stevie B looks at me like *What are you possibly going to say to that?* But I go for broke. "Are you the Margaret Campbell who was at the quarry with Levi Tanner when he went missing twenty-three years ago?"

A full minute ticks by, and Ms. Campbell hasn't moved or said anything, so Stevie B whispers, "Do something, Nell."

She still has the door open a few inches, with one of those safety chains in place. I'm afraid she'll slam the door shut and we'll lose our chance, so I pull up a picture of Finn on my phone and hold it up for her. It's one I took on Monday when Finn was in the hospital. She's wearing a green gown covered in puppies and kittens, and she has tubes and wires sticking out of her arms and nose, and she's hugging her doll. I keep holding my phone up as I say, "Her name is Finn Wilder, and she's gonna die."

Margaret Campbell hesitates, then closes the door. And I don't know if that means *Get out of here; I'm calling the police,* or if she's closing it to release the chain. But then I hear the chain moving, and she pulls the door all the way open and waves us inside.

She's a ghastly pale-gray color, and her hair is disheveled and sticking up in spots, like the mangled feathers on a dead pigeon. "My husband will be home soon," she calls over her shoulder as we follow her toward the back of the house. "He can't know you were here, or that I spoke to you."

The whole place is dark. There's stuff piled everywhere and dishes stacked up in the kitchen like no one's been cleaning up. She's wearing slippers and an untied bathrobe with pajamas underneath.

She sits down at the kitchen table and points at the chairs across from her.

"How much do you know?" she flat-out asks, just like that, as we take a seat.

Not sure how to play this, I say, "We know enough."

She kind of sighs and slumps in her chair.

"How much do *you* know?" I try, not even sure if we're talking about the same thing.

She stares off, not making eye contact, as she seems to think about that. "Too much, and not enough," she finally admits, and then she gets up to fill the teakettle.

I'm wondering if I should say something more to keep the conversation going, but she beats me to it. After she sits back down, she looks right at me and asks, "How long ago did Cole Wilder leave?"

I freeze.

Stevie B freezes.

"How'd you . . . ?"

She doesn't let me finish. She leans in close and eager, looking a little on the wide-eyed scary side when she whispers, "I saw her. Two days ago. At the high school."

I figure Stevie B's gonna say something, but he doesn't. He just fixes his eyes on her and doesn't move.

"You saw *who* at the high school?" I force myself to ask.

"Charlotte," she announces. "I saw Charlotte at Clawson High School. The same girl who came for Levi Tanner twenty-three years ago."

Then the kettle whistles loud and shrill, and Ms. Campbell gets up and makes us tea.

37

Mr. Marcus told us in seventh-grade science that we can't feel the Earth spinning around its axis and whirling around the sun because of something called Einstein's equivalence principle. Then he said that it's not just the earth that we can't feel moving, but the whole universe. He explained that the sun and the stars and the planets and the whole shebang are hurling through the cosmos at close to half a million miles per hour, and we can't feel that either. "Half a million miles an hour!" he said a second time, then a third—like even he couldn't believe it.

Mr. Marcus told us that the reason it doesn't feel like the planet we are standing on and the universe it's part of are careening at half a million miles per hour through space is because we're moving too, at exactly the same speed. And because we can't see anything that isn't moving along with us, we feel like we're standing still, when we're not.

I haven't remembered much of anything we learned in school, but I remember that. Mostly because as soon as he said it, I knew Mr. Marcus was dead wrong about the whole we-can't-feel-it thing.

Because *I* could feel it. Not all the time, but sometimes. Sometimes I could feel everything spinning by me, leaving me behind or hurling me forward, the lights and air and sounds whirling by my face in a whoosh and a blur, leaving me spinnin' dizzy and looking for something to hold on to so I wouldn't go flyin' off into the dark. And right now, sitting here with Stevie B and Ms. Campbell, with Cole gone and Finn's life ticking down on some doomsday death clock I set on my phone, is one of those times when I feel the sheer force of the universe flying through space.

I'm so dizzy I grab the edge of Margaret Campbell's kitchen table, white-knuckle the peeling Formica, and inhale sharply. I can tell that Stevie B feels the earth spinning fast and the universe hurling through space too, because he grips the table the same as me.

And then he makes a noise that I can only describe as sounding like the air coming out of the whole universe. It's not a loud, shrill shriek, or a low thump-thump sputter, like a balloon might make as it flies around the room deflating in some last-gasp death dance; it's more like a high-pitched death hiss that only I can hear. Like the universe just sprang a microscopic pinprick of a leak, and him and me, we're being sucked through it into a black hole that only we know about.

Margaret Campbell examines her hands as a small bird lands on the kitchen windowsill and peers in at us, its little head twitching from side to side as its pecks at the mullions. "I used to know Cole's dad and mom. Yours too," she says, staring at the bird for a moment. "Both of yours," she clarifies. "We went to school together. Haven't spoken in twenty-three years. Not many of our classmates kept in touch because of what happened with Levi at the quarry, but my sister works up at the hospital and I know the Wilder girl's been real sick since she was born. In and out of the hospital.

"Anyway, after I saw Charlotte, I called the high school asking who was absent this week. Cole Wilder was on the list. I remember the three of you running in a pack in middle school. So when you showed up just now and held up that picture and told me her name, I just put two and two together."

She says that, and it's like my head explodes, creating a big-bang universe-expanding cosmic mess. Ms. Campbell's watching me and Stevie B now—but she's not watching us like she's checking to see how we're reacting. It's like she knows what she's saying is true and she doesn't need us to confirm it.

"I was supposed to be at play practice at the middle school this afternoon," she tells us. "It's *Romeo and Juliet*." She looks up at that bird pecking at the window when she adds, "It's kind of perfect, if you think about it."

"How do you mean?" Stevie B asks, and it's the first thing he's said since we stepped inside the house.

She seems surprised by the question and shrugs. "It's ironic, I guess, that of all people, I would be in charge of directing a tragic love story that ends horribly for everyone."

"Cole's been gone for almost two days," I blurt out, desperate to steer the conversation back to what's happening now. "He left with Charlotte on Wednesday."

Stevie B shifts in his seat like he's uncomfortable. Like I said something I shouldn't have or I gave us up. But I need answers, and I don't want a tragic love story for me and Cole, so I just keep talking. "You were dating Levi, right?"

"We were going to . . ." She doesn't finish. "Well, that was a long time ago. Before . . ." She looks down and sighs. "Well, before *everything*." Then she changes direction. "The picture you held up before. Cole's sister. How old?"

"Five," Stevie B whispers.

"How long?"

I open the timer on my phone and hold it up for her to see. What's left of Finn's life is ticking down fast, burning through my heart. "Just over twenty-four hours," I say, and Ms. Campbell starts telling us about Levi and Charlotte, like bleeding out this story is just something she has to do.

"Me and Levi used to jump into the quarry all the time. Ben was our best friend, and Levi's brother was terminally ill. Then Charlotte showed up with newspaper clippings and medical information from the future, saying that little boy didn't have to die. She said she could save him."

Stevie B shoots me a look.

"What happened?"

"Levi left with Charlotte by jumping into the quarry. I begged him not to go, *begged* him, but he went with her to the future to retrieve medicine. And me and Ben stayed behind."

She averts her eyes. "We stayed here in Clawson. And we lied to the police, and we lied to our families and friends."

"Did Levi come back?" I ask.

"No. But *I* knew and *Ben* knew he didn't drown in some tragic accident, and we've carried that truth with us, and that lie, all this time. Until now."

The three of us sit there at her table, not talking for a few minutes, just hurtling through space, dizzy as hell from the truth of this.

"Levi's little brother. Did he live?" Stevie B finally asks.

Ms. Campbell doesn't answer right away. She watches that little bird peck at the mullions.

"What happened to Levi's brother?" I press.

Still no answer. She stares at the bird and then down at her hands.

I try again. "The plan was that Levi would bring back medicine that would save his brother, right? 'Cause that's what Cole's doing. Trying to come back from the future with medicine to save Finn."

Ms. Campbell says, "Levi didn't come back, and his brother died.

Levi's brother *died*. Just three days after Levi left with Charlotte."

The air gets sucked out of the room. I get hot, and the kitchen starts spinning.

Stevie B shifts in his seat.

I mumble, "Finn."

Then I have a flash of Cole smiling, my head firing off a string of memories—images and thoughts. Cole and me up at the quarry jumping. Us kissing. Finn playing . . . I turn to Stevie B, begging him with my eyes to say something or do something to fix this. To change those words and this truth so I can live with it.

"So Levi," Stevie B says. "His brother died, and you never saw Levi again?"

Ms. Campbell turns away. We wait. But when she doesn't answer, she gives us the answer, and that thing my mom says, about knowing stuff and listening to it, is screaming in my head.

"You saw Levi?" I cry, on the brink of yelling. I stand, nearly knocking over the chair I was sitting on.

She still doesn't answer. And I *know*.

I know she saw him.

Levi didn't come back, but she saw him!

The truth of that is all over her face.

I lean forward and say it again. "You did! You saw him. You saw Levi!"

Stevie B grabs my hand and pleads, "Nell . . ."

"Where'd you see him? When?"

Her phone pings. She picks it up off the table and reads a message. "You have to go. Now! Ben is on his way home already. If he sees you, if he asks, you can't tell him what we talked about! Just say you're helping with the play." She stands, takes our cups and puts them near the sink, then hurries toward the front of the house, her bathrobe splayed out behind her as she runs. "Hurry! Come on!

Don't say anything. No one can find out we were lying about Levi and the quarry . . . I don't want any trouble."

We catch up to her at the front door. I want to hear more, but we have no choice. She pulls the door open and tries to push us out. Her breath comes fast, hands trembling, eyes wide; she's pleading with us to go.

"Tell me about Levi, and I'll leave you alone," I say. "He's not here, but he's not dead. You saw him!"

Stevie B's already outside, on the front steps, and Ms. Campbell has me pushed halfway through the door. I stand my ground and practically beg, "Please tell me. Tell me about seeing Levi!"

She doesn't answer, so Stevie B asks, "Did you jump? Did you try to join him?"

"Many times. Now leave!"

"What happened?" I ask. "What happened when you jumped?"

"I couldn't do it. I didn't make it."

"Why'd you stop trying?" I plead.

And Margaret Campbell says, "Because Levi comes to me."

38

My heart leaps out of my chest. I step back into the hallway.
"Levi? Levi comes to you? From the future?"

"Yes."

"When?"

"Random times."

"How?" I ask. *"How* does he come to you?"

No answer.

"Does your husband know?" I try, my voice quaking.

We wait, but she doesn't say anything else.

"Ms. Campbell?"

Nothing.

Then she asks, "Do you know what the multiverse is?"

Stevie B takes a step back, says, "Oh God . . ."

I say, "No."

"There are universes parallel to ours. An infinite number of universes, where we all live an infinite number of alternative lives. Together, those universes make up the multiverse. Some people can travel between those universes. Others can't."

"Can you?" I manage to ask.

"No. But Levi can."

"He can . . . what?" I need clarity. I need to understand!

"He can travel from one world to another," she says. "But there's something else. He can also break through the barrier *between* those worlds. It's not here and not there when he comes to see me. It's not now and not then. I see Levi in a liminal place between the universes."

"Levi?" Stevie B questions, almost yelling. "Levi does all of this?"

"Yes."

"Oh God!" Stevie B says again. "So Levi, when you see him . . . how does he . . . ?"

"Like I said, some people can cross over. In certain places. There are *ripples*."

"So Levi's not dead?" I ask.

"No."

"But you're saying this is more than just time travel?"

"Yes. There's the future and the past—time travel. And then there's sideways—the multiverse. But then there's in between—the liminal place."

Stevie B is bent over, his hands on his knees like he might pass out.

"Tell us how it works," I say, "and when, and—"

"When Levi comes to me, he's not *here* like we know it. He's dreamlike. Levi explains it by saying he enters my consciousness. So I don't have him, but I didn't lose him completely either. I can't describe it any better than that, and I've said enough. Too much. You have to leave. Please! That's all I'm going to tell you."

I watch as she hurries toward the kitchen. Stevie B grabs my hand and pulls me out the door. "Nell, come on. We have to go!"

I take giant strides to keep up as he drags me along. Then I glance back at the house one more time before I climb into my truck and turn the engine on.

39

As we fly out of Ms. Campbell's driveway and head up her street, Stevie B's freaking out, slamming his fists, saying nothing that makes any sense.

"What are you thinking?" I finally ask when we get close to town. "About what Ms. Campbell said."

He glances over at me, pale and bug-eyed and done-in. "Shit, Nell! I don't know! What are you thinking about what she said?"

"I'm thinking we're not in Kansas anymore. Like *really* not in Kansas anymore."

"So where are we, then?" he asks, his eyes drilling right though me.

"Fuck if I know," I say. I look out the window at Jilly's Gas 'n Go and Judson's Dry Cleaners and Macy's State Street Diner. "If it makes you feel any better, technically speaking, we're still in Clawson. Like *physically* in Clawson."

"Well," he snaps back, "then Clawson isn't what it used to be."

"Do you think maybe she's just . . . lost it?" I ask. "You know, had a full-on lights-out systems meltdown?" I glance at Stevie B, hoping to see an improvement, but he's still gape-mouthed and shaken. "Maybe one of those deals where the power's out at the central station, the hard drive's on the fritz, and the backup generator's fried?"

"No. I do not," he says, like he's sure. "All that stuff she said, Nell?" He shakes his head. "We can't be having a shared hallucination. You and me? Maybe. You and me and Cole? Maybe that too. But *not* you and me and Ms. Campbell, the middle school English teacher. And *certainly not* you and me and Cole and Charlotte and Ms. Campbell, the middle school English teacher, and Ben Wallace, the Clawson police sergeant. We can't be having some kind of psychotic group event."

"Why do you think Levi didn't come back with the medicine his brother needed?"

"Dunno, Nell."

"Do you think that means Cole isn't coming back for Finn?"

"I don't know! But it's not looking good, Nell."

We drive in silence for a few minutes before I ask, "And what do you make of what Ms. Campbell said about parallel universes and seeing Levi in some in-between place?"

He doesn't answer. He just stares at the dashboard.

When I stop at a red light, he says, "I have to show you something."

He's scrunched up on the seat, balled tight like a fist, his hair messy and sticking out everywhere, his face drained of color. "I have to show you something. *Now*, Nell. It's important. Just . . . pull over. Please."

"Let me check on my mom first. It'll take five minutes. We're almost at my house. Then you can show me."

"Nell!"

"Just let me see if she's home," I plead. "It's after five. If her car is there, then . . . she's okay."

He keeps staring straight ahead like he's in a trance. "If something happened to your mom, Nell. If she shot Wozniak . . ."

"Don't. Go. There." I put my signal on and turn left on Millbank, headed in the direction of River Bend and my house.

At the next stop sign, I pull my phone out of my pocket and put it on the seat between us. I have the timer open, showing Finn's life counting down at high speed. That's happening no matter if the phone's tucked in my sweatshirt pocket or sitting right here where I can see it. But right now I *need* to see it to give me the strength to make the promise I am about to make to myself:

I will not let Finn die.

And I will not leave Cole wherever he is.

That will not happen.

I say that over and over in my head as I turn onto my street, and as I drive past the stand of pines on the right and the post-and-rail fence on the left. I say it again as I slow down when I pass the Franklins' fallin'-down barn.

But as soon as I round the bend and crest the hill, I see there's trouble ahead. We're high up enough to see the yellow lights of the prison vehicles and the red and blue swirling lights of the squad cars parked in front of my house.

Stevie B sits up. "Is that . . . ?"

I brake hard and do a U-ey—turning the truck around as fast as I can, pointing us north, back toward town, as another squad car flies past us, headed in the opposite direction.

"I can't go home," I tell him. "If it was just police cars, then this could be about Cole, and they could be looking for you and me. But prison vehicles? That's for my mom."

He glances back over his shoulder. "Maybe it's not what you think—"

"What I *thought* was that my mom was *probably* involved in the transport of that prisoner. And what I now *know* is that she *was,* and that they tested her or searched her locker and caught her with drugs. Which means she's been arrested and they're searching the house. Otherwise, there wouldn't be all those prison officials there right now."

"You don't know that!" Stevie B tries.

"Yeah, I do. I *know* that! I know she was one of two guards on the medical transport team at Manville. And I know what they do if you're found under the influence at work when you discharge your weapon and someone dies. And I know what they do with an underage kid who has no parents. And I can't be *that* kid. Especially not now. Not with Cole and Finn and Charlotte, and everything else we have going on."

I remind myself to drive slowly, to not go over the speed limit, to use my turn signals, to not draw attention in case they're looking for me. "Will they be looking for me?" I ask, squeezing the steering wheel tight, tears sprouting from my eyes. "Do the cops look for kids if their parents have been arrested?"

"Maybe," he says, "but I don't think so. I don't think they're expecting you to be on the run, Nell. They probably figure you'll show up at home on your own."

When I turn onto Main Street, he asks, "Where we going now?"

"Cole's house. Then the quarry. I made myself a promise, Stevie B. I will not let Finn die. And I will not leave Cole wherever he is. That will not happen."

"Yeah, but—"

"So right now, I have to see Finn—*have* to—and then I just need to think. And hide. And no one will find us at the quarry. We have to figure out what to do."

"Pull over," he says.

"Why?"

"I hear you about Cole and Finn. And I'm real sorry about your mom. But just pull over. I told you before—I have to show you something, Nell. It's real important. So pull over, please!"

"Show me later, when we get to the quarry."

"No," he says. "I need you to pull over. Right now! It can't wait. I need to tell you now, before I change my mind."

When he says that, my uh-oh meter goes from kissin' the red zone to straight off the top of the gauge. From high-throttle over-drive to engine fire. I turn to him with my *Oh, no! What now? Don't do this to me* face, and I see that he means it—like *really* means it—so I swerve around a pizza delivery car and a FedEx truck, then pull into the parking lot across from the Quicky Mart and park the truck.

"Okay," I say firmly. "Tell me what you have to tell me."

Stevie B looks down at his hands and says, "He comes to me too, Nell."

40

I feel my blood thump-thumping and my breath catching in my chest, forming a big knot of worry—new worry to add to all the old worry that's already piled up sky-high. I somehow muster up the strength to ask, "Who? Who comes to you?"

Stevie B's all drawn and pale when he says, "Levi. Levi comes to me." And he's looking at me like he's real sorry he had to say it.

I stare at him blankly, blinking and thinking, *I did not see that coming,* but I manage to blurt out, "What the fuck, Stevie B?"

"I thought it was just me dreaming," he adds. And he looks like he's real sorry he said that too.

"You thought *what* was just you dreaming?"

"The visions I've been having of Levi."

"*Visions?* You have visions of Levi? *Levi Tanner?*"

He nods. "I didn't know what else to call them until Ms. Campbell said that thing she said about some in-between, liminal space and him entering her consciousness. And that's a good way to describe it."

"When? When does he come to you?" I ask.

"Sometimes at night, when I'm sleeping. But mostly when I'm awake. Mostly when I'm drawing, I guess."

"How long has it been happening?"

"I don't know exactly. But the last two years or so, I guess."

He tells me that, and my breath catches in my chest again. "You've been dreaming about Levi Tanner—*Ms. Campbell's* Levi, the kid who went to school with our parents and jumped into the quarry and didn't come back—for the *last two years?*"

"That's what I'm saying. I'm just not sure it's dreaming."

"What the hell, Stevie B? Are you sure it's him?"

"Absolutely certain."

"How often?"

"All the time, Nell." Then he leans forward and starts rummaging through his backpack.

I know what he said a few minutes ago, about how we can't all be having a shared hallucination, especially not one that is this specific. But even still, I'm sitting here wondering if all of us—me and him and Cole and Charlotte and Ms. Campbell and Sergeant Wallace—*are*. And I'm trying to figure out where this is headed, wondering what the hell Stevie B could possibly have in his bag that would explain any part of the woo-woo, paranormal shitstorm we're experiencing.

Then he pulls out his biggest sketchbook, the one he transfers his best drawings to. He sets it on his lap and starts flipping through the pages, sending the smell of chalk dust up into the air and staining his fingers black before he settles on one drawing in particular and points at it like it'll explain everything.

I take the sketchbook from him. "Jesus H. Christ, Stevie B!"

It's Levi, all right. Levi's face, exactly as it looks in the photo in my mom's yearbook. Ms. Campbell's Levi, age seventeen.

I examine his jaw and his hairline. The shapes of the two scars:

the zigzag scar on his cheek, and the half-moon above his right eye. But it's not only these specifics that get me; there's something else about this drawing. It's that thing artists do when they capture someone's face with only a few lines and you know exactly who it is right off, even though you can't explain what part of the drawing did it—if it's the eyes, maybe, or the jawline, or the shape of the mouth, or the way the hair falls, or how the cheeks are hollowed out, or something else altogether. But whatever it is, it's those tiny details that make the drawing recognizable as *that* person and no one else, and Stevie B captured that in this sketch. It's Levi Tanner, through and through—there's no doubting it.

I look back up at Stevie B, wide-eyed and awestruck, to see what he's gonna say, and he's staring out the front windshield, looking torn to shreds.

"Until you showed me your mom's yearbook yesterday, I thought me seeing that face when I was sketching was me dreamin' and imagining, Nell. I thought Levi was someone I made up in my head and that it was normal for people like me who draw to have visions and get ideas and see faces. And then I thought it was normal to conjure up details like those scars and that jawline."

He looks over at me real quick and adds, "But then I saw that yearbook photo yesterday and I *knew*, Nell. I *knew* something was *really* wrong, 'cause I see him in my head and he comes to me when I work. It's more real than dreaming and less real than normal living, but it's something. I see that now. And I drew this picture a couple of years ago, and I've been drawing lots of pictures of Levi, and other things too—things Levi compels me to draw—for a long time now."

"So he's what? Your muse?"

"Something like that, I guess."

I turn back to the drawing, trembling, not sure what any of this means, and he says, "There's more too."

I was afraid of that. 'Cause lately it seems like there's *always* more. Then Stevie B reaches over and turns the page of the sketchbook to show me another drawing. He looks away as soon as the page opens, like he can't bear to see my face or that drawing either.

I glance down, scared of what I'll find, and what's sitting there in front of me, in pen and ink and charcoal, is a picture of me and Cole and Levi. The three of us, together.

We're standing on top of the quarry—the jumping-off place— the sheared-off rocks of the cliff wall dropping below us on both sides. We look like superheroes. Real pumped-up metropolis-saving comic-book-worthy badass superheroes. We look fiery and fierce, with our hands on our hips, in tight shirts and pants, and masks over our eyes. I have a red-and-yellow lightning bolt flaming across my cobalt-blue shirt. Cole is in all black. Levi is in bright yellow, and he's got these blue lines shooting out of his eyes, like lasers. Cole seems to have some kind of spear in his left hand, and his knuckles shimmer, like they're made of ice or diamonds—or energy, maybe. Our muscles are well defined and bulging under our shirts, our eyes focused and piercing, the whole universe spread out around us, dark and sparkly and infinite.

I glance at the bottom of the page, and I see Earth below us, a curve of hazy blue and green sitting some distance beneath our feet. I lean in and examine the picture up close, taking my time to scrutinize every detail like I'm searching for clues.

All three of us appear content and certain—happy, even—and me and Cole look to be the same age as Levi. It's like Levi didn't age a day from his yearbook photo and we didn't age a day from today.

"When did you draw this?" I ask, feelin' like I've got the hooves of a wild mustang stampeding in my chest, pounding the breath right out of me. I think about what Cole said all those times: *Special things are coming for us, Nell. I know it!* And I'm wondering if this might be it.

"I drew it over a year ago," Stevie B reports, his voice blunt, but with relief bleeding through his words like it feels good to let them out. "Look," he adds, turning the page and pointing to the date scrawled in tiny numbers on the back of the drawing.

"Well, maybe you'd seen Levi's yearbook picture a few years back and you just, you know, took parts of it without remembering?" I throw that thought out there, like bait on fishing line, hoping to hook something more normal to explain this.

He shakes his head. "I never saw your mom's yearbook before yesterday, Nell. I'm sure of it."

"So why didn't you say something about this to me yesterday, then?"

"I didn't know what to make of it at first. And then you freaked me out when you went and stuck your head in the tub, Nell."

I turn back to the drawing. "Your parents probably have that yearbook too, you know. So maybe you saw one of theirs and don't remember." I'm wanting more than anything for that to be true, but he sits up a little and faces me, saying, "I swear, neither one of my parents has a yearbook, and if they do, I've never seen it. Plus, it's not normal imagining when Levi comes to me, Nell. I see that now."

"Are you sure?" I ask. "Like full-on die-on-a-poison-sword certain of that?"

"I'm absolutely certain it's him."

"So . . . what?" I ask, thinking about the picture he drew two years ago of me wearing the necklace. "You're saying Levi comes to you and shows you the future . . . or something?"

His shoulders fall. "I'm not sure. But maybe. I think it's that thing Ms. Campbell said about people breaking through from the future or from some parallel universe and entering some liminal place, but whatever it is, Levi . . . he comes to me too!" Then he asks, "Why me, Nell? Why does he come to me?"

I don't answer him. I look back at the sketchbook. At the drawing of me and Cole and Levi. Then Stevie B turns the page, and it's the same sketch again with all the same details, but in this one there's someone else with us. A fourth person, standing off to the side. She's bigger than us—looming, almost—and drawn more hazy, like he used more chalk or charcoal and less ink and pencil, and smudged her more than the rest of us. I examine her closely, then glance up at Stevie B.

"That's . . ."

I don't say her name. Not at first. I look down again, running my fingers over the lines of her face.

"I didn't know who it was when I drew her," Stevie B says. "I didn't know who it was until today, Nell. I thought I made her up too. But I can see it now. Clear as day."

I study the girl's eyes, the wave in her hair, the shape of her nose. "It's Finnegan," I whisper.

"All grown up," Stevie B adds.

"Maybe this means that Finn's gonna live. If this means anything, if you *can* see the future, maybe it means she won't die tomorrow!"

"I hope you're right, Nell, but that's a pretty big conclusion to draw from something I sketched two years ago. I mean, I know what I said about visions and Levi coming to me, but these are only *drawings*, and it's Finn's *life* we're talking about here."

"So what do we do?" I ask.

"I don't know. But it feels like maybe I have information about the future—you know, like I said, *inside of me*. And I don't know how to tell which parts are real and which parts maybe I made up. So I don't know what I'm supposed to do with it."

I study the sketch with Finn in it for a while. "If all of this is true, all this stuff that's been happening to us—the time-travel and multiverse stuff—how many people do you think know about it?"

"I don't know, Nell. But why us?"

I look out the window at Clawson. At normal people living their normal lives. Doing laundry at the Suds 'n More and filling their cars up at the Gas 'n Go and going to their jobs. "Do you remember when we were five, in Ms. Kinley's class in kindergarten?"

"Just barely. Why?"

"When me and Cole were by the cubbies, putting our coats on one day, he said, 'Special things are coming for us, Nell.' That's a weird thing for a five-year-old to say, don't you think? And he kept saying it, all the time, all these years, like he had to remind me."

"And you think maybe this is it? The special thing that Cole saw coming for you?"

I don't answer. I look again at the picture Stevie B drew of me and Cole and Finn standing with Levi, all of us looking so strong and certain, like we're about to save the world. Me feeling *not* strong and *not* certain and *not* capable of saving myself, let alone anything or anyone else. I sit here trying to make sense of what is happening but come up sixty seconds short of a minute.

Then, out of the corner of my eye, I see a Clawson police cruiser pull into the parking lot. The cop's driving real slow, crawling almost, like he's looking for someone.

"Did he see us?" I ask as I pull onto the main drag, narrowly making the light.

Stevie B checks over his shoulder then says, "Not yet, Nellie."

41

"Are you okay?" I ask after I check my mirrors one more time to make sure we're not being followed by that cop car.

"Not really," Stevie B admits. "This is a lot, Nell."

I reach over and grab his hand.

"What do you think we should do now? Just *wait*?" he asks, sounding a little desperate. "Just keep waiting for Cole to come back, or not come back. Or for the cops to come get us, or . . ."

He keeps holding my hand and listing every bad thing that could happen, and I keep driving east on Main Street. "Look," I try, when he pauses, "it's after six on Friday . . ."

"Cole said he'd be back by now, Nell."

"That's why I think we should go to the quarry to wait for him. So when he gets back, if he needs help, we'll be there."

"You still think he's coming back?" Stevie B asks.

"It's not looking good, but it's the only thing I *can* think. And like I said before, I want to stop at Cole's house first."

"What for?"

"I have to see Finn. With what Ms. Campbell told us about

Levi's brother dying, I *have* to. I know maybe it doesn't seem important considering everything that's happening, but I promised I'd take her moon catching tomorrow night. And it's just . . . tomorrow might be . . ." I don't finish, and Stevie B says it for me.

"Too late. Tomorrow might be too late."

I turn onto Cole's street, and Stevie B sinks down in his seat. He keeps sitting there looking like he's flat-out busted and he's given up completely.

"Don't quit on me," I tell him. "You can't quit on me."

"I'm not quitting, Nell. I'm just falling apart a little."

"Fair enough."

After I pull in to Cole's driveway, Stevie B's still scrunched up and closed off, tucked in tight against the passenger side door.

"Want to come with me?" I try.

"Nah. You go, Nell. I need some time."

Two minutes later, he's sitting in the truck and I'm standing on the Wilders' front stoop, feeling about as bad as a person could feel—until Finn pulls the door open and everything bad flies out of my head 'cause she's breathing fine and she's smiling like all that's good in the world is right here on her doorstep.

"I'm here to go moon catchin'," I whisper like it's a super important, top secret mission.

"It's not even Saturday, Nell!" she whispers back.

"Some moons need catching sooner than we think, Finn."

Cole's mom comes to the door, and she looks real happy to see me too. So it's this tiny moment where everything feels normal, even though the three of us are about as far from normal as people could possibly be.

Finn runs off to get her stuff, and Mrs. Wilder hurries outside to talk to me. "I wasn't at work when it happened because I had Finn at the doctor, but I heard about your mom," she says in a hushed voice. "You okay?"

"I think so," I tell her, full-on lying.

"Have you seen her?"

"No. Not yet. The cops are at my house now, so . . ."

"You want to stay here tonight? I could make some calls maybe. See what I can find out."

Finn is back now, with her sneakers on the wrong feet. For some inexplicable reason, she's wearing swim goggles and mittens. She's holding a flashlight in one hand and carrying the moon-catching net in the other when she starts whinin' at her mom. "You go back inside. Me and Nell have a secret project."

Mrs. Wilder says, "You girls have fun. Make sure to watch her breathing, Nell, and I'll make those calls."

She heads inside, and me and Finn stand on the front steps. I'm looking up at the sky for a minute, and Finn's talking in circles about something I'm not listening to, 'cause I'm too busy thinking about how damn big my problems are.

"How many moons are there, Nell?" Finn asks when she finally finishes her story and looks up at the sky too.

"Hundreds, Finn. Eight planets, and hundreds of moons. Cole taught me that." I bend down next her, trying not to cry and trying not to laugh as she peers back at me wearing those goggles. "How many moons do you think we can catch with that net of yours?"

"All of them," she whispers, like she really believes it.

She steps off the stoop and starts swinging her net, and we manage to pull Titan and Rhea from their orbits around Saturn. And in less than ten minutes, we have all ninety-five known moons of Jupiter spinnin' in our pockets.

"You know," I tell her, "Saturn has tiny moons called moonlets, which are like baby shepherd moons, holding Saturn's rings in place. Cole taught me that too."

"Cole knows everything about everything in the sky, Nell."

"You sure are right about that, Finn."

"Is he coming home soon?"

I say, "Cole's coming home tomorrow," but I don't dare look at her when I say it.

She wraps her arms around my legs and hugs me hard, and I hang tight to that moment, unsure about everything in this world except for the hold that Cole and Finn Wilder have on my heart. "Come on. Let's walk around back and swoop that net of yours some more."

By my count, we manage to snag every last moon in the universe, Finn putting each of them in her pockets, one after another, like they're spinning pixies we can't see except for in our imagination.

"Cole says there's an invisible magic force that holds all the moons and planets together so they won't fall out of the sky and they'll never be apart."

"That's called gravity, Finn."

"He says it's called 'heartstrings' for you, me, and him."

"What do you mean?"

"Cole says you and me and him have invisible heartstrings holding us together forever so we'll never be apart."

And when she says that, my heart downright melts.

+ + + + + + +

I take her back inside, and Mrs. Wilder sends her to get ready for bed. "I just heard from Carol Stewart," she tells me in a hushed voice after Finn runs off. "Looks like your mom's been arrested, Nell. I don't know what's true and what's not, but they're saying it was drugs in her locker. I'm so sorry, honey."

She says that, and it damn near knocks me down. I mean, I *knew*, but now I *know*, and somehow that feels a whole lot different. I manage to say, "I was pretty much expecting that," and she looks like she was pretty much expecting it too.

"My offer stands if you want to stay over, Nell."

"Thanks. That means a lot. It really does. But Stevie B's waiting for me in the truck, so I should go. But maybe I can put Finn to bed first?"

"You sure?"

"Yeah," I tell her. "I figure Finn's the best medicine for me right now."

Mrs. Wilder says, "Amen to that," and I head up to Finn's room and climb into the bed next to her.

She hands me the Shel Silverstein book—the one with the dog-eared cover and the moon-catching poem she loves. I read that poem over and over again until Finn's eyes close. Then, under her breath, she starts reciting it from memory right along with me.

"I've found what I sought and I finally caught
The moon in my moon-catchin' net. . . ."

I don't sneak out of her room until those spun-sugar words stop falling from her lips and I hear her breath come long and slow and steady. I stay a few minutes longer even, just to watch her chest rise and fall.

"She's out cold," I whisper to Mrs. Wilder, who's drinking tea and hunched over some bills at the kitchen table, me feeling bad about not telling her more. Me feeling bad about what I fear may have happened to Cole, and what may be about to happen to Finn, and what I know about Charlotte and the quarry and everything that's happening to all of us. I feel all of that practically begging to burst right out of me, but I don't have the heart to destroy a person like that, so I go ahead and tell her that Cole'll be back tomorrow and that me and my mom'll be okay. Me wanting—*needing*—to gift her one more day of peace before we see what tomorrow brings. Then I thank her again for offering for me to stay over before I head back outside.

Stevie B doesn't say a thing when I climb into the front seat next to him, but he shows me a picture he drew of me and Finn holding hands, the two of us flying past the house, with a dozen moons shining over our heads. We're leaping over a small hill, Finn with the moon-catching net clutched in her hand, awe and wonder plastered on her face.

I stare at that picture, crushed by the possibility that Finn Wilder may die tomorrow. Not knowing if she'll ever be cured and be able to run and jump and fly over hills like Stevie B drew her.

I'm trying not to break down and cry, trying not to think, but I'm crying and thinking anyway.

"I guess it's your turn to fall apart," Stevie B says.

I figure he's right, but I don't tell him what Mrs. Wilder told me about my mom. I hand the sketchbook back to him, saying, "Thanks for that picture. For all the pictures."

"That superpower you asked me for a long time ago?" he says. "The giant magnet to hang on to people you love? It's your heart, Nell. I see that every day."

I lean over and hug him real hard. Me fitting in his arms like they're Cole's. Like right here and right now, they're the safest place in the entire universe.

"It's good, what you just did with Finn," he whispers. "It's really something."

I squeeze my eyes and wipe away my tears as I let go of him and turn the engine over.

I figure tonight Finn Wilder fell asleep with her pockets full of imaginary moons and all those invisible heartstrings holding us together, and Mrs. Wilder thinks that Cole will be coming home tomorrow, so that *is* something.

As I turn my truck out onto the road and head toward the quarry, I feel those heartstrings pulling real hard inside my chest, and I decide, *Damn it all, no. Something might be something, but sometimes it's not enough. Even though it might be all that we have.*

Then I convince myself that this mess we're in right now—with Cole gone and Finn's death sentence, with the whole Stevie B and Levi thing, and my mom arrested—is flat-out *not okay and not enough.*

It's not enough for Cole. Or Finn. Or Mrs. Wilder. Or my mom.

And it's not enough for Stevie B.

Or for me.

I tell myself that sometimes those heartstrings pull so hard they give you the strength to fix the stuff that's not enough.

Then I tell myself that Nell Bannon is brave enough to do just that: to fix the stuff that's not enough.

As I drive toward the quarry, I tell myself that over and over again until it sticks.

42

Fifteen minutes later, when I pull in next to Cole's truck at the quarry, Stevie B announces, "I looked it up when you were moon catching with Finn. The seeing-faces thing? I'm not the only one who has it."

"What do you mean?"

"Other people, Nell. It happens to them too."

"What kind of other people? Like psychics? Or palm readers or quacks?"

"No. Like real, legit regular people. And science people."

"So these regular people and science people, they believe in visions or déjà vu or seeing stuff in your head before it happens?"

"It's called 'precognition.' It's seeing things, *future* things. Faces you've never seen before but are real. Then there's something else called"—he pulls up a screen on his phone—"'synchronicity' and 'the collective unconscious,' that says that we're all connected across space and time. I've been reading, Nell, and there's something else real scientists—like actual *physicists*—believe. It's called . . . Hold on." He pulls up a new screen. "'Entanglement. *Quantum* entanglement.' They looked at these tiny particles—photons, I think—that were close once but are really far apart now. Like *really* far apart. Like billions of light-years apart in the universe. When they made a change to one of them, it changed the other one. Those photons, Nell? They communicated somehow, then changed each other instantaneously, even when they were light-years apart."

"How?"

"Nobody knows, except to say they're entangled somehow."

"So you read science articles now? Like brainy—"

"Pretty much comic books. I found one called *Totally Random*, written by a physicist, that explains the entangled thing. It's a made-up story about how the initial position of two coins that are put into something called the Super Quantum Entangler PR01 alters the probability of coin-toss outcomes. Which means the coins communicate their initial position—heads or tails—to each other somehow. Those coins are entangled, Nell. The author made up the entangler machine, but the science behind it is real."

"So what are you saying? That you and Levi . . . and Ms. Campbell and Levi, you're . . ."

"I'm saying we're far apart in the universe—we might not even know each other—but we're entangled, somehow. It's like we have crossed wires. Like we communicate in some way even scientists can't understand. Like those coins in the Super Quantum Entangler PR01. That's the only way I can explain it. Ms. Campbell called it 'crossing over.' But it's communicating with someone you shouldn't be able to communicate with if you just believe in the normal stuff we already understand."

"So . . . your drawings . . ."

"I think they're real, Nell. Maybe not all of them, and maybe not some of the superhero stuff, but a lot of them. I think this stuff I'm drawing, it's gonna happen. In some cases, *has* happened. So I think the universe isn't what we think, Nell. I mean, I showed you a picture I drew of Charlotte standing at the quarry wearing Cole's grandma's necklace before I'd even *met* Charlotte. Before I'd ever *seen* that necklace. And then we saw what I drew. You and me, we *saw* it. So the Levi pictures? The pictures of you and Charlotte and Cole and Levi and Finn? They're real. I can't explain it better than that, but somehow they're real. Somehow we're entangled."

It gets all quiet, and the air doesn't move, and he doesn't say anything else. He just stares out the window at Cole's truck.

"You know what Cole told me, Stevie B? He said the universe is bigger than we think."

"Yeah, well. He's right."

"So you think you're like Levi, then? You can cross over?"

"Yeah. I do. I don't like it, and I don't understand it, but I do. Or maybe *I* can't, but *he* can, and he's telling me things."

I look over at Cole's truck too.

Stevie B asks, "Why me, Nell?"

I don't answer. Instead I ask, "Is there any chance you have a drawing of Cole climbing out of the quarry on a Friday night or a Saturday morning, him holding a pill to cure Finn?"

"Wish I did, Nell."

"Yeah. Me too."

"So you believe me? All that stuff I told you? I need you to believe me. 'Cause otherwise—"

"Yeah, I believe you. *Of course,* I believe you. Especially about the Super Quantum Entangler PR01."

Stevie B smiles the tiniest bit.

I glance out at the woods. Cole's truck sitting there empty. The whole world looking big and dark. "How long till Saturday at five?"

"It's going for eight on Friday," Stevie B tells me. "So a little more than twenty-one hours."

I check my phone, hoping to see some message I missed from my mom—*anything* from my mom—or a miracle message from

Cole, telling me he borrowed someone's phone and he's home. But there's nothing.

"You know, Nell, you never told me what happened that night when you and Cole jumped into the quarry and something went wrong."

I figure he's bared his soul, telling me all the stuff he told me about him being entangled and crossing brain wires with Levi, so I owe him. "That night when we jumped, we were on the south side, very close to the rocks," I begin. "And we went *deep*. Deeper than normal. I was out of air, but somehow it felt okay—at least at first. So I grabbed hold of the rocks. Cole did too. It was like Charlotte said: a stone ladder. And we climbed farther down, and then, I don't know, I guess I must've blacked out. At least, that's what I *think*—or *thought*—anyway. I remember coming to, and I was alone—no Cole. Just all this water. I was completely out of air, lungs exploding. So I started frantically swimming to the surface. It took forever—at least that's how it felt. And when I finally made it to the top, I was freaked-out. Like *really* freaked-out, because Cole wasn't *anywhere*. Not in the water, and not on the rocks. And my lungs were burning. Like *on fire* burning. I called his name over and over, and I dove back in again and again, but I couldn't find him. So I kept diving in and crying and shaking . . ."

I can't finish, and Stevie B's staring at me.

"And?"

"I eventually went home."

"Shit, Nell! Where was Cole?"

"I don't know."

"Did you call for help?"

"No. I was fifteen. And alone. And afraid. And it was almost morning by the time I quit searching for him, and we weren't supposed to be out, and I was confused about what had happened and exhausted and cold, and I thought maybe he *left* me—I shouldn't have thought that, but I did—so I just . . . ran home."

"And did what?"

"Nothing."

"Well, I guess it worked out okay, because Cole's been here the last two years, but that's shit-for-brains, Nell!"

"Yeah, but after is when it got weird."

"Meaning what?"

"Cole showed up at school the next day and claimed he didn't remember anything happening—said I made it up. He insisted that we didn't even go to the quarry and we didn't jump that night."

"Do you think you time-traveled?"

"I certainly didn't think it back then, but now? I think maybe I came close."

"What about Cole? Do you think he time-traveled?"

"I don't know. Maybe he traveled back to a few hours earlier that day, couldn't understand what happened and freaked out. That's what I'm kind of thinking right now. Which would explain why he said the whole thing didn't happen, I guess."

"Do you think you could find the place on the south wall again? The stone ladder?"

I stare out at the trees and don't answer.

"Nell?"

I still don't answer, but that doesn't mean I don't *know* the answer.

I just sit there thinking, *Yes. I could find my way back to the south wall and that stone ladder. And, yes, I remember. I remember every detail like it was yesterday. And I could find the stone ladder on the north wall too, if I had to.*

"I've been thinking, Nell. You know what Cole said to you when you were five and in the cubbies, how something special was coming for you? Like you guys were supposed to do something important? I think he was right."

"Because . . ."

"Look." He opens his sketchbook and flips through to the page he showed me before, with me and Cole and Levi and Finn. "What are you doing in this picture?"

"We're all dressed up like superheroes standing in outer space."

"Yeah, but what are you *doing*?"

I peer at the sketch. "I don't know."

"I think I might."

Stevie B has this look I've never seen before. It's a look I've never seen before on *anyone*. He seems serious and scared—but there's something else too. It's like he's enthralled or exuberant or . . .

"Go on," I say.

"I think you might be trying to find a way to save everyone. You know, *escape* some bad thing that happened." He flips through the pages to the front of his sketchbook and shows me another drawing. "I drew this two years ago. When I was fifteen."

It's a picture of the black sky.

Outer space. No people.

But the black of infinity isn't empty and bleak; there's extraordinary detail. It's vibrant and charged and bursting with energy. It appears to go on forever, in all directions. The sky is studded with stars. Rimmed with streaks of bright color. There are rings around the planets, luminous moons; a comet tail sails through the dark.

He turns the page again. Shows me a similar picture. But this time, there's a tear—the dark sky is ripped wide open near the edge, leaving a gaping, shattered hole torn right through the fabric of the universe. And beyond, it isn't dark; it's beautiful. Filled with even more color and light. I pull the sketchbook closer, and I'm thunderstruck with awe. Speechless at how this picture makes me feel and what it may mean. It seems vast and optimistic. Looking at it actually makes me feel hopeful. Which makes no sense. I mean, how could I be hopeful in this life and in this moment?

And yet seeing this picture, I feel powerful. Infinite, even.

Stevie B takes the sketchbook from me and turns the page again, then hands it back.

It's the same picture of outer space with the planets and the color and the tear in the dark sky, but me and Cole and Levi and Finn are in it. And this time, in *this* picture, Stevie B is with us. He's standing side by side with Cole and me. The three of us have peeled back the dark of space to open a pathway out.

We ripped the hole in the universe. *We* made the tear. *We* appear triumphant.

Then Stevie B turns the page again, and it's the same drawing. The same drawing as the one before, and the one before that. But just like in all the others, something new is added.

This time, in *this* sketch, there are people pouring through the hole we tore in the fabric of the universe. Lots and lots of people, in a trail that doesn't appear to end.

"What are they doing?" I manage to ask.

"I don't know," he says. "But I think we're saving them."

"How do you know that?"

"I don't know *how* I know that, Nell. But I *do*. bvThis," he adds, pointing at the sketch with the ripped-open sky and the people pouring through it. "I just *know*. I mean, I *can't* know it. But I do."

"What's on the other side? Where are they going? Do you know?" I ask.

He nods, then turns the page.

It's the same drawing but zoomed in on the view through the tear.

I recognize it immediately. The lay of the land. The gentle turns of the river. The church spire. The Hendersons' barn. The hills in the distance . . .

I look at Stevie B. His face is calm for the first time in days when he says, "It's Clawson, Nell. It's home. I think we're bringing them home."

43

I slide the sketchbook onto the seat between us, feeling humble and small. Then I glance out the window at Cole's truck, wondering what to believe, as images flash through my head: Stevie B's drawings. Ms. Campbell at her kitchen table. Cole and Charlotte jumping. Finn swooping her net. Then Cole standing next to his truck, dripping wet, his hands shaking. Cole, climbing in and driving home, hugging Finn. Her laughing, playing . . . living.

Then another image: Cole's body floating face down in the quarry.

And another: His truck choked by vines, abandoned and covered in dry leaves, surrounded by cops searching for clues to what happened to him. Me and Stevie B in handcuffs. Finn's funeral . . .

Layers and layers of possible outcomes. *Infinite* options, each clouding out the one that came before. "Do you believe in free will?" I ask.

Stevie B appears startled. "Of course."

"What about destiny? Do you believe in destiny?"

"That too."

"That makes no sense," I tell him. "You can't believe in both."

"Maybe you can," he says. "Maybe we *have* to."

I think about that. "Yeah, maybe." Then I start gathering my stuff. "Let's go."

"Where to?"

"The jumping-off place."

"What for?"

"To wait for Cole."

＋ ＋ ＋ ＋ ＋ ＋ ＋

When we arrive, we sit on the rocks and I put my phone between us so I can see the timer. Finn's death clock is running down at high speed, devouring what's left of her life a fraction of a second at a time.

"How long?' he asks.

"A little under twenty hours."

"How come we're up *here*, Nell? And not down below by the pool of water Cole would swim out of?"

I snap, "'Cause this is where I want to sit." Then I reach into my bag and pull out Charlotte's counting device and start a second timer.

I tell myself it doesn't mean anything. But it does. *It means everything.*

I set it to 960 seconds, just like Charlotte did. Then I watch as it starts ticking down. 959, 958, 957 . . .

Me staring at the numbers, mesmerized, holding my breath as time disappears. Me knowing what I promised myself:

I will not let Finn die.

And I will not leave Cole wherever he is.

That will not happen.

"Why do you have Charlotte's timer?" Stevie B asks, his voice tinged with alarm.

I don't answer that. Instead, I blurt out, "My mom was arrested. She shot Wozniak. They found drugs in her locker. Cole's mom told me back at the house."

Stevie B sighs. His shoulders fall. "I'm sorry, Nell. Real sorry." Then he hugs me. And it's one of those hugs that's trying to fix something that's way past fixing.

I wipe away my tears and go right back to holding my breath, and then when I can't do it—can't get past two minutes without air—I say, "You know who I feel like right now?"

"Who?"

"Alice."

"Hot Alice from my homeroom?"

"No. The girl who falls down the rabbit hole and swims in a pool of her own tears, then meets up with a white rabbit and plays croquet with the hotheaded queen."

"So you're talking drugs. Like in the Jefferson Airplane song?"

"I was thinking about the book, not the song, but yeah. *That* Alice. The one in Wonderland . . . And drugs."

"Why?"

"'Cause that's what they're gonna think, if we tell them what happened."

"Who?"

"Everyone. The cops. School. Our family and friends."

"That we were high?"

"Yep. All of us. Badass bad-trip chasing-the-dragon *Alice in Wonderland* Jefferson Airplane high. And you know what else? They're all gonna think we killed Cole."

"Cole *and* Charlotte," he says.

"Good point. She's missing too. Thanks for pointing that out."

"Sorry, Nell."

"Well, if you think about it . . . technically, she *can't* be missing. How can a girl with no name, no home, and no past actually be missing?"

"Dunno. But she is. At least as far as the school and the cops would be concerned," Stevie B states before he asks, "Do you still believe Cole is coming back?"

"I'm scared he might not. Levi didn't."

"I was afraid you were going to say that."

"Yeah, me too. Cole said he'd be back Thursday. Friday at the latest. It's Friday, Stevie B. And Friday's almost over and he's not here."

"But what about that thing I told you about Charlotte being Cole's great-granddaughter?" he asks. "How that means Cole *has* to come back so she can be born?"

"Don't know, but maybe she lied about the being-related part and faked that necklace somehow." And then I think, *Or maybe Cole needs my help to get home,* but I don't say that out loud.

"And the rest of it?" he asks.

"You mean, is Finn gonna die and are we gonna do something like rip a hole in the sky and save all those people?"

"Yeah."

"I have no clue."

"Me either," he says.

"You know all that stuff about the multiverse? I googled it back in the truck. You're right about the scientists, Stevie B. Big scientists believe in that stuff too. Not only what you said about seeing things from the future and all of us being entangled. They believe the infinite-world parallel-universe people-having-multiple-lives-in-multiple-universes thing too."

"I figured," he says. Then he glances in the direction of my phone and Charlotte's counting device sitting there between us. "How long, Nell?"

"Just under two minutes."

"No. I mean, how long does Finn have? How long till Saturday at five?"

"Nineteen hours and thirty-seven minutes," I say, and then I pick up my phone and Charlotte's timer, walk over to the edge of the flat stones, and peer down at the water.

"Open your sketchbook," I call to him. "The older one."

He pulls the book from his bag. I walk back over and sit next to him.

"There's a picture I saw . . . I never told you I saw it. It's me draped on the rocks, climbing out of the quarry. The one where I look so—"

"I know it," he says right off as he flips through pages, his fingers coated in chalk dust. "Here."

I take the book from him. "That's the one," I whisper as I catch his eye before we both turn to scrutinize the drawing. "What's that? In the background?" I ask. "Against the rocks?"

He studies the picture some more. "It looks like . . ."

"A bag," I offer. "I didn't pay attention to it before, but it's a bag. It's *Charlotte's dry bag*, Stevie B! Look at the zipper. The white tag on the side. They're the same. Why would I have her bag?"

"Nell . . . It's not that clear. It could be any bag."

"No. That's *her* bag, Stevie B. And there's only one reason I would have it."

"Nell, no."

"You said it, Stevie B. You said the stuff you draw, some of it *happens*. Some of it's real. So . . . maybe . . . maybe I'm supposed to be here, climbing out of this quarry carrying that bag—Charlotte's bag, with the medicine in it for Finn—because *Cole* can't. Maybe you drew it to warn me. To tell me to—"

"Nell, no. Don't say it."

I don't say *jump*. I don't say anything. I just keep staring at that drawing.

"Shit, Nell. What are you thinking?"

"I'm thinking that it'd be ironic if I spent most of the last seventeen years thinking I was meant to do *nothing* in this life when I was really sent here to save Finn, and maybe Cole, and maybe even to rip a hole in the sky to save people I don't even know. People who might not even be born yet. I mean, that's a mind-bending gasket blower if you ask me."

He doesn't say anything, so I add, "You know, I keep hearing this song playing over and over in my head."

"The one your mom always plays?"

"No. A different one. The one Cole sings a lot." I find the song on my phone and hit PLAY, and Lauren Daigle starts to sing "Rescue." It sounds otherworldly—her voice, those words—rising up like that in the dark woods, right here next to the quarry:

> *I will send out an army to find you*
> *In the middle of the darkest night . . .*

The wind gusts, sending my hair blowing and leaves rustling, and Stevie B turns the music off, then whispers, "Nellie, no."

I grab Charlotte's counting device as I walk over closer to the quarry.

"Where you going?" he asks as he follows me.

I don't answer.

He reaches for me, calling out, "Nell, no!" This time it's closer to a yell.

I pull away and say, "I'm just gonna look." Then I step up onto the higher rocks and move to the edge. I peer down at the water, then close my eyes.

I can see everything: the silver slips of moonlight dancing on the surface like minnows.

I can feel everything: Cole standing next to me. Finn living.

Those heartstrings holding tight and pulling hard.

I can hear everything: Cole whispering, "Special things are coming for us, Nell. I know it."

I open my eyes and look up at the sky, then down at the water beneath me, and I imagine Cole singing that Lauren Daigle song, switching the words up like he does.

Stevie B is next to me now. I'm clutching Charlotte's counter when I whisper, "I have to."

"Nell, no," he begs, those words all bruised and achy.

He knows. We both know what I have to do.

He's got his hand beneath my elbow. The rest of him is all tangled up in my head and heart when I say, "It's Friday night and Cole's not back. And Charlotte lied to Margaret Campbell and Ben Wallace because Levi didn't come back home with medicine like she told them he would. And Levi's brother died! So, Charlotte's lying about some of this, which means I have to warn Cole and I have to bring him home. I'm worried he won't make it back on his own. And I can't sit here and do nothing and let Finn die."

"What about your mom?" he asks.

"It breaks me to say this, but I can't help her now. I mean, it just *breaks* me, Stevie B. Right in half. But it's out of my hands. I'll be back. I'll be back by tomorrow, and I'll try to help her then."

"Nell, please . . ."

"I have to," I say. "I have to rescue Cole. And save Finn."

44

I pull my sweatshirt over my head, toss it to the side, shiver in the October air, then kick my sneakers off. I'm standing near the edge of the jumping-off place, clutching Charlotte's timer in my hand as I peer over the ledge. "Nell, no!" Stevie B begs when he realizes that sweatshirt and sneakers off means I'm really doing this—and I'm doing it now. He grabs hold of me with both of his hands, then stumbles and loses his balance as I pull away. I move back again, and he matches my step, then leans in and kisses me. And it's not a chaste on-the-cheek asking-permission friend-kissing-friend could-possibly-be-more-but-maybe-not kiss—not even close. He wraps his arms around me, pulls me in, tilts my chin up, and *really* kisses me. And the most confusing messed-up part of this whole thing isn't that I'm about to jump into the quarry and risk drowning myself in an attempt to time-travel to rescue Cole and save Finn; it's that I kiss Stevie B back.

And my side of the kiss isn't a chaste I'm-being-polite friend-kissing-friend could-be-more-but-maybe-not kiss either.

Not even close.

When I pull away, I whisper, "Don't kiss me like that." But it's not convincing. Not to me. And not to him.

"Then don't kiss me back like that," he says.

"Let's not . . ."

"Let's not what?" he whispers.

"Let's not dissect it."

"Okay," he says.

I look down at the water as the Lauren Daigle song plays on repeat in my head.

"Then I'm coming with you," Stevie B declares, and he starts pulling his sweatshirt off.

I watch him, and I'm feeling an ache so big when I plead, "You can't."

"Why not?" He inches closer as he unbuttons his shirt.

"I need you here."

"*Why?* Why do you need me here?" He drops his shirt onto the ground and starts to unbutton his jeans.

"Finn. You have to stay here to take care of Finn."

It takes him a minute to pull apart what that means, but then he says, "Nell, no!"

"We'll be back in time, I promise. Me and Cole. By five tomorrow. If we're not here before three, take my truck, go to Cole's, and pick her up. I already told Mrs. Wilder it would be you babysitting, not me."

"When? When did you tell her that, Nell?"

He seems scared. Desperate, even. And I feel like I've betrayed him when I admit, "I texted her from the truck."

"So you knew you were gonna jump? You planned this? Before you even looked at that picture of you climbing out of the quarry with Charlotte's bag?"

"I had to . . . *Have* to! That sketch of me with that bag? I'd seen it before. And seeing it again? Well, it made me certain."

"And where am I supposed to go with Finn? And what do I do when . . . ? I don't want that responsibility! How do I save her, Nell?"

"By letting me go. Look. I figure you should drive to the hospital at three, as soon as you pick her up. Wait in the parking lot. So if she stops breathing, you can—"

"Jesus, Nell!"

I watch him standing there. Vulnerable and lost. He's one leg of a triangle that doesn't sit right with the other two missing. "I'm sorry. I'm so, so sorry. But I have to."

"Hold on," he says, looking resigned. "If you're doing this, *really* doing this, there's another picture you need to see." He steps away, barely letting his eyes leave me, then grabs one of his sketchbooks, flips through and stares at a page before he climbs back up on the rocks and hands it to me.

It's me and him, standing exactly as we are now. At the quarry, on the rocks, at night. His arms are wrapped around me, mine around him. We're entwined. Kissing. *Really* kissing. Passionately. Exactly like we were a few minutes ago.

I can't tear my eyes away. The detail is extraordinary. I'm wearing Cole's family necklace, just like I am now. My shoes and sweatshirt are lying off to the side—the same shoes and sweatshirt I was wearing today, the folds of the fabric, the creases and shadows, the same as they are now.

His sweatshirt and shirt—exactly what he had on too.

"When did you draw this?"

He points to the date. "Almost a year ago."

"But how do we know which drawings are *real*? And not just something you made up?"

And Stevie B says, "Because the real ones? The pictures that are real? They happen, Nell. We watch them happen."

I think back to the drawing of me climbing out of the quarry with Charlotte's dry bag sitting behind the rocks and I have never been more certain of anything.

I have to jump.

45

I turn to face the quarry. Then I look down at the black water and the unknown.

I think about free will and destiny. About believing things we know in our hearts to be true, even if we don't fully understand the how or the why.

Then I think about jumping, and everything Charlotte said. How where I am now—the north side—will take me to the future. The south side to the past. I think about that high-tech map she showed Cole, with the stone ladder.

I hear her voice—measured and controlled—pointing out the handholds, explaining about seconds and timing and breathless cold.

Eight minutes down. Enter the tunnel. Eight minutes back up.

I focus on the details. The outcroppings to watch for. The warm current running on the eastern side. The icy pool. The bright white light . . . I remind myself to use the timing device as a guide. And to count. *One, one thousand, two, one thousand, three, one thousand . . . Get to ten, then start again. Repeat that pattern forty-eight times. For* sixteen minutes. 960 seconds. 480 on the way down, 480 on the way up.

My heart screams, *But I've never jumped alone!*

So I imagine that I have my arms wrapped around Cole's back and my legs hitched up around his waist and my eyes closed tight, my face buried in the warmth of his neck. Then I clasp my hands and hold them high above my head like the spires of a church, and I swear, I can feel Cole here with me, like we're entangled across space and time.

"Nell," Stevie B whispers, "you're the bravest person—the *fiercest* person—I know."

I take a deep breath and center myself, feet and head and heart.

Stevie B says something more, but I don't hear it.

I take another slow, deep breath. Whisper, "I'm sorry." To Stevie B. To my mom. To Finn.

I'm sorry for leaving them. Leaving them to face losing me.

I'm sorry for my choice and my destiny.

But I don't look back.

With a final, single breath, I fill my lungs with air.

And then I do it.

Feet first. Heart second. Head a distant third.

I jump.

46

I pierce the water as sharp and straight as a needle and begin to count as soon as my face goes under.

One, one thousand. Two, one thousand. Three, one thousand . . .

I get to ten, then start again.

I plunge deep, deeper, deepest. Clutching Charlotte's device, I reach for the north wall, hear Charlotte's voice as she pointed out each part of this journey to Cole: *Find the stone ladder under the ridge. Locate the handholds. Use the counting device. Watch the screens . . .*

I am precise.

As I climb down, the pain of wanting to breathe hits fast— sooner than I thought it would. And it hits hard—arriving with bursting pressure in my chest. Then panic sets in as I glance up toward the surface.

Six, one thousand, seven, one thousand . . .

I focus on counting as I descend farther. I hear Charlotte's words: *Get to ten, then start again! Then do it again. And again. And again.*

Find the warm current on the eastern side.

Count!

I pace myself. Glance up toward the light one more time, then down toward the dark water below me. I try to block out the pain as I continue to descend. I watch the screen and count.

I hit the icy pool. Feet first, then torso. I pull hard with my arms as I lower myself using the stone handholds, like Charlotte said: as a ladder.

The markers: all there, exactly like she said they'd be. I count.

The icy cold sends pain shooting through my limbs, and there's a numbness I haven't felt before. I try to push past it as I descend.

I wonder if I'm going to die.

But I am relentless. I count.

I push past two minutes, then three. An eerie quiet settles in. I keep at it. Count to ten, then start again. Match my count and my location to the one on her device. Adjust and correct when I mess up. *One, one thousand, two, one thousand . . .* over and again.

I grab hold of the outcroppings—sharp, slimy, cold—as I make my way deeper. A red light pulses on Charlotte's timer, marking my location along the wall. I close my eyes. Open them. Panic. Close them. I count!

Pressure in my chest and ears. *Ignore it!*

I push past everything: the pain, the thoughts in my head.

The water feels silky-smooth but still ice-cold. Head- and brain-numbing. Then, pockets of warmth. I pop my eyes open: Green murky water. Gray stone. *It's not so bad.* I begin to feel . . . calm.

I move lower.

Then something . . . new.

I see a bright white light—not above me, but *beneath* me. I fight hard. Tell myself, *Don't black out!*

I'm long out of air. But . . . I'm okay.

I glance toward the sky again. It's not there.

I am deep enough that I can no longer see up. I panic for a moment—breathless, starved for oxygen, truly alone. I want to shoot to the top and gasp. Claw my way out of this. But I know that I can't. I hang on to one thought: *Find Cole!*

When I reach *ten, one thousand* for the forty-eighth time, I check the red, pulsing light once again, confirm my location along the wall, then press myself up against the stones, just like Charlotte said to.

And then . . . *whoosh!*

I'm no longer vertical.

Horizontal. On my back, face up. Moving fast.

Sharp, searing pain. Bright light. I extend my arms and turn. I see things. Images flying by: Flashes of people, old and new. Memories, then places I've never seen . . .

I hear Mr. Marcus's voice from seventh-grade science. *We're traveling at half a million miles per hour! Do you know how fast that is?*

I do now. Faster, even.

Then suddenly, it's eerie and quiet. My hair floats around my face in slow motion. My chest aches. The images are gone.

I'm vertical again. There is no more color. Just darkness.

I check Charlotte's device—it reset just like she said it would. There's a needle pointing up, like a compass.

I start to count all over again.

One, one thousand, two, one thousand . . .

I need air. Can't get any.

Four, one thousand, five, one thousand, six . . .

Same 480 seconds for the ascent. Same count to ten, forty-eight times.

I tell myself, *Don't panic! Pace yourself. Be precise!*

Again, I find the metronome in my head. Match my numbers, my location on the wall, to that on the screens. *One, one thousand, two, one thousand, three, one thousand . . .*

The rise to the top feels like an eternity, my lungs exploding. It gets worse, the closer I get to the surface. I climb.

I'm cold. So cold.

Then suddenly it's warmer.

I want to blast up or sink down, drift away. End this.

But I don't.

I find strength. *Three, one thousand. Four, one thousand. Five, one thousand . . .*

Every time I get to ten, I start again. I have to repeat that pattern forty-eight times on the way up, just like I did on the way down.

I tell myself, *It's almost over. I can do this.*

I can reach the surface.

I can rescue Cole and save Finn.

After

1

When I burst through to the surface, it's with a gasp. A big-
bang genesis breath. A universe-being-born primal breath of life.

Muscles weak, aching, I gasp again. Spin around. Breathe.

I am somewhere. I just don't know where.

No, that's not it. I know exactly *where* I am—in the pool of water
at the bottom of the quarry. Only I'm not certain *when* it is.

It takes every ounce of strength I have to swim to the edge. My
lungs burn with a new kind of fire. I know if I don't get out of the
water fast and dry off and warm up, I will die.

I heave myself halfway onto the rocks, water spilling off me in
ribbons and sheets; I lift my head, blink a few times.

I rub my hand over my face, try to focus. Nothing appears different than it was before I jumped.

Nothing *is* different.

It's the same gray, flat stones under me as I drag myself out of
the water, then sink down onto the rocks.

I look up.

It's still the same felty blue-black sky I saw when I left a little over sixteen minutes ago. The same crescent moon and the same stars that shimmer overhead. Cole's stars and Cole's sky.

But I don't know the year.

I breathe as I glance around and take in the sameness: the trees and the underbrush, the rock outcroppings. I inhale the sweet and cloying butterscotch of the pines, slowing the pace of my breath before I haul myself even farther up onto the rocks, only to collapse again.

Head spinning, muscles weak, I put my head down and listen.

It's the same forest sounds: The brush of wind in the branches, the rustle of leaves overhead, the last of the crickets and cicadas and katydids. A chorus of tree frogs, a scuffle in the brambles. My own breath.

I lift my head, look around again. Take inventory. I have no change of clothes. In a matter of minutes, I will freeze.

I turn my eyes up toward the jumping-off place. I call Stevie B's name once, then again. And I wait.

No answer.

So no Stevie B.

Which is my first real clue—my first real proof—that I'm not *when* I was.

The second one comes when I look down at Charlotte's device, still clutched in my hand.

A single word flashes in neon green: **ARRIVED**.

2

I tell myself, Get up! Move! I lift my head, squint, then see something sitting in the shadows on the side of the path.

A black strap. Canvas against stone.

I climb to my feet; they feel like frozen stumps. Water falls off of me as I stumble forward.

It's Charlotte's dry bag tucked behind the rocks!

I ask myself, *If the bag is here, does this mean they made it?*

I make my way closer, fall to my knees. Muscles twitching, fingers numb, I unzip it.

Dry clothes.

When I see them, I start to shake violently. I dig through the bag.

Lots of Charlotte's clothes, papers, more devices, and then . . .

Cole's favorite sweater. A pair of his sweatpants.

Warm tears spill onto my cheeks. *Did he leave them for me?* I wonder. *Did he know I would come for him? Or did he just pack extra clothes for himself?*

Then more thoughts.

Bad thoughts.

Or does this mean Charlotte lived and Cole didn't? He didn't pack clothes for me; they were for him. And he didn't need them because . . .

Panic overwhelms me. I quickly look around. See something else lying off to the side. Shiny and black.

I make my way over and pick it up.

A wet suit!

Relief.

Then panic rises again: *There's only one.*

I frantically search for the second one, scanning, squinting in the dark. I don't see it. I scour the ground around me a second time, then a third, hoping . . .

But I see nothing.

I examine the wet suit I'm holding but can't tell if it's hers or his. Can't remember what they each looked like.

I hurry back to the dry bag, search inside for clues.

Who lived?

And who didn't?

I can't tell. There's so much stuff.

I tell myself to *Stop! Stop thinking.*

Then that thing Steve B said, the thing about Cole needing to survive for Charlotte to have been born means Cole *has* to be alive. But that means . . .

Tears well up in my eyes. They're unexpected. *Maybe Charlotte didn't . . .*

Stop! I tell myself again. *Don't catastrophize. Just find Cole and you'll find out what happened to Charlotte. Maybe . . . Maybe it's not what you think!*

Survive.

I strip off my wet clothes and put on the dry ones. Cole's clothes, to give me strength. I check around and in the bag again. No socks. No shoes.

I start to walk. Barefoot. Up the steep hill, then the two hundred yards through the woods to where we always park.

My thoughts are cloudy. Confused.

Everything still looks the same: The slope of the hill to the east. The dirt path winding through the woods to the road. The towering pines. I thank the moon for its sliver of light.

But I can't think clearly. Random thoughts hit me like stray bullets. They hurt.

I should have told Stevie B to check on my mom. *In case. I don't. Make it back.*

I spin around. Glance in the direction of my house. Who would be there seventy-seven years from when I left?

More thoughts. Bad thoughts.

I should have told Stevie B about the Narcan in the cookie jar.

I shouldn't have kissed him back.

I'm glad I kissed him back.

Stop! I tell myself again. Just put one foot in front of the other and walk toward the road.

+ + + + + + +

I get to the parking area. Limbs still frozen blocks of ice. Head still swirling.

It's empty. The parking area is empty.

I don't know what I expected to find. Cole's truck maybe? Seventy-seven years from when he left it?

My truck sitting next to it? Rusted out and covered in debris?

I look down at my legs and arms and torso. Run my hands over my face and hair. I am still seventeen. This gives me comfort. I don't know why. Or what I expected.

I hear Cole's words in my head. *It's bigger than we thought, Nell. Way bigger.*

I hear Stevie B's words too. *You're the bravest person—the fiercest person—I know.*

Then I keep moving. I take one step, two steps, three steps forward, not sure where I'm going or what I'll find.

3

I hear Cole's voice. A steady drumbeat of words. I told you, Nell, special things are coming for us!

Is it in my head? Or real? I don't know. I'm confused. Disoriented. I keep stumbling forward along the path. My feet bare, I feel every twig and stick. Every pebble. They hurt.

I start thinking about what I read about oxygen deprivation.

Ten minutes without air: Lots of brain cells destroyed. Recovery unlikely.

Fifteen minutes: Recovery all but impossible.

So this is what impossible feels like.

Then Cole again, calling to me. *Don't be afraid, Nellie Bannon. It's you and me against the rest of them.*

"What is this place?" I call out, my words a huge effort. Then, too exhausted to take another step, I drop to my knees, like a single leaf as the seasons change. Soft and unheard. Floating.

Cole's voice again. He sounds surprised. *Why, it's Clawson, Nell!*

I look around. No Cole. He's just thoughts in my head.

I try to say something else, but I can't form words. My head's cloudy. My face numb.

Cole's voice is gone.

He was never here.

I have never felt so alone.

I look up as clouds roll in front of the moon and block the light. Then I collapse in a heap on the ground.

4

When I open my eyes, the sky is clear again. The stars are bright. I glance around to get my bearings. I can't tell how much time has passed, but as soon as I try to lift myself up, I see movement. Something—no, *someone*—a guy, definitely a guy—off in the distance.

Fear rises. Hope does too.

He's walking toward me.

Heart pounding, breath coming in fiery bursts, I mumble, "Cole." Then I outright scream his name.

He stops.

I raise my hand to wave.

It's hard to see. He moves, and I lose him in the shadows. I attempt to stand, to get a better look—to make sure he sees me— but I sink back down, my legs too weak.

He appears again, still coming toward me. As he gets closer, he starts to run.

It's Cole! Has to be Cole!

He makes his way a few steps closer. Then . . . something's not . . .

He's the right age, but something is off. His gait . . . His size? *Something* isn't right. He appears . . . different.

I watch him come closer. My heart sinks, then races in a flurry of beats.

He's . . . shorter. Thicker.

It's not Cole. My instinct is to run. Get away. Hide!

I attempt to stand again. Fail. Fall back onto my knees. Fear overwhelms me as he approaches.

He's close. *Too* close.

I lean back, feeling trapped. Too scared, too weak, to defend myself.

And then he calls out, "Nell?" Softly, at first, and then with more urgency, "Nell?"

He knows my name. How does he . . . ?

A few more breaths, and he's standing over me.

I'm sitting now. I try to inch away. Resist.

He bends down. I can't see his face.

I'm afraid of what will happen next. He attempts to lift me up. I fight back. He says, "It's okay."

He seems gentle. I tell myself, *He knows my name!*

I try to speak again. Manage to ask, "What year is it?"

He says, "2101."

5

So . . ."

"The future," he confirms. "You traveled to the future."

"Who are you?" I ask.

He doesn't answer, but his face looks familiar. I can't place him. It's too dark to see, and I can't think.

I whisper, "I know you. I . . ."

"Try not to talk. You have to conserve oxygen. Cole asked me to check all the paths leading out of the quarry once every hour." He's struggling to pull me up onto my feet.

So he knows Cole. And Cole's here. Alive!

"Who are—" I start to ask again, but he shushes me.

"We have to hurry. Get you warmed up."

"Where's Cole? What happened to Charlotte? Where are you taking me?"

He's half carrying me as we make our way toward the road, but he doesn't answer.

A few minutes more, and I see a silver car, sleek and low-slung, in the distance, on the side of River Bend. Where Cole and I park sometimes.

We stumble down the hill. He helps me into the front seat, then walks around and gets in on the driver's side.

He sees me trembling and puts the heat on high by voicing a command. It radiates immediately, with no noise. No button. No fan. Another command, and the car starts driving itself. I think, *The future. I'm really in the future.*

He offers me water in a long silver cylinder.

It's not cold. It's meant to warm me. I drink it as he clips something onto my finger. "Checking your oxygen levels," he explains.

I sink into the seat. He grabs a blanket from the back and lays it over me. The seat is heated, the blanket made from some heavy material I've never seen before. I still shake.

"Tell me about Cole," I manage to say.

He doesn't answer.

"What about Charlotte? Is she okay?"

Still, he says nothing.

The device on my finger beeps. A red light flashes. He takes it and says, "No wonder."

I wait for him to explain. He doesn't.

I study his face, then whisper, "I know you."

He smiles. "Not possible."

Then it comes to me. Who he is.

In the light from the dashboard, I see them: the scars.

The half-moon above his right eye. The zigzag shape on his cheek.

They are fainter now, but they're there. Just like Stevie B drew them. Just like the photo in my mom's yearbook.

I examine his profile, then mumble, "Levi? Levi Tanner?"

6

He seems surprised. Pleased, almost.

I'm not sure what I feel. Fear? Relief? Panic?

I say, "Yearbook. Stevie B." Not sure if he'll know what that means. But he nods as if he does.

My tongue feels thick, my thoughts slow. I ask about Cole again. Then Charlotte. "There was only one wet suit."

My words are slurred.

He doesn't respond.

"You're not dead," I say. Then I feel ridiculous. Confused.

"I knew your mom and dad," he comments.

"Ms. Campbell . . . Margaret, she . . . loves you. Even now." The words, they surprise me. I feel embarrassed for saying them.

He smiles, then commands the car to pull to the side of the road, and he takes out a small device and starts typing.

He tells me to rest.

I try to say something more. But no words come to me.

I try to fight it, but I can't.

My eyes close, and I black out.

7

When I wake up, we're driving again. We're still on River Bend Road, near the quarry, and it's still dark out—I don't know how long I've been asleep.

"What time is it?"

"A few minutes after ten p.m."

"What day?"

"Friday."

I mumble, "Finn."

He says nothing.

I look out the window, my head a little clearer. Everything appears the same. Somehow it's 2101, I'm seventy-seven years in the future, but it looks the same. It's just woods and houses, and it's so familiar. *It's home.*

We make a series of turns and head toward town. I fade in and out as I try to keep my eyes open. I tell myself, *Pay attention! Stay awake! You don't know how far he's taking you. Memorize the way so you can get back to the quarry on your own if you have to.*

On Main Street, the traffic lights are different—strange. They seem to change automatically as we approach. I try to sit up. Then I slump back down again, cold and weak and exhausted.

The buildings . . . We pass by so many new buildings. Taller buildings. Sleeker buildings. Everything is shiny and new. Henley's Drugstore, the pet store and the bagel shop, Jilly's Gas 'n Go. Judson's Dry Cleaners and Macy's State Street Diner—all gone.

Levi sees my face as I peer out at the world. "Tech boom. Biotech. AI—artificial intelligence. Machine learning. Robotics. Cybersecurity. A lot changes in almost eighty years."

"The prison?" I ask.

"Still here. Different, though."

He doesn't offer more, and I don't ask.

We leave town, turning left on Waverly, then right on Parker. Levi keeps looking at a palm-sized computer as the car drives. A small drone passes next to us. Then another.

"Where are we going?"

"I'm taking you to Charlotte and Cole."

A flash of relief travels through me. "So she survived? Charlotte made it?"

"They both did. Injured, though."

"How bad?"

"You'll see for yourself in a few minutes. They're waiting on the far side of the quarry." He glances down. "Your feet. They're bleeding." He swivels his seat around and roots through the stuff on the back seat—jackets, sweatshirts, computer devices—until he finds a pair of shoes and hands them to me. "You're going to need these."

They look strange. High-tech red high-tops—more like half boots. With all sorts of Velcro-like self-sealing pockets running up the sides.

"Waterproof, for storage," Levi offers.

I have a flash of Cole . . . His red Converse sneakers coming in through my window. The cubbies in kindergarten. Me saying, *Boys can't wear red shoes.*

Cole always wears red shoes.

"Cole asked me to bring them. He said he didn't leave shoes for you back at the quarry."

I put the shoes down, too tired to put them on, certain now that Levi's not lying to me; he's seen Cole. There's no way he'd know about the bag at the quarry or the missing shoes unless he's seen him. And Charlotte survived! "The second wet suit," I say. "I couldn't find it. I thought . . ."

"I had to carry her back without her changing out of the wet suit first. She was hurt. Cole too. And things got . . . messy."

I watch another drone sail by the car. This one bigger than the others.

Levi comments, "They're used for deliveries and surveillance." Then he voices a command, and the small electronic device sitting on the console lights up. It projects a map onto the windshield. Then data—numbers and letters—stream across the glass.

I try to make sense of it but fail. "What do all those numbers and letters mean?"

"Too complicated to explain now," he says, lifting the gadget from its console. "But this device is everything," he says. "It provides all the knowledge we need to understand the workings of the world."

"So like my phone?" I ask.

"No. Self-contained. Not network-dependent. More like . . . a better brain."

I try to think about what that might mean. Then my fingers reach for the necklace.

He's watching me. "Charlotte told me about the necklace. How it exposed her identity."

"There's only one," I say. "But then there were two, because she brought it back with her, so . . ." My voice trails off. I can't remember or find the words, or put them in the right order.

He smiles. I feel overwhelmed.

I try to explain again. "Something about continuous sets of something or . . ."

"Spatiotemporal locations."

"And a cat," I add. "I don't remember, but it has something to do with a cat."

He laughs a little. "The Cheshire Cat from *Alice's Adventures in Wonderland*. In the story, the cat leaves, but his smile stays behind. Back in the day, the concept of that intrigued physicists. Inspired conversations about the paradoxes of time travel."

I think about Alice, the book . . . Can't remember the cat, or the smile. I say, "Me and Stevie B . . . we were just talking about that book . . ."

I feel ridiculous again. I'm making no sense.

I look at him and start thinking, *Something about him feels wrong.* I manage to sit up more, examine his face. He should be . . .

"How old are you?" I ask. My voice sounds stronger. Even to me.

"You must be feeling better," he comments.

"You should be older! If you were seventeen when you left Clawson, plus the twenty-three years since then, you should be . . ." My head is clearer than before but still fuzzy, and I can't do the math.

"Forty," he says. "You're thinking I should be forty."

"But you look . . . seventeen. *My* age."

"I am seventeen."

"So . . . you get to stay seventeen forever?"

He doesn't answer.

I search his face again.

And his eyes do that thing like Charlotte's do—they change

color, his from burnt sienna to hazel, then to boiling black. I almost say something about his eyes. I want to ask what that means. But he commands the car to pull to the side of the road and shut down, and I can't think.

"One thing at a time," he says. "Now put those shoes on. We have to walk for a bit, and your feet are still bleeding."

I look down at my feet. Then at the shoes.

"No sizes or laces," he informs me. "They stretch to fit everyone. Kids love them." He adds, "Check out the sides, on the inside. There's plenty of space to store stuff. Keys, electronics . . ." He slips one of his devices into the side pocket of his right shoe. Then takes another device from the console and stashes that one too.

I study his face. Wonder what it would be like to be seventeen for twenty-three years. I have a flash of what Cole said to me: *I don't know what "forever" means anymore, Nell.*

Then I put the shoes on, wondering if that's how Charlotte kept Levi here.

Maybe she promised him he could be *seventeen forever.*

8

Levi leads me up a steep, rocky path that's almost completely overgrown with brambles. I follow close behind, feeling stronger, head a bit clearer, as he holds the branches back and we step over fallen limbs. Using the portable electronic device he had in the car to project a hologram in the airspace in front of us, he maps our way. I've never entered the woods on this path, or from this side of town, and I don't recognize where we are until we round a curve and the clouds shift, allowing just enough moonlight to stream down so I can now see the quarry off to my right. I stop and look across the water, all the way to the flat stones of the jumping-off place, as Levi leaves the path and drags a pile of brush to the side. He calls me over, then waves for me to follow closely. We make our way to an opening in the rock face that's hidden behind more brush, maybe three feet across and five feet high.

"What is this place?"

"You'll see."

I glance back over my shoulder in the direction of the quarry. "Why didn't we walk?"

"It's farther than it looks. Plus, you were in no condition to walk that far."

I hesitate. He puts his hand on my upper arm. "You want me to take you to Cole, right? This is the only way."

I step through the opening behind him into a tunnel. Except for the light coming from the device he's holding, it's completely dark, the ceiling so low we have to scrunch down and duck.

We continue for thirty, maybe forty feet, and then a cavernous stone room opens up before us.

I look around. Taking it all in as my eyes adjust to the light.

There's an electronic humming sound, banks of computers, piles of stuff everywhere. Levi walks over to a computer and starts punching keys. Then he begins stuffing things into a dry bag.

I try to get my bearings.

It's obvious that this isn't some random meeting spot. There's so much stuff. Gadgets, wires . . . clothes. Wet suits. Equipment. Light comes from glowing boxes—some kind of lanterns placed all around. I ask again, "What is this place?"

Levi says, "It's one of our base camps." He sees me eyeing one of the computer banks and adds, "All of this is lithium-powered."

I'm about to ask where Cole is when Levi walks over to a cot tucked into a nook and bends down. There's someone lying there.

My hands sweat; I feel dizzy. I step closer. I see a flash of hair, then a foot and an arm. The person sits up. Levi moves to the side . . . It's Charlotte, not Cole.

She's bruised and scraped up pretty bad. But she's alive.

I feel a pang of relief. Tears fill my eyes. I wipe them away.

She looks surprised when she sees me. "You shouldn't be here," she mumbles. "But I'm glad that you are."

I step closer. Feel a rush of something so big I can't name it.

Levi says, "I found her on the south path."

"You coming here like this complicates things," Charlotte states, still eyeing me. "But maybe in a good way." She shifts her position, clearly in pain. Then she turns to Levi. "Recovery?"

"Not great when I found her. But pretty good now."

"So she handled the walk from the car?"

"Like a champ."

"Any problems? Interference?"

"Couple of drones. That's it."

"Delivery or surveillance?"

"Delivery."

"So . . ."

"We're safe."

Charlotte turns and looks at me again. "You're lucky you're alive. We almost didn't make it."

"Where's Cole?" I ask.

"Sleeping in the back," she says. "Levi will get him when he's finished with what he's doing."

I watch as he unwraps a bandage on her leg.

"How bad is he hurt?" I ask as I take inventory of Charlotte's injuries—bruises, scrapes, mostly. Her left leg is immobilized in some kind of brace.

"You'll see him in a minute."

I step closer to her. She's wearing a T-shirt and sweatpants. Levi replaces the bandage, then starts adjusting the brace. Charlotte leans forward to help him . . . And that's when I see it.

The rose-colored heart-shaped birthmark sitting under her collarbone.

Just like I have.

Exactly like I have.

Exactly like my grandma had.

I stare at the birthmark, thinking, *One chance in a million.*

My eyes tear up again. I mumble, "You're . . ."

She sees my face flash with shock, then soften. "What is it?" she asks, sounding alarmed.

One in a million. That's what my mom said the doctors told her— one chance in a million that me and my grandma would have the exact same heart-shaped birthmark in the exact same place. Now Charlotte has it too.

"Nothing," I manage to say. "It's nothing."

But it's everything.

It means she's mine.

It means Charlotte isn't just Cole's.

She's *ours*.

9

As I stumble back, trying to process this—Charlotte is mine, *she's Cole's, she's mine, she's ours*—I see movement near an opening at the far end of the cave. I turn to look and . . .

Cole is standing in the doorway.

He's leaning against the wall, his eyes on Levi and Charlotte—he hasn't seen me.

He's hurt, bandaged. He takes a step forward. He's limping, but he's here and he's alive!

A wave of relief and a rush of heat run through me, but I don't move—can't move.

He's scanning the room slowly, taking it all in . . . Then his eyes land on me and stop. He blinks, then turns his head to the side—recognition, then disbelief and confusion.

A thousand thoughts fly like sparks between us. Gratitude and relief and fear and hope wash across his face, across my face. And we don't move and we say nothing at all, because nothing needs to be said when something so impossible has happened that even the stars in the night sky aren't big enough to hold it.

Then I race to his side and tuck into his arms and get a chill when he whispers, "Nell," then, "Nellie," as I exhale his name. We say everything that needs to be said with hardly a word. Then, with all these feelings burning hot in my heart, he pulls me away and leads me into the back room, kissing my face and thanking me for coming for him and asking if I'm hurt. I put my finger to his lips to quiet him as we stumble over to a cot, where he pulls me down.

He's not wearing a shirt, and his chest is covered in bruises and scrapes that look tender and sore, so I try not to touch him but I need to touch him, so I run my fingers over his lips as tears stream down my face and he tells me to hug him even though everything hurts except for his heart.

I want to slow down time, or stop it completely and live this moment with just the two of us, me and Cole. Not here in some strange cave in some distant time, but in our time, in our home, under *our* night sky. I want him to tell me about the bigness and the promise of the universe, him pointing up at one of the constellations, me pretending I can see Cassiopeia or Orion, Jupiter shining beneath Leo or the bright stars of the Northern Cross as he traces his fingers along my skin, touching me like he's touching the sky. But I know that can't be—not now, not here, not with Charlotte and Levi in the next room, and not with him so hurt and Finn dying and the clock ticking and ticking and us needing to get home—so I whisper, "We need a plan, Cole. And we need to hurry."

"I know that," he says.

"How bad are you hurt?" I ask as I lie there with him.

"I'm better today," he tells me. "Better because you're with me."

"Your lungs?"

He takes a deep breath. "Improving, I guess."

"What happened when you jumped? How'd you get so injured?"

"Charlotte said it just happens like that sometimes. We got

unlucky. We nearly drowned. My dreams, Nell. I had nightmares about drowning like that my whole life. Are you okay?" he asks, looking me over, like he thinks he can see the parts of me that are hurt and broken with his eyes.

"I'm fine now," I tell him, only lying a tiny bit as I examine the bruises and cuts on his chest and arms, tracing my fingers in circles around them.

He mumbles, "I can't believe you're here." Then he pulls me into another hug, and I ask, "Can you jump? With me jumping with you?" I'm afraid of what he's going to say.

But Cole whispers, "Finn," and I have a flash of her face, her sneakers on the wrong feet, her smile . . . I think about moon catching and invisible pixies and Stevie B back at home holding my phone, staring at Finn's death clock as time keeps ticking down.

Then I kiss Cole to hide my tears: Little kisses over big tears and even bigger fears. Kisses that cover his cheeks, then his lips, then his neck. And my heart feels like it might pound its way free from my chest and explode when he says, "I missed you."

"It was only a couple of days," I tell him, and he says, "It felt like years. Seventy-seven years, to be exact."

I smile the tiniest bit, saying, "It felt like more than that, Cole. It felt like forever."

"I think you're right," he says. "It might have been forever, Nell." Then he kisses my cheek, then my neck.

And I don't want to but I have to, so I ask him again, "Can you jump, Cole? You didn't answer me before."

"I can jump," he says. "Will jump. Have to jump with you."

And I whisper, "Finn."

We lie there next to each other for a minute before I ask the other thing I'm afraid to ask but have to ask. "You and Charlotte? Did you steal the medicine?"

He glances toward the doorway. "No. Not yet. We were too beat-up. Charlotte and me, we were in rough shape—still are." Cole tries to sit up, but he slumps back down, wincing in pain. "Today was the first time I could get out of bed and walk—the first time I've been awake for more than an hour or two."

"But we don't have much time, Cole. It's Friday, close to midnight, I'm guessing. So there's only . . ."

"Seventeen hours," Cole says, looking away.

"Has she brought it up? Charlotte. Stealing the pill?"

"Neither one of them has said anything about it," he says, "and I've been afraid to ask. Afraid I'd never get home. Never see you. Be too late to save Finn." Then Cole adds, "They told me stuff, Nell. Not about the medicine for Finn. About the universe." His voice is soft. He's scared, I can tell.

"Told you stuff like what?" I ask.

"It's bigger than even I thought, Nell. *Way* bigger. And the quarry? This whole thing? It's bigger than time travel too."

"What do you mean?"

"They said the universe, it's made up of these repeated patterns. We might not notice them, but they're everywhere in nature. In lightning bolts and rivers and coastlines. In ferns and the trees that branch in the same patterns as our arteries and veins. In the spirals in pine cones that are repeated in flower petals . . . And they said these patterns, they're *everywhere*. They're in math and music. In physics and chemistry. In the smallest things and the infinite things. Then they told me that the whole of the universe is a pattern that repeats itself too."

"What does that mean? And what does it have to do with—"

"They're saying that the universe *replicates*. There are an infinite number of universes, Nell! Universes just like ours. Some really different. Some close to the same. And they're saying we're in *all* of them. We don't know it, but we have infinite lives, Nell. All of us. In all of those other universes. Then they said that some people can travel between them. And *they* can. Charlotte and Levi can time-travel and travel between all those universes."

I think about where I am. How I got here. I think about Finn, Stevie B, his drawings. What he told me about Levi.

I think about my mom, then say, "I don't care about all that."

"What do you mean?" Cole asks, sitting up a little to study my face.

"I only want one. One universe. One life. One you. One me. One Finn. One Stevie B. One mom. One time. *Our time.*"

He pulls me in close. "Me too, Nellie. I want one universe. One life. One you. One me. One Finn. One mom. One time. *Our time.*"

"Don't forget Stevie B."

"Never." He brushes the hair off my face.

I glance around the cave, then think about the reality of where we are and what we have to do. "Can we talk about normal stuff, Cole? Not repeating patterns and tree branches and multiple universes, and not Charlotte and Finn and the rest of it? Just for a few minutes."

"Normal *normal* stuff?" he asks, and that little smile of his appears on his face.

I touch the corner of his mouth.

"Or normal *pretend* stuff?"

"Normal pretend stuff."

"Like that trip we want to take?"

"No," I say. "Take me home and show me the stars."

Cole slides down onto his back, raises my hand toward the ceiling and slowly swoops our fingers up and down and across like we're scrawling a message through the air.

I rest my head on his shoulder. "Which stars are you showing me?"

"The three stars of the Summer Triangle."

I close my eyes. "How far away are they?"

"Over a thousand light-years."

"What are their names?"

"Altair." He swoops our hands. "Deneb." He moves them again. "Vega," he whispers.

"Tell me again," I say as our fingers dance across a pretend sky.

"Altair . . . Deneb . . . Vega . . . ," he repeats, his voice soft and slow and hypnotic.

"Say that again."

"Why?"

"I love your voice."

"I'll name the stars for you every day when we get home. I promise."

"Every day forever?"

"Every day beyond forever."

"Is that a thing?"

"It's *our* thing now, Nell. Beyond forever is our thing now."

"Tell me their names again. I don't want this moment to be over."

He whispers, "Altair . . . Deneb . . . Vega . . . ," as our hands trace an invisible sky and I know for certain that we are not separate at all and never have been. That me and Cole have always been part of each other, even though we have barely lived.

He drops our hands from the sky, but keeps mine cocooned in his.

I whisper, "It is . . ."

He continues, "We are . . ."

"Seventeen," I breathe, "like a song . . . ," and Cole traces the heart-shaped birthmark beneath my collarbone when he adds, "Musical notes and lyrics that go so perfectly together . . ."

"They should never be played if not side by side . . . ," I say.

"Or one on top of the other," Cole adds right before Charlotte and Levi appear in the doorway and we quickly sit up as I mumble, "It's time for us to figure out how to get home."

Then Cole tells me what he always tells me when we talk about going to faraway places. He says, "Going home is the best part, Nellie."

10

Me and Cole sit there on the edge of the cot, shoulders and thighs touching, fingers entwined, as Charlotte hobbles over to us on crutches and hands us each a bottle of water. Levi gives her a small computer device, and she punches some keys, as I drink the entire bottle of water, then take the first deep breath since I got here that doesn't burn like hot coals. "Watch this," she says. "It'll explain a lot."

A hologram appears, just like the underwater map she projected at the quarry and just like the map Levi used to guide us through the woods. But this time, she shows us a modern, teeming city of sleek, silver glass buildings and beautiful courtyards with fountains and flowers. At first, the images cover the entire wall. Then she presses another button, and they fill the room. Surround us in 3D. Swallow us, almost.

"Clawson's a city," I say, recognizing landmarks and vistas, and feeling a little breathless as the images engulf me.

I stand up, spin around, taking it in. Taking Clawson in. Then taking Cole in as he sits on the cot, watching me. Taking Charlotte in as she stands across the room. The reality of who she is to me. To us. Who the three of us are to each other.

"This is Clawson now," she says. "You only saw a small portion of it on the ride here." Then she clicks another button, and there are more images: more beautiful towering glass buildings and more parks, then a meadow full of flowers.

"That's the field up off of Lyndhurst Road," Cole comments as a small girl runs through, maybe five years old. She's laughing.

"My niece. It's footage from a few weeks ago," Charlotte comments.

Then there's another child running behind her. Chasing her. And he's laughing too.

"One of Levi's relatives," Charlotte tells us.

The pictures fly by, faster and faster. Moments. Faces. People. Charlotte keeps clicking, and the projection keeps changing. Old people, then more children, running, laughing, playing. They appear around us, one image after the other, in rapid-fire succession. I follow the people and places as they move around the room. I reach out to touch them. Cole reaches out to touch them. They look so real.

Charlotte appears mesmerized. Levi as well.

My fingers reach for the spot where the birthmark sits beneath my collarbone. When I glance up, I notice that Charlotte's eyes have followed my hand. *I wonder if she's seen mine.*

I wonder if Cole has seen the heart-shaped birthmark she has under her collarbone.

If he knows for sure that Charlotte isn't just his, that she's mine.

And . . . ours.

"Now cut to twenty years later," Charlotte continues. "Twenty years from now, 2121." Her voice is shaky. "This is your Clawson in the near future."

New images appear. *Lots* of images.

Clawson is depressed, run-down. Destitute.

"Now look at twenty years after that. 2141—so forty years from now—one hundred seventeen years from your time." She clicks again, puts up another set of pictures. "If Finn and the others were all to die . . . we get this."

Clawson's burned to the ground, with buildings smoldering, garbage everywhere, desperate people, homeless and in rags . . . It's painful to see.

"Now take a look at New York. Chicago. Los Angeles," she says. "Rome. Paris. Hong Kong. Nairobi. Seoul. Shanghai. Tunis. Delhi." She clicks and clicks. "They're all the same."

"They're burning. The world is burning," I say.

"This will happen everywhere. *Has* happened everywhere. And *we're* going back in time trying to stop it."

Levi steps closer to us and explains. "Before things got too bad, a group of futurists—specialists in statistics and theoretical physics—ran simulations to see what might have led to a better outcome. The one that worked the best was when they altered the composition of the population. But not by eliminating specific people. By *saving* specific people. They used artificial intelligence to isolate people from the past who, had they lived longer, would have played a part in preventing this catastrophic outcome for the world."

"So you're saying they did *math*?" Cole asks.

"Computers did," Levi says. "They calculated who needed to live to alter the outcome."

"It started out as a hypothetical math experiment at a university think tank. But then the first time portal was found, then the second, and that math moved from theoretical to possible," Charlotte explains. "And Levi's brother and Finn Wilder are two of those people."

"Two of the people who need to be saved if we don't want the world to burn?" I ask.

"Exactly."

"In *our* universe?" Cole asks.

"Yes," Levi confirms.

"And they can save the world from what you just showed us," Cole says, "just by living?"

"Correct," Charlotte says.

"But Levi's brother died," I point out.

Charlotte and Levi exchange a look. "We need to save eighty-two percent of the people on the list. Not all of them. And we haven't been able to save everyone."

"Like Levi's brother?"

"Yes. And as you just saw with me and Cole," Charlotte offers, "time travel isn't easy—or always safe. What we're attempting to do is difficult."

"So . . . you save eighty-two percent of the people who need to not die . . . ," I start, trying to piece everything together.

"We save them," Charlotte continues for me, "and it goes from this"—she shows us cities around the world burning—"to this."

Beautiful, prosperous cities fill the room. "This is a computer simulation of the expected outcome if we are successful in saving at least eighty-two percent of the people on the list."

"In our universe?" Cole asks again.

"Yes," Charlotte confirms. "And the scientists behind this work are confident that if we can pull this off . . . if we save enough of the people we need to save, instead of burning cities and Armageddon in 2141, we get beautiful farm fields, high-tech businesses, thriving, peaceful cultures. And not just in Clawson. It's being done all over the world."

"The other time portals," I say. "Where are they?"

"Twelve locations so far. Scattered around the world," Levi tells us.

"So why isn't the quarry cordoned off?" Cole asks.

"Because in 2101, we're the only ones who know about it."

I turn to Levi. "Why didn't you come back to save your brother and be with Margaret?"

"I was injured getting here. Just like Cole and Charlotte were. But worse. It took me a full year to recover. My brother died before I could return."

"So you stayed?"

"By the time I recovered, everyone at home thought I was long dead. So I stayed here to help save the world."

"And hop between universes? And stay seventeen forever?"

He nods.

"And you still see Margaret?"

Levi pauses. "In a way, yes."

"And Stevie B. You stayed here, but you go to see Stevie B in some weird . . ." I don't finish. Don't know how to finish.

Levi hesitates again but then says, "Yes."

Cole flashes me a look. "Nell, what are you talking about?"

I tell him, "I'll explain later," then I turn back to Levi. "How is it that there were two people in Clawson, New York, whose deaths had to be prevented? That seems like a lot of important people from one Podunk town."

"Clawson became a tech hub, so the people living in Clawson, even the non-tech people, ended up having a greater mathematical chance of impacting global outcomes."

"We saw that pattern repeated in other tech centers around the world as well," Charlotte adds.

"What is Clawson a tech hub for, exactly?"

"AI and biotech mostly," Levi says.

"And there are three. Not two," Charlotte says.

"Three what?" Cole asks.

"Three people from Clawson who can't die if we want to save the world. Not two."

"Who's the third?" he asks.

"Me," Charlotte says. "I'm the third."

11

"If all of this is true," I say, "then why are you in some shitty cave, like you're hiding out? Why aren't you in some fancy building with giant computer screens and—"

"Because in *this* time, in 2101, very few people know anything about what we are doing. And even in later decades, there are people who don't think we should be attempting this at all," Levi tells us. "So for now at least, we have to hide."

"So there are people who *want* our world to end?"

"They don't think we should interfere," Charlotte says. "So, in a sense, yes."

"So you're doing that thing you talked about," I suggest. "Creating a causal loop by going back in time and selectively changing things?"

"Exactly."

"But you're okay with that because . . ."

"Because," Charlotte says, "we've seen what happens if we don't." She clicks the device again and images of the burning world spin all around us.

"If there are multiple universes, *infinite* universes, why do you care about ours?"

"Because I live there, in your universe," Charlotte explains. "I want to live."

"And people we love are there too," Levi adds.

"So Finn's . . . what?" Cole asks. "Some kind of famous scientist or brilliant genius or mathematical—"

"I can't tell you specifically," Charlotte tells him, "but I will say Finn's a pretty regular person."

"I don't get it," I say. "What exactly does she do to save our world?"

"Stop trying to understand everything, Nell. Because you won't be able to," Charlotte warns. "None of us can. Just understand this: We're all dominoes tumbling. One into the next, throughout time. And some of us matter in extremely important ways, even though it may not seem that way to us during our lifetime."

"Show her Finn's line," Levi says.

Charlotte flinches. "No. It doesn't matter now, and it's too much information for them to process."

"Show us," I press. "Show us what he just said. Her 'line.'"

She flashes an annoyed look at Levi, but then clicks some buttons and a diagram appears with Finn's name on the top.

"It's her lifetime connections," Levi offers.

"It looks like one of those family trees," Cole comments.

There are hundreds, maybe thousands of names. "Finn will know all these people?" I ask.

"Some only indirectly—*most* indirectly," Charlotte says, still sounding put-out. "This person would become Finn's college roommate," she says, pointing. "He's someone she would date," she comments, pointing to another. "But most are strangers— strangers she would interact with. Just minor acquaintances."

"All of our small interactions can potentially alter history," Levi explains. "Even the incidental ones. And collectively, that can manifest as significant change."

"They have a name for it," Charlotte says. "It's called the butterfly effect."

"It just means that the impact of a small thing can cascade and magnify disproportionally," Levi explains, "manifesting a much larger event somewhere far away—or years later."

"So that list," I say. "The list that shows who died but needed to live. The change-the-outcome people? Finn Wilder is on that list, and now—"

"We save eighty-two percent or more of those people, and we'll stop what you just saw."

"So, is it working? How many have you saved? Have you saved eight-two percent of the people or . . ."

"Let's just say we're close."

"And the people on that list who you don't save? The other eighteen percent?"

Charlotte hesitates. "They are . . ."

"Are what?" I ask.

"Acceptable losses," Levi tells us.

"That doesn't *feel* acceptable," I shoot back, eyeing both of them.

Charlotte looks away.

Levi stares at his feet and says, "We agree."

I turn my attention to Charlotte. "You said 'would.' Not 'will.'"

Cole looks at me, questioning. "Nell?"

"Just before," I start to explain. "Charlotte said, 'This person *would* become Finn's college roommate.' And 'He's someone she *would* date.' She kept saying 'would.'"

Cole rises to his feet.

"Enough," Charlotte says. "My leg hurts. I have to lie down, and you two have to sleep. Both of you."

"Hold on. What aren't you telling us?"

"Sleeping," she says, "is not optional. You have to get home by tomorrow and get back to Finn. And you both have to heal."

"I didn't come here to sleep, Charlotte," I tell her. "I came here to save Finn and rescue Cole."

"That's fine, Nell. But you can't do either of those things until you rest and recover more. Plus, like I said, sleeping's not optional."

"We gave you something," Levi admits. "In the water. To help you sleep. It will knock you out in about"—he looks at our empty water bottles and then at his device—"three minutes."

Charlotte adds, "Best if you two lie down before you pass out and get hurt."

"First, tell me why you said 'would.' Is Finn one of the eighteen percent who you don't save? Is that why you said 'This person *would* be her college roommate' and 'This is someone she *would* date?'"

Then I get dizzy and stumble forward. The room starts spinning. Cole grabs my elbow. Everything appears to be moving in slow motion.

The world turns black.

I pass out before Charlotte can answer.

Saturday

12

When I wake up, my is head pounding and my mouth is horribly dry. I'm lying on the cot and Cole is still asleep next to me. I stumble to my feet, trying not to disturb him, then walk over and peek through the opening to the main room. Levi is at a computer, working. Charlotte is standing over him on crutches, I have no idea what time it is—or even what day it is.

Cole wakes. Mumbles, "Nell . . ." Then he sits up on the edge of the cot and says to me in a hushed whisper, "Stay here. Don't go out there yet."

"I'll be right back."

He calls after me, "Nell, wait."

I ignore him and walk over to Levi and Charlotte.

"How do you feel?" Levi asks as soon as he sees me.

"Almost normal," I report, only half lying. I turn to Charlotte. "Do you have a non-drugged water?"

She hands me a bottle. "It's not drugged. I promise."

I take a sip, then down the entire thing. "What are you doing?" I ask.

"Monitoring the quarry for interference. Here. Eat this," she adds, handing me a plastic tube with some kind of goop in it.

"What is it?"

"Disgusting," Levi says.

"Seriously?"

"Yes. Seriously disgusting, but nutritious. Eat it," Charlotte says. "You're going to need your strength today."

"What time is it?" I ask as I rip the end off and squeeze the goop into my mouth. "Baby food," I say. "Gross-tasting baby food."

"It's nine thirty-five, Saturday morning," Levi reports.

"We have to get you and Cole back home," Charlotte states. "I think he's finally strong enough. And with you here to help, maybe he can handle the jump."

"What about Finn?" I ask.

Levi and Charlotte exchange a quick glance. "It's too late," Levi reveals. "Let's save you and Cole and hope that saves Charlotte."

I stare at them as I process what they're telling me. "You're saying Finn's an 'acceptable loss'? One of the eighteen percent you have the leeway to *not* save?"

Neither one of them answers, and I know.

"Does Cole know that?"

"I do now," he calls over, and we all turn to watch him limping toward us.

"Well, that's a hard no from me. An absolute not-gonna-happen," I tell them. "We *have* to save Finn."

Cole slips his arm around my shoulder and says, "We're not leaving here without the medicine for Finn. And if I did the math right," he continues, "you, Charlotte, won't exist if I don't go back to where I belong. So I'm guessing you want that to happen. Plus, you're one of the people from Clawson on that list. So you *need* me to go home so you'll live to be here and do this—save our universe."

"What do we have to do to save Finn?" I ask. "Just tell us.

Because we're not going back without doing it."

Levi looks eager to salvage this. Charlotte looks frustrated and desperate. "Trust me," she says, "I want to save Finn as much as you two do. Look at what I risked to *try* to save her! But it's already Saturday morning, going on ten. Finn has a little over seven hours. That's it. And we don't have the medicine. We missed our chance. I was in no shape to take Cole to the lab, and he was in no shape to break in and steal it. I'm still not mobile *now*. It's out of the question. I'm sorry. Really, really, sorry. And I didn't want to tell you. But, please, now that you know, let's save you two. Let's get you home in time to say goodbye to Finn."

"No," Cole says.

"I second that," I say. "Not happening."

We're at a standoff. Levi is looking back and forth between the three of us, waiting to see what's going to happen.

"*I* can do it," I announce. "I can steal the pill for Finn."

"How?" Levi asks.

I lock eyes with Charlotte. "Same way I stole your phone and all that stuff from your bag. What's the setup at the lab? During the day. Right now."

She looks defeated.

"Just tell me. Is it open? On Saturday?"

"Yes."

"And?"

"Fancy lobby. Reception sign-in desk. Banks of elevators . . . My mom's lab is on the third floor. That's where the medicine is."

"Security?"

"Tons. It's a drug company with high-value medicine and proprietary research. Espionage is a huge problem in the pharmaceutical industry. Discoveries can be worth billions."

"But they know you, right? Front desk? Security guys?"

"Yes."

"So maybe we don't *break* in. Maybe we *walk* in. Right through the front door and steal the pill."

"How are we going to do that?" Charlotte asks.

I look over at Cole before I say, "A bump-and-run with mustard." Cole smiles.

Charlotte asks, "What is she talking about?"

"We cause a distraction," Cole explains. "Then, when everyone is preoccupied, Nell steals the pill we need."

"How?" Charlotte asks. "You make it sound easy. Like you can just walk in and do it."

"We'll figure out the how, and all the details. I can do it. I've been training for this my entire life."

"Where?" she questions.

"Henley's Drugstore," I tell her.

"And the Gas 'n Go," Cole says.

I smile. "And in the Clawson High School cafeteria. Think about it, Charlotte. It's way easier to walk in through the unlocked front door and dupe people than it is to break into a high-security building at night. Isn't that what you originally planned? Some kind of off-hours locked-door break-in?"

"Yeah, but you can't just walk in and steal expensive pharmaceuticals like you're shoplifting lipstick. And I can't be involved. I could go to jail. My mom would lose her funding if I was implicated. People would die. The world needs her medicine. She saves millions of lives!"

"So we don't get caught," I say.

"*We?*" Charlotte questions.

"You and me," I explain.

"On the plus side, Nell's seventeen," Levi comments. "It's a good cover. No one will suspect she's there to steal anything if she's with you."

"The crutches are a great touch," Cole adds.

"Yeah, but she's not beat-up enough to cause the kind of scene I want when we enter the building," I tell him.

"I don't understand," Charlotte says.

"You're the mustard," I tell her. "I'm the bump. After, we run."

Charlotte suddenly looks like she gets it. "I'm the mustard. Like in the cafeteria when you took my bag. *I'm* the distraction. And I need to be a *big* distraction."

"Exactly."

Levi appears interested. "Keep talking, Nell," he says.

"Me and Charlotte show up this morning. We walk right into the fancy lobby and stagger up to the reception desk. I'm holding Charlotte up. She's a mess. We make her appear more hurt than she is, and she acts it." I turn to Charlotte. "You said the guards there will recognize you?"

"Definitely. They all know me." I get a flash of excitement, because she sounds interested. Like maybe it could work.

"How many guards?"

"Three. Bobby, behind the front desk is a receptionist, so he's unarmed, but there are three armed guards. Two in the lobby. One in a back room watching the interior hallway and exterior security cameras in real time."

"How busy is the lobby?"

"Pretty busy. Delivery people. Employees coming and going."

"Even on a Saturday?"

"The lab operates seven days a week. Over eight hundred employees."

"So what would happen if we staggered in, like I said? Me holding you up? You, with your black eye, leaning into me like you're half-unconscious?"

"What black eye?"

"The one Levi's going to give you in a minute. What will the response be?"

Levi looks startled at that suggestion but then jumps in, saying, "Think about it, Charlotte. You haven't been home since you returned with Cole. Your mom hasn't seen your injuries."

Charlotte shifts her weight on the crutches. "As soon as we walk in, the guard at the door will recognize me and assess the situation as problematic. He'll come running over."

"You insist you have to see your mom," I suggest. "Act woozy and disoriented."

Cole asks, "What will the guard do?"

"He'll call up to my mom. Then he'll alert the other two guards."

"Will they ask Nell for ID?" Levi asks.

"Maybe," Charlotte says. "They might want to retain her for questioning, in case they think she did this to me . . ."

"If she did it to you, she wouldn't be walking you in, and you wouldn't be clinging to her," Cole offers.

"Cole's right," Levi says. "Under the circumstances, they'll probably just ask Nell to leave. Say they've got it from here. Then what do you do?"

Charlotte suggests, "I'll hold on to her. Act scared."

"Then . . . ?"

"My guess is he'll take both of us up. I don't think the guard'll peel me off of Nell if she's holding me and I won't let go. I'll do what Nell and Cole said—act all woozy and disoriented and clingy."

"Where will they take you?" Cole asks. He's got some energy in his voice now, and he's looking better than yesterday—better than a few minutes ago. Stronger.

"They'll take us up in the elevator to my mom's lab. I'll insist on it."

I flash Cole a smile. *Charlotte's in!*

I pick up one of the disgusting food tubes from Levi's desk and hand it to Cole. "Eat this. You're gonna need your strength."

"Is your dad around?" I ask, turning to Charlotte.

"No. He's in our Switzerland office all week."

"Will your mom definitely be there?"

"Yes. She's always there."

"How many other people in the lab?"

"Best guess? One tech."

"Are there security guards on the upper floors?"

"No, they use swipe cards to open doors. And biometrics—face and palm-print recognition. But the guard will use his to get us through," Charlotte says. "So *then* what?" she asks.

"The guard brings us to your mom's lab. I tell her what I told the guard. That I found you beat-up like this . . . and you asked me to bring you here."

"Found me where, though?"

"Lying on the side of the road?" Cole suggests.

"Which road?" Levi asks. "We have to nail down the details so the story sounds believable."

"Nowhere near the quarry," Charlotte mumbles. "Let's say you found me on North Alder. I have a friend who lives near there."

"Okay."

"When?"

"This morning."

"So we're strangers? And I found you lying on the side of the road?" I ask.

"Exactly."

"So what are you going to say happened to you?" Cole asks.

"Beat up? Mugged?" Levi tries.

"E-bike accident," Charlotte announces.

"Perfect. Where's your bike?" I ask.

"Gone. They run people off the road and steal bikes all the time for the lithium batteries."

"No, Charlotte. I mean where's your bike *really*?"

She points to the corner of the cave, where there's a bike leaning against the wall.

"Okay, good. Make sure it disappears."

She nods.

"Then what?" I say. "The pill for Finn . . . How do I get it?"

"My mom has them showcased on a display shelf with all the other recently approved medicines behind her workstation. She uses it for inspiration—and to impress clients."

"Labeled?"

"Of course."

Charlotte shifts her weight again and winces in pain. "She'll be tending to me. She'll probably send for the medical staff. We have two nurses on-site. She may send the lab tech to get bandages or whatever to clean me up. You ask for water. I don't think she'll get it for you. I'm guessing she'll send you to the sink by her workstation to get it yourself. Next to the sink are bottles of drinking water. On the counter behind the sink you're going to see the pills. Look for a vial labeled 'LR-009' on the bottom shelf—recent FDA approvals are on the lowest shelf with these big display labels, so it'll be easy to spot. The hard part is you'll have to open the bottle without anyone seeing and only take one pill. She'll know right away if the whole bottle is gone. But I don't know how you can possibly open—"

"I'll figure it out," I say.

Cole flashes me a look of worry, then asks, "Are you sure the medicine inside is real, Charlotte? Not fake, for display purposes?"

"It's definitely real. They're all real."

Levi looks at Charlotte. Me and Cole do too. We're waiting for her to say yes.

"What about security cameras?" I question.

Charlotte nods. "Tons of them. They're everywhere. But they

only monitor exteriors and hallways in real time. The in-lab footage is saved for ten days and only reviewed if there's a suspected incident. The guard in the back security office will probably come to the front entrance when we go upstairs. So they won't likely see *any* real-time footage until you've left anyway."

"So even if they figure it out and check the footage inside the lab and see me open the pill vial, we'll be long gone," I comment.

"And if they use facial rec, Nell won't exist," Levi offers. "And you'll be off the hook, Charlotte, because of your injuries. Even if someone does figure out it was Nell and the whole thing was a setup, it'll look like you were a victim. The thieves targeted you, ran you off the road, then Nell brought you to the lab acting like a Good Samaritan. Nell here stole the meds, and you had no idea."

"Are there cameras on the road where you're claiming the accident was?" Cole asks.

"No," Charlotte says, looking more and more committed. "The pill you're stealing? It costs over a million dollars, and health insurance doesn't cover it. So the theft is believable, even outside the context of what we're doing with it."

"Plus," Levi adds, "if it goes smoothly, maybe no one will notice for months that it's gone, and maybe they'll never connect the two incidents."

Charlotte looks at each of us. Me first. Then Levi. Then Cole. Then she asks, "Levi, is there enough time to pull this off and get them back before five?"

"Just barely. But yes."

She sighs. "Fine. I'm in. Levi will drive all of us to the lab, then he waits with Cole in the car. Nell will hightail it out of the lab as soon as she takes possession of the pill. I'll stay with my mom. Levi then takes you two straight to the quarry. You two jump. Then Levi, you go home or come here to the cave, but don't contact me. I'll catch up with you in a few days. And Nell? If something goes wrong," Charlotte warns, "you're on your own. I can't help you, and I'll stick to the story that we just met today when you found me lying on the side of the road."

"Got it."

"Can you pull it off?" Levi asks. "Like *really* pull it off, Nell?"

Cole and I lock eyes. "Cole taught me how to steal stuff when we were little. He told me there were two rules."

"One," Cole says, "don't take anything you don't absolutely need."

"And two," I continue, "don't hide it anywhere obvious. Then he made me practice over and over again and taught me how to work alone and how to work with a partner."

"But most importantly," Cole adds, "I taught her how not to get caught."

Charlotte smiles. "Sounds like we have a plan."

Cole leans in close and whispers, "Thank you for coming to get me, Nell."

"I had to," I tell him. "I'm way better at jacking pharmaceuticals than you are."

"There's only one problem," Levi announces, glancing down at one of his devices. "We have to go soon. We're running out of time."

"How long?" Charlotte asks, wincing again as she walks off.

"Exactly six hours and twenty-two minutes till Saturday at five."

Charlotte starts firing off instructions. She tells me and Cole to go to the storage room next to the bathroom for supplies—food and clothes, whatever we need. She tells Levi to find us wet suits and pack the dry bag then find an airtight, waterproof container for the pill.

Before I go to get ready, I turn to Levi. "How's your swing?"

"What?"

"Your swing? The black eye? Remember? I need you to punch Charlotte."

"No!" Levi protests.

"Not too hard," I suggest. "Just hard enough to give her a black eye. She's pretty scraped-up already, but for Charlotte to be the mustard, she has to look more beat-up than she is."

13

Levi outdid himself—or else Charlotte bruises easily—because he gave her a major shiner. A red and deep-purple half circle beneath her right eye and a just-might-need-stitches cut above the brow as well.

"Jesus," I say when I see it. "You didn't have to do such a good job."

Levi acts defensive. "I thought the cut above the eye was a nice touch."

Charlotte seems delighted. She's looking in the mirror when she comments, "I think this might actually work, Nell." She's changed into dirty, ripped clothes and looks the part of a recently-run-off-the-road high-speed bike-accident victim.

"You set?" Levi asks after Cole comes hobbling in. "Feeling up for the jump?"

"Absolutely," he says.

But watching him, I'm worried. He's still limping pretty bad and now he's coughing a fair amount. And I'm doing the impossible math in my head.

Chance of us getting away with stealing the medicine? *Impossible.*

Likelihood of me and Cole surviving the jump? *Impossible.*

Odds of us getting back in time if we do survive? *Impossible.*

Cole asks, "Can you do it? Can you pull it off, Nell?"

"No problem," I tell him. "Easy-peasy."

"Dry bag is all set," Levi reports to Charlotte. "It's packed with clothes for both of them, wet suits, a counting device. Oh, and triple-waterproof packing for the meds and—"

"How are we doing for time?" Cole asks, and I freeze up. It took over two hours to pack up and plan.

Charlotte says, "Four hours and fourteen minutes."

14

We have to cause a bigger commotion," I whisper as I lean over Charlotte, who's lying on the floor of her mother's lab all of eighteen minutes after we stepped out of the car in front of the building.

Everything worked as we discussed until we got upstairs, and then the plan quickly unraveled. There was no way for me to get to the medicine the way Charlotte described.

Right now, Charlotte's lying on the floor—because she claimed to be too dizzy to stand. I'm hovering over her, holding an ice pack against her eye, there's no lab tech in the room, the guard is by the door on the phone, and her mom—my granddaughter—is now at the sink wetting a cloth. They've been watching me too closely, and I haven't been able to get anywhere near the medicine display. When I asked for water, the guard walked over and got it for me.

"Like what?" Charlotte whispers back.

"A bigger distraction. Hurry. Stand up and stumble. Say you're gonna be sick. I'll hold on to you. We'll walk over toward the medicine and cause a scene over there. A *big* scene. Just improvise."

Charlotte rises to her feet. I stand with her, holding her up as she calls out, "I feel sick."

Her mom glances in our direction, turns the water off, and says, "Lie back down."

Charlotte ignores her, and we move toward the sink. Charlotte says, "I'm going to throw up."

I have my arm around her waist as her mom rushes forward. We push past her in a hurry. Charlotte sways and staggers a few steps. I fake trying to catch her, then we both crash backward in between the sink and the medicine display that's behind it. On my way down, my arm swings out, and in one swoop I knock over the display.

Beakers, pipettes, and plastic pill bottles all fall to the floor. Glass shatters. Charlotte's mom yells something to the guard as she rushes toward us. Charlotte's splayed out on the floor, not moving. Blood is trickling down the back of her head. She hit it on the counter—for real. Her mom bends down and hovers over her. The guard makes a call, then comes running.

I'm on all fours, my back to them, a foot or two away from Charlotte and her mom. I start coughing, crawling through the broken glass and pill bottles, moving away from the fray. I pick up one bottle, read the label, drop it, then pick up another . . . then another. Finally, I retrieve the right bottle from the floor, double-check the label—LR-009—unscrew the lid, remove a pill, then recap the bottle, the whole time waiting for Charlotte's mom or the guard to yell out and stop me. But neither of them does. I struggle to my feet, slipping the pill into my sweatshirt pocket.

I turn to face them. No one notices. They're too busy reviving Charlotte.

I tell myself, *Distraction's over. It's time to run.*

I stagger, lean on the counter, brush myself off. Announce, "I should be going. You don't need me here."

Charlotte's mom calls over her shoulder, "Hold on. I don't even know your name. We can get you . . ." She glances up at me. "You're bleeding too," she says. "Your arm. You cut your arm. Just give me a minute." She turns back to Charlotte, who has opened her eyes.

The guard is now on the radio again calling for maintenance and asking where the ambulance is. He's yelling.

Charlotte sits up. I want to say goodbye—thank her. Maybe learn more about my granddaughter too. But I can't. I turn and walk toward the door.

I push it open. Her mom calls out, "Hold on," one more time. I ignore her. Walk past the people in lab coats hovering in the hallway, hungry to know what has happened. They watch me but don't approach.

I walk past the elevator—and step into the stairwell. I take the steps two at a time down a flight, my hands trembling. I start to count. *One, one thousand, two, one thousand, three, one thousand . . .*

I reach the second-floor landing. Race across it. *Four, one thousand, five, one thousand . . .* Eyes on the door to the hallway. It stays closed. *Six, one thousand . . .*

I hurry down the second set of steps, still counting. I'm expecting the doors to fly open, men with guns. *Seven, one thousand . . .*

I'm expecting to be grabbed. Stopped. Arrested. *Eight, one thousand . . .*

I reach the ground floor. Approach the door that opens out to the lobby. Expect something—the door to be locked or alarmed— maybe an encounter with a guard. But there are no locks, no alarms. And no one comes for me when I pull it open.

I scope out the massive, bright space. Note the guard by the front entrance. *Nine, one thousand . . .* The EMTs running, pushing a gurney toward the elevator bank. The receptionist on high alert. *Ten, one thousand . . .* He's on the phone, pointing, directing someone toward the back of the building.

People are huddled in groups, whispering.

I take a deep breath, step out onto the white marble floor, and I count. *One, one thousand, two, one thousand, three, one thousand, four* . . . The whole time, every step, I'm expecting to be stopped. *Five, one thousand* . . .

I'm just seconds from freedom. *Six, one thousand, seven, one thousand* . . .

I'm a few feet from the exit. There are multiple doors. I decide on the one farthest to the right—farthest from the guard. *Eight, one thousand* . . .

I walk toward it as my hand reaches into my pocket. *Nine, one thousand* . . . I search for the pill. Find it. Run my fingers over the smooth outer coating. I'm gentle; it's fragile. I don't want to wipe off any of the medicine it holds. I will my hand not to sweat, not to tremble, not to make a mistake. It's so small. How can something so small be so big? I remove my hand from my pocket so slowly, so carefully, thinking, *Don't drop it. Don't break it. Don't lose it* . . . Me thinking, *I broke the rule. I hid it somewhere obvious.*

Ten, one thousand . . . I glance to the left. The guard by the main door is now busy directing police upstairs. I put my head down. Lift my hand to the door handle. *One, one thousand, two, one thousand* . . .

I can taste it: freedom and home. *Three, one thousand* . . .

I pull the handle, and . . .

It won't open.

Four, one thousand . . .

An alarm goes off.

Five, one thousand . . .

I look up and back over my shoulder. *Six, one thousand* . . . No one looks my way. The alarm—it's not very loud. It's a warning, not a scream.

I try again. The door doesn't budge.

A man steps next to me. I freeze. He's so close I can feel his warmth. I'm thinking, *This is it. It's game over.*

But he smiles. Holds his palm up to an ID reader.

The door sweeps open. He waves me through.

Seven, one thousand, eight, one thousand . . .

I step outside, where cold air and sunlight hit my face.

Nine, one thousand . . .

The man exits behind me, rushes past. *Ten, one thousand . . .*

I watch him disappear into the people milling about the courtyard.

He may have just changed the world, I think. That single seconds-long encounter I had with a stranger could have saved Finn Wilder's life and stopped the future world from burning and he'll never know.

I hurry down the steps, away from the building, heading toward the car. I feel the pill in my pocket again. I run my fingers over its oval shape, the smoothness of its surface, in awe of the power it holds.

In this moment, I know how big the universe is and how important I am to its survival.

How important we all are.

I am transformed.

I am still Nell Bannon. But I am not the girl I knew.

I am bigger and better than that; *more than I ever thought.*

I am the girl Stevie B draws.

And she is infinite.

15

I climb into the waiting car, smile, and they know.

"Let's go," I say as I hold the pill up for Cole to see and tears well up in his eyes and mine.

He whispers, "One lung from me and one from you," then kisses my cheek as Levi commands the car to take us to the quarry.

I hand the pill over to Levi and he places it inside a plastic envelope then puts that inside a waterproof pill bottle, which he slips inside a small waterproof bag that he stashes in a zipper pocket inside the dry bag.

I down two full bottles of water as Cole holds my hand and Levi checks to make sure no one is following us.

As we drive, I tell them what happened in the lab with Charlotte. Then Levi opens up and tells us things. Things about his world and ours; about him and Margaret. About how much he misses her. How he wishes his life had been different.

"What about your eyes?" I ask softly after he stops talking and turns to stare out the car window. "Your eyes and Charlotte's? Why do they change color? And why are you still seventeen?"

Levi turns to face me, but hesitates before he answers. "If you travel between universes, there are cellular changes that alter eye color and aging."

"Can you explain about the other universes?" Cole asks.

Levi hesitates again, studying Cole this time like he's trying to decide how much he should tell us. "Every decision we make presents options," he starts. "Turn left or turn right? Take one job or the other? Date this person or that person? When we make our choice it plays out in this universe. But each of the options we *didn't* select spins off an alternative universe where that scenario plays out. It's based on something called *many world theory* and it's an infinite form of fractal patterning on the largest scale."

"And somehow you can travel to those alternate universes?" Cole asks.

"Yes."

"How?"

"Some of those universes are accessible through gateways."

"Gateways?" I ask.

"Access points through black holes."

Cole says, "So, it's like you can . . ."

"Universe hop," Levi confirms.

"Why do you do it?" Cole asks.

"Because in some of those universes, I can see my brother alive. I can observe me living with my family. Me living with Margaret. It's a way to be with them."

"But you're just watching?" Cole tries.

Levi says, "It's more complicated than that. And it's all that I have."

Cole squeezes my hand.

"You and Nell don't need to know any of this," Levi adds. "You need to get home and save Finn. That's it."

"There *is* some stuff we do need to know," I say gently. "And you only have a few minutes to tell us."

"Fair enough," Levi responds. "Fire away."

"Stevie B's drawings?" I ask. "They came from you, right?"

I feel Cole tense up next to me.

"Yes."

"Why'd you . . ."

"I had to."

"Had to what?" Cole asks.

"I had to plant ideas in Stevie B's head. Compel him to draw . . . specific things."

"What's he talking about, Nell?"

I don't answer him. I press Levi, "Why?"

"Because you wouldn't have jumped to save Cole without seeing those drawings first, Nell. So . . ."

"You showed him what to draw . . ."

"Exactly."

"But you didn't time travel to see him. And you didn't universe hop. You kind of . . ."

"Entered a liminal space," Levi offers.

"Why not time travel? Be there with them for real?"

"It would change too much."

"And the people you visit in that in-between place, Margaret and Stevie B, they . . . know you're there with them?" I ask.

Levi nods.

I think about what Margaret explained, and how Stevie B freaked out when he realized he hadn't just made Levi up.

Cole asks, "What did Stevie B draw, Nell?"

"The future," I tell him as I stare out the car window. "He drew the future." I flash back to the picture Steve B drew of me climbing out of the quarry, dripping wet, with Charlotte's dry bag sitting in the background, and I know Levi is right. *Those drawings did play a role in me jumping.* Then I think about the sketch Stevie B drew of us dressed like superheroes—the one with all of us standing together above the earth with the rip in the sky and the people pouring through that pathway out, and all of a sudden, I'm wondering if this is the end of something or only the beginning. I turn to Levi, "Are you done with Stevie B? Are you and Charlotte done with *all* of us?"

Levi doesn't answer, so I push harder. "This is it, right? We go home and cure Finn and you and Charlotte stay here. She doesn't come back to Clawson, we don't time-travel, and you don't visit Stevie B anymore? We're done here. Right?"

Cole is glancing back and forth between me and Levi trying to figure out what I'm talking about as I wait to hear the answer. But Levi doesn't offer one. The car makes the final turn into the parking area near the quarry and the engine shuts down with a *CLICK* before a screen on the dashboard flashes ARRIVED.

Levi finally says, "Look, I've spent my life wishing I'd made it back in time to save my brother and wishing I had a life with Margaret. Wishing I had *one* life, in *one* universe, the one we are standing in right now. You two have that chance. Don't blow it by wanting to know a whole bunch of stuff you don't need to know."

"You didn't tell us if you're done with us," I challenge.

But he's already climbing out of the car. "Tell Stevie B his art is important—*save-the-world* important. And tell him to go to art school." Then he grabs the dry bag and shuts the whole conversation down.

Cole steps out of the car and grabs Levi's arm. "If Finn dies, I'd do it too. The universe hopping thing. I would totally do it."

Levi nods slightly, then starts walking toward the south side of the quarry.

As we trail after him heading up the path, I'm still wondering what he meant by saying Stevie B should go to art school, and I'm still wondering if that means we're gonna be called on to do more in this save-the-universe plan. But when we catch up to Levi and he starts talking again, he's not discussing that—he's telling us that we should try to run, and Cole can't.

As Levi hurries ahead, I ask Cole, "Do you think this is it? We save Finn and they're done with us?"

"The only thing I know for sure, Nell, is that if we don't make it back and we don't save Finn, there'll be no *us* to help anyone with anything."

And I know he's right.

I also know we might not make it back alive because Cole's struggling and breathing heavy, stopping to rest and using his hands to steady himself, leaning on the cliff walls as Levi calls out instructions—tips about rock outcroppings, pockets of cold water, breathing and not breathing, about precision and timing, and never telling anyone what we know or what we saw.

"As long as Finn gets the pill before five o'clock today, she'll be okay, right?" Cole asks—and Levi confirms—each time we stop so Cole can catch his breath.

When we arrive at the jumping-off place, Levi pulls me aside and says, "This is on you, Nell. To get him home." Then he hands me the dry bag, and me and Cole put our wet suits on. We climb up onto the highest point, inch close to the edge, and gaze down at the water. Cole mumbles, "Finn," then turns to Levi and says, "Please thank Charlotte for us."

I secure the dry bag to my back, thinking about everything Cole and I have, wondering if we can do this. If *I* can do this. Wondering if we're going to make it back in time—or make it back at all.

Levi steps up next to us and hands me the counting device. "You're all set, Nell. The timer's preset for where—and when— you want to go. I added a three-second delay as a countdown to the jump."

I check the device, say, "It's eight minutes after four."

Cole says, "That means we have fifty-two minutes until five," then he takes a couple of big, deep breaths.

Levi says, "You can do this," and Cole hugs him.

I say, "Thank you." Levi steps down, and I take Cole's hand.

We turn to face the quarry.

I think about how brave and strong I now am and whisper, "I will hold you and keep you safe forever."

Then I hit START on the device.

We jump on three.

16

We pierce the water, straight and sharp, as one. Limbs entangled, toes pointed, hearts beating fast. The splash and bubbles follow us down in an explosive rush of force. The water's so icy cold it feels like glass cutting my skin.

I start to count. *One, one thousand . . .*

Colder than I remember.

Two, one thousand . . .

I open my eyes.

Three, one thousand . . .

Darker than I remember.

Four, one thousand . . .

I get to ten, then start again.

We travel down as far as the jump alone will take us, then use the stone ladder to climb lower. I check the device. Recalibrate. I reach for the outcroppings on the southern wall and, pulling with my arms, keep going down. Cole holds on to me as I count.

Six, one thousand, seven, one thousand . . .

I am precise. I get to ten, then start again as we descend. I tell myself, *Forty-eight times on the way down. Then forty-eight on the way back up.*

My lungs burn, want to burst. There's pressure in my ears. I ache. But Cole holds on to me, as I hold on to the dry bag and Finn's medicine. To life.

I check the device, then adjust. I do it over and again. When we get close to the tunnel, I loop my feet around Cole's ankles and pull him in close. We press ourselves flat against the stone of the southern wall, fighting the pull of the current and the drift of water. Limbs knotted, I check the device again—both screens. Eight minutes exactly. Location spot-on. I feel the stone wall give, and we're instantly turned with force from vertical to horizontal. We fire into the tunnel fast, feet first, as if through a chute.

Together. We're still together. I won't let go. Cole squeezes me tighter.

Then blinding, vivid, bright light surrounds us. Colors, loud noise, music. I see my dad. My grandma. My mom. I see Cole. Finn. Stevie B. And more people. Lots of people. Babies. Children. People I know and don't know.

Then I feel my limbs ripping from my torso, from Cole's torso. I try to fight back—holding tight to Cole now, to the bag—as I feel myself stretching, elongating . . .

Water rushes by. There are stars above me in an inky-black sky, watery light, followed by colors again, pastel this time. And people, more people, new people. It's haunting. It feels like we're being carried by energy, or flying with wings of light.

And then, a different force, and we're flung upright again. Followed by a slowing and a calm. Murky water surrounds us. My hair floats in a halo. No beautiful colors. Just shades of cloudy green and gray.

The other side.

Cole's face is blurry and distorted, but he's still with me. He squeezes my hand as I start to count again. *One, one thousand . . .* We climb together. *Two, one thousand . . .* A quick glance at Charlotte's counting device, then we're staring into each other's eyes. For a flash, I see grit and fight looking back at me, but then Cole's lids close and I fear he's too weak and won't make it. *Three, one thousand . . .* I push on knowing wherever, *when*ever, this takes us, we are side by side, entwined beyond forever in space and time.

I count. *Four, one thousand, five, one thousand, six . . .*

17

When our heads rise above the surface of the water, I've got the dry bag strapped to my back and I'm still holding on to Cole with one arm, fighting to keep the two of us afloat. Cole is ashen and drawn, coughing up water, as I gasp for air, my lungs burning after the first breath and the second and the third. Cole is clearly struggling—choking and slipping back under the surface. Tears spring to my eyes, but I tell myself, *I am strong. I can do this.* I slowly drag him, drag the bag, with all I've got, toward the quarry's edge.

I grab hold of the rock ledge, then manage to pull Cole in close. Out of breath, with cloudy thinking and fiery lungs, I slip the dry-bag strap off my shoulder, swing my arm, then launch it onto the flat rock, barely making it without my head going under. Then, still holding on to Cole's arm, I drag myself halfway out and lie sideways on the rocks.

I try to pull him out, but I can't. "You have to climb, Cole! I can't lift you," I cry.

He reaches up. Holding on to the quarry stone, he manages to hoist himself partway as I climb up the rest of the way then reach down to lift his legs and his torso, near deadweight, out of the water. He lies there on the rocks, coughing and choking, taking in big breaths as I roll him onto his side, away from the edge, then collapse in a heap next to him.

I mumble, "Finn."

He whispers, "Altair . . . Deneb . . . Vega . . ."

"I love your voice," I say.

He says, "Welcome home, Nellie."

I force myself to sit up, unzip the bag, and check for Finn's medicine. Hands shaking, I hold up the inner bag with the pill in it for Cole to see. His eyes barely open, he gives me a thumbs-up. "What time is it?" he chokes.

I glance at the device. It's getting so close to five, I don't want to tell him. "No idea. But we have to hurry."

I quickly pull out dry clothes for both of us. Weak and exhausted, minutes from freezing to death in the October air, we change out of our wet suits.

"We have to move," I tell him. We hold on to each other as we make our way as best we can toward Cole's truck, our legs heavy, muscles burning, but both of us recovering much faster than we did after the first jump.

Then right before we round the bend to the parking area, fear strikes fast and hard. I'm petrified that it's already after five. Petrified his truck will be gone, or Stevie B won't be where he's supposed to be. Or Finn will be too sick—or worse.

I ask Cole, "Are you still talking to God?"

He doesn't answer. We take a few more steps and see Cole's truck sitting there and he mumbles, "More than ever before."

"Good," I say, hoping we're not too late. Hoping the truck will start. Hoping . . . "Keep at it" I tell him, as we continue down the hill. "Finn's with Stevie B," I add as we climb into the cab. "I told him to bring her to the hospital and wait for us in the parking lot. Just in case."

"Why isn't she with my mom?" Cole asks, alarmed.

"Your mom had a work thing. I was supposed to babysit."

He removes the keys from under the visor, his hands shaking.

"So I had to send Stevie B, because—"

"You had other plans," Cole says as he turns the key and the truck roars to life.

"Yeah. Pretty important plans."

"It's 4:44," Cole announces after he glances at the dashboard clock.

"That means we have . . . ," I say, but I can't do the math, my thinking still cloudy and slow.

"Sixteen minutes to get to the hospital," Cole says. Then I reach for the heater as he shifts into reverse and floors it.

18

When we pull into the hospital parking lot in Cole's truck, it's pitch-dark—and almost five. We spot Stevie B in the middle of the empty lot across from the emergency room doors, looking like the last man standing after an apocalypse, and our hearts soar, then tumble, then rise again when we pull up closer and see he's holding something in his arms. Cole mumbles, "Finn," and my breath catches in my throat, 'cause her name comes out of him sounding more like a whimper than a word. We don't know for sure what's gonna happen next, but the whole thing feels so dramatic. Stevie B standing there holding Finn like that, looking all shell-shocked and beat-to-shit. His mouth open, eyes big and wet, shirt untucked, hair sticking up. Finn not moving at all.

Cole doesn't even shut the engine off. He takes the pill envelope and a bottle of water I found on the back seat, then flies out of the truck, leaving the door hanging open, racing to take Finn from Stevie B's arms.

When Finn Wilder lifts her head and reaches out to him and Cole gives her the pill, it's 4:54—six minutes before five.

It's not until I watch Finn swallow that pill that I can finally breathe again.

I climb out of the truck and walk over to them, feeling weak and coughing, but with my heart damn near exploding.

Stevie B's looking around dazed and confused. Like he's not sure what just happened or what to make of it. Cole is sitting on the pavement hugging Finn, making her drink more water, and checking her mouth over and over to make sure she swallowed that pill.

The four of us are quite a sight. Me and Cole and Stevie B separated from each other, but forever tied together, orbiting Finn, like moons around a planet. And I can't help but think about all that stuff Stevie B said about us being entangled, and what Finn told me about those invisible heartstrings holding us close.

+ + + + + + + +

When me and Stevie B sit down on the curb on the other side of the parking lot to give Cole some time alone with Finn, I announce, "It's after five on Saturday, Stevie B. And Finn's breathin' fine, like a normal kid, and Cole's here with her. And you and me, we're okay too, so I'm figuring that right now, this moment, in this world, is just about perfect. So thank you for everything."

He says, "Of course."

"You know," I tell him, "I met Levi Tanner in person, and he told me that your art is important. Like change-the-world important. He knew your drawings would convince me to jump . . . *That's* why he came to you. And they changed how I see myself and how I see the world too."

We both look over at Cole with Finn. "We wouldn't have made it without you. I want you to know that."

Stevie B sits there for the longest time before he says, "So Levi's alive and this is all real and . . ."

"Yeah. Pretty much. And Levi said he wants you to go to art school."

Stevie B is real quiet for a few more minutes, and then he asks, "Did he happen to say which one?"

So I elbow him and he elbows me back, and it turns into a whole thing.

"You know," I tell him after we settle down, "I'm gonna add Charlotte's name to my Brave Bitches List. Right next to mine."

"So you two are friends now?"

I smile. "Something like that. Your name too, Stevie B. I figure you should be on the Brave Bitches List too."

"After this?" he says, glancing over at Finn. "I should be right up there on the tippy top."

I reach for his hand and hold it.

"And you and me, Nell?" he asks.

"Not in this universe, Stevie B."

"Yeah, I figured," he says, looking over at Cole.

Then I tell Stevie B more about what I know and what I saw. The short SparkNotes version for now. I mention the mind-bending stuff Cole and Levi told me about infinite universes and us having multiple lives. "You know, somewhere out there in one of them, you and me have a life together. Probably infinite lives together in infinite universes. You and me, young, old, rich, poor, sick, healthy, spinnin' through space and time together, with no end and no limits. Just not here," I whisper, "Not here in this world."

He hugs me, and his lips brush my cheek, and I turn my face away. "This here," I continue, looking over at Cole holding Finn, "this universe, is written for me and Cole."

Cole walks over, holding Finn's hand, and I stand up and brush myself off. "Since you guys are all okay," I announce as Finn hugs my legs, "I have to go and see about my mom."

"I can take you, Nell," Stevie B offers.

"No, I'll take you," Cole says. "We can all go."

"Thanks," I tell them, "but I should go myself. I *want* to go myself. And if you're up for it, Cole, Stevie B can fill you in on what happened while you were gone."

Then Finn asks if we can all go moon catching and pixie hunting, and Cole promises, "Every day."

I'm walking toward my truck when I hear her ask, "Every day forever?"

So I call back over my shoulder, "Every day beyond forever, Finn."

+ + + + + + + +

As I climb into my truck, I figure, me and Cole and Stevie B and Finn and my mom and dad and grandma—even Charlotte and Levi—all of us, all of the stars in my universe, we're entangled now, wherever and whenever we are in space and time, each impacting each other in ways we'll never understand. And I figure that means it's just like my mom always says, *We know stuff, Nell. We don't know how we know it or where it came from, but we know it.*

I figure Charlotte and Levi were right too, when they told me that we don't have to understand everything.

And Cole was right all along as well: There *is* magic to this life.

And now I know that the magic is us, in the here and now.

And that it's precious.

I might not know much, but I know that.

After After

Two Weeks Later

We took down those inmate pictures from my bedroom wall today.

Cole said, "You were building yourself a prison, Nell. Even if you couldn't see the bars."

He was right. And I can see those bars now. Clear as day. They were built by me out of fear. Fear as strong as steel and barbed wire, same as a life sentence.

It was a lot of work, and messy as hell, taking those bars down. But scraping all those pictures off the wall felt like a weight lifting, or a moving-up ceremony of sorts. Cole helped. Stevie B too. And Charlotte helped in her own way, by showing me how big the world is, and how much I matter. People like me, people who think they're *nothing*, don't always get to see that. Meeting my great-granddaughter, seeing how I'm tied to others who aren't even born yet, changed me.

When I think about everything Charlotte and Levi said about me not needing to know everything, about how we're all interconnected, about how we matter to the future in ways we don't understand, I know I'm going to do something with my life. So, these days, I'm not lookin' for that new tree to plant my ass under when high school ends in the spring. I'm looking for something I can grow into, not sit under. Something I can *do or be*. I'm searching for some version of myself I couldn't see before all this happened—one closer to what Stevie B sees and draws, than how I saw myself.

I also realize that me and Cole and Stevie B aren't a triangle that doesn't sit right if one side is missing.

I was thinking too small when I thought that, too.

We're part of something much, much bigger. Something with infinite sides that doesn't sit right if any of them are missing.

I looked it up, and it's something mathematicians call an *apeirogon*.

I see the importance of each of us now, spinning through the infinity of space and time together.

And I know that I'm connected to the past and future.

That I am infinite.

And I matter.

My passport came in the mail today too.

"Look at this," I say to Stevie B, holding up that envelope with the US government return address.

I rip it open, then hand him the passport, and he flips to the page with my picture and asks, "Who is she, Nell?"—like this was another one of those expired passports I got from strangers on eBay and we were playing that game.

"Her name is Nell Bannon, and she is brave and fearless. Someone important," I tell him. "Someone who just might go somewhere and do something big someday, to set the world right."

"Cool," he says, flipping to the blank pages where the country stamps are supposed to go. "But she hasn't gone anywhere yet."

I smile. "Maybe she has. And, don't worry, she will."

And I mean it.

But I'm in no hurry. I know I'll use that passport someday. *Many* somedays, even. Go many somewheres. Do something. *Many* somethings.

And I know I will always and forever have something to come back to right here in Clawson. With no limits and no boundaries defined by space and time. Or by me. 'Cause Cole was right about something else too: It's the people that tie you to a place.

And I've got better people than most. I know that now.

+ + + + + + + +

When I show up at Cole's at six o'clock, he meets me at the door and swoops me into a hug, pushing me back out onto the front steps so no one will hear what he has to say. "Finn's cured," he whispers. "It's exactly two weeks since she was supposed to die, and her blood work and oxygen levels came back completely normal today for the first time in her life. The doctor called it a miracle."

I peek in at Finn racing around the kitchen and I'm thinking about that man in the lobby at the lab who opened the door for me, and how one little thing that seems like nothing can change everything.

"How's your mom?" Cole asks. "What happened?"

"She's doing okay," I tell him. "The shooting was officially ruled justified at today's hearing. The other guard corroborated my mom's story. He stood up in front of the panel and explained that Wozniak tackled him, got hold of his gun, and posed a grave safety risk to the transport team and to the public."

"I'm so happy, Nell. What's next for her?"

"Medical leave," I guess. "Rehab. They're still working out the details. But no prison time."

Finn steps outside, and Cole picks her up, points up at the stars, and starts singing that Blake Shelton song my daddy used to play.

"When you love someone, they say you set 'em free
But that ain't gonna work for me . . ."

I gaze over at the two of them, wondering again if Cole saw the heart-shaped birthmark sitting below Charlotte's collarbone. Wondering if he knows that she's not just his. That she's mine. And ours.

I don't plan on asking him or telling him, though. And I don't think about whether Levi will visit Stevie B or if Charlotte will show up looking for us to time-travel to save someone from Clawson again. I figure it's like Charlotte said: We don't need to know everything. But I do know this one thing for certain: Standing here next to Cole and Finn, her healthy, my mom doing okay, all of us with the stars and the moon shining over our heads, feels like home.

It feels like family.

And it feels like forever—beyond forever, even.

+ + + + + + + +

When Finn gets sent to bed, I ask Cole if he wants to jump.

He looks at me surprised. "Charlotte and Levi told us not to," he warns, but I pretty much know we're gonna jump again anyway.

"They just don't want us time-traveling," I tell him, "because it's dangerous."

And Cole gets that smile of his where the corner of his mouth turns up and his eyes get crinkly, and then he gets all soft-looking. And me and him, we don't say another word. We just head to his truck and drive up to the quarry.

Then we follow that path through the woods, just the two of

us, Cole singing the Lauren Daigle song he loves so much, mixing up the words like he does. Him singing about being lost and getting found.

Then we ditch our sneakers and our phones and climb up onto those rocks, and I hitch my legs around his waist, and Cole whispers, "I want *this*, Nell. You and me. One precious life, right here in this universe."

Then right before we fill our lungs with air, he warns, "Stay far away from the quarry walls."

And then we jump.

Feet first. Hearts second. Heads a distant third.

The two of us holding our breath just long enough to go nowhere at all, but where and when we already are.

Right here.

Right now.

Home.

Author's Note

Sixteen Minutes is a work of fiction, but much of the underlying science—the possibility of time travel, the potential existence of parallel universes, even the concept of the multiverse—is based on respected work from highly reputable theoretical physicists and mathematicians.

From Einstein's theories of special relativity and general relativity to Hermann Minkowski's work on the geometry of space-time and its relationship to speed, as well as gravity tunnels, the Cheshire Cat effect (inspired by Lewis Carroll's *Alice's Adventures in Wonderland*), many-worlds theory, traversable wormholes, closed timelike curves, quantum entanglement, and fractals (those repeating patterns in nature and math that Cole told Nell about in the cave), much of what is in the book is based on either proven facts or viable theories—new and old—in physics, quantum mechanics, and string theory.

Of course, because *Sixteen Minutes* is fiction and was written to entertain and inspire, I took great liberties picking and choosing which theories to run with, which to stretch and bend, and which to unabashedly ignore, as that is the purview and stomping ground of a fiction writer. *We get to make stuff up.*

But, for those who would like to learn more about the actual theoretical science of time travel and the possible existence of parallel universes and the multiverse, I would encourage you to consider reading nonfiction books like *The Hidden Reality* by Brian Greene and *Time Travel in Einstein's Universe* by J. Richard Gott. Or Steven Hawking's *The Theory of Everything* and Brian Cox and Jeff Forshaw's *Why Does E=mc²?* Read about time-travel paradoxes, the simulation hypothesis, and M-theory. Read about precognition: Carl Jung and synchronicity and the collective unconscious. And if you're interested in a deep dive, try reading about quantum entanglement. But maybe start with the book that Stevie B read: *Totally Random: Why Nobody Understands Quantum Mechanics (A Serious Comic on Entanglement)* by Tanya Bub and Jeffrey Bub. And don't let its graphic format fool you; the 2022 Nobel Prize in Physics went to three scientists for their work in the field of entanglement and quantum mechanics:

> One key factor in this development is how quantum mechanics allows two or more particles to exist in what is called an entangled state. What happens to one of the particles in an entangled pair determines what happens to the other particle, even if they are far apart.
>
> —The Royal Swedish Academy of Sciences
> Nobel Prize press release, October 2022

But beyond all of the science, and perhaps most of all, I hope *Sixteen Minutes* has given you newfound respect for the wonders of the universe. I hope this story has convinced you that the universe is bigger than you might have thought and that our lives matter in profound ways—even when we think they don't. And I hope you will consider the possibility that all of us are entangled in ways we may never fully understand.

Then I hope you jump.

Feet first. Heart bursting. Head, a distant third.

Acknowledgments

For me, writing a book feels like a solitary sport. A long distance cross country run where I spend a considerable amount of time wearing sweatpants, completely alone with the people and places I make up in my head, trying very hard to get to a destination I'm not entirely sure I will ever reach.

Then when I hand my manuscript in and sprint over what I think is the finish line, a whole team of real people—professional book people—swoop in and inform me that the finish line I *thought* I had crossed is not the end of this book journey at all. It's only the beginning.

Those professional book people then promptly lace up their running shoes and escort me and my not-quite-finished story toward the actual finish line, and in the process help transform those typed pages and imaginary characters into a plot perfected, pacing corrected, tweaked and polished, brilliantly packaged and superbly branded book that they then get into the hands of readers.

So, I have come to understand that even though book writing

begins as a solitary sport spent with imaginary people, book publishing is very much a team sport populated with real people other than me. And it is here, in these acknowledgments, that I get to thank that team of real book people who helped guide *Sixteen Minutes* over the *actual* finish line.

First and foremost, I owe a debt of gratitude to my agent, Molly O'Neill at Root Literary, for seeing the power and wonder in this story early on, for finding it a home at Penguin Random House, and then for working by my side to transform it into a finished book. I'm grateful for your direction and guidance, Molly, and for your stellar knowledge about both the publishing industry and the craft of writing. I have the utmost respect for your love of language, creative insight, calm demeanor, and tactful, persuasive nature—and of course, for your superhero-level overall awesomeness.

I am equally indebted to my editor, Stacey Barney at Nancy Paulsen Books. Plot guru, character dissector, insightful poker and prodder, questioner of all things even remotely questionable, thank you, Stacey, for finding holes that needed filling, roads that led nowhere, and for reeling me in and pointing me in the right direction when I wandered too far off course. And thank you for having patience when I wanted to ignore everything else to frolic mindlessly in pretty words. But most of all, thank you for providing me with the platform and space to do my very best work.

I am grateful as well to the entire extended behind-the-scenes team at Nancy Paulsen Books and Penguin Random House who ran those last miles by my side. I am thankful for your collective expertise and support, and I am in awe of your creativity and professionalism. I am indebted to Theresa Evangelista for her brilliant cover design, to Pablo Hurtado de Mendoza for the artwork, to Elizabeth Johnson for such a thorough and precise copyedit, to Cindy Howle, Jenny Ly, Emily Rodriguez, Nicole Kiser, Cindy

De la Cruz, Amanda Cranney, Felicity Vallence, Shannon Spann, Lizzie Goodell, and a huge thank-you as well to all the other talented back-of-the-house team members I have not named but who helped bring *Sixteen Minutes* from words on paper to shelf-ready, looking so singularly spectacular.

To the larger book community, the vital pre- and post-publication world of reviewers, bloggers, librarians, teachers, booksellers, and, of course, readers—thank you for all the support and love you give to books. Stories shape our lives, and sharing those stories with others as writers and educators and book lovers allows us to explore what matters most about our humanity. I thank each and every one of you for finding the books that touch your heart, for reading and cherishing them, and for being the engine that gets those books into the hands of others. You are an integral, foundational part of the publishing world, and it is my sincere hope that *Sixteen Minutes* will be one of those magical, thought-provoking stories you recommend to others.

I also owe a debt of gratitude to my family. As always, it has been an honor and joy sharing this book journey with you. Thank you for loving Nell, Cole, Stevie B, Charlotte, and Finn, and for allowing them to live with us for so long. I am fully aware of how much space they have taken up in our lives—and the fact that at times it felt a bit like we had adopted very demanding imaginary children who we then let run amok in our house, so thank you for putting up with them—and with me.

And finally, for everyone who has read *Sixteen Minutes*: It has been my greatest honor to have been invited into your heads and hearts and to have shared these ideas and this journey with you. And even though most of us will never meet, I believe that if *Sixteen Minutes* holds any truth at all, it is that those of us who have shared this story are now entangled across space and time for the simple reason that this book brought us closer together, if only for a brief time. It is my sincere hope that *Sixteen Minutes* took all of you to a distant time and place, then brought you safely back home. Because, as Cole Wilder tells Nell Bannon, coming home is the best part of every journey.